SIRENS OF THE PAST

A TIME TRAVEL ROMANCE

SPIRITS THROUGH TIME

AIMEE ROBINSON

AMR PUBLISHING LLC

To Eric and Scott

SPIRITS THROUGH TIME SERIES

Charmed by the Past

Sirens of the Past

Forged by the Past

CHAPTER 1

Dick was about to die. He was sure of it. What other possible outcome could there be?

After all, he was falling. As in, *the* fall, the great fall he imagined for one who had lived a life of degradation such as he would experience before they crash-landed onto the fiery rocks of Satan's hell. His stomach floated inside of him, as if his organs had become untethered. His knuckles scraped the craggy confines of the well shooting him down toward his final reward.

Dick tried to right himself, tried to reorient his body so up was up once more. A tightness in his neck constricted his movement as he made one last attempt to glance back at the man surely responsible for ending his life.

Jacob Bellamy. His former friend and fellow runner in his infantry regiment. They'd fought together in the Great War. Well, "friend" was a loose term. Dick would have been better off making friends with a German grenade. And in many ways, he had. After all, it was Bellamy's wartime charge that had propelled Dick to run headfirst by himself toward a German-riddled machine-gun nest during their time in France. The resulting solo advance on Dick's part had rewarded him with a shell explosion mere feet from his head and cost him his hearing on his left side and a scarred, pockmarked face a mother wouldn't even love.

True to all he'd heard about near-death experiences, his mind raced with images of recent events.

Hunting down Bellamy at his cabin off Lake Roland.

The slice of Dick's knife across Bellamy's back before he dragged his former friend to the old well outside the cabin.

The murderous intent that fogged Dick's head as he snaked the well's pulley rope around Bellamy's neck.

Dick's closed eyes sealed shut more tightly. Sweat-slicked hair plastered against his forehead as his descent's speed increased. His final recollections replayed behind squinted eyelids.

The clang of the metal pulley as the rope snapped, freeing Bellamy. Dick's attacking weight no longer supported by his immobilized foe beneath him.

His loss of balance over the lip of the well. Bellamy's cold fists that gripped his ankles and raised them in the air behind him. The abrasive scrapes along his midsection and thighs from the stone and grit brushing over him for the last time. The moonlight that illuminated a curious green patch of dust on his trousers before he plunged into total darkness.

A muffled moan slipped out of Dick's lips. His eyes flew open as he panicked.

He was falling. Trapped in terrifying helplessness. Horrified by the unknown anticipation of when he would crash into the surface of the water at the base of the well. And then . . .

Nothing.

No sounds of splashing water. No scorching pain or snap of his neck. Just a cold hardness beneath him and heavy darkness weighing him down.

Actually, that wasn't entirely true. Upon closer inspection, blossoms of pain began to slowly flare up throughout his torso. A reflexive deep inhale confirmed the small pockets of painful fire spreading throughout his chest.

Hell. He was definitely in hell. The brief iciness at his back quickly subsided and made way for the horrors of his life to feed off his soul in full force. Because why should death treat him any better than life had?

Harsh clicks broke through the silence as Dick's teeth chattered in the cold, though his insides burned white-hot. Memories bombarded him with images of a debased life.

Blood on his knuckles from the fights he couldn't resist.

Fat pockets lined with stolen money.

Whiskey. Women. Spoils of war . . .

A brief shiver racked his body. Sudden and invasive chills licked up his spine. Like a flower petal under the blazing sun, his skin tightened. The shocking frozen tension encased his muscles, causing clenched fists and stiffened limbs. Never would he have imagined hell to be so cold, but it made sense. Fire was predictable in its torture and quite lackluster. It moved fast and furiously, scorching everything in its wake without regard for fanfare. All bite and no bark.

A frozen hell was more tortuous. Ice crept slowly, like a bottom-feeding predator, and left a trail behind for its victims to fear. Solid tombs of last breaths immortalized. This would be his new eternity.

Dick winced as he shivered again, the sharp movement deepening the growing ache in his chest. But just as he released a slow exhale through his pursed lips, he slammed them shut in shock.

A faint humming flitted through his war-ravaged hearing. He turned his good ear to the sky to assess better. No, not a hum. More like a deep, melodious taunt. Not high pitched and screeching, as he would have expected from other damned souls in hell with him. This was beautiful, light, and enchanting. It whispered through the frozen cracks in his battered shell of a body.

An angel.

"Sir . . ."

There it was again. Beautiful.

"Sir? Are you all right?"

Figuring then was as good a time as any to finally crack an eyelid, he slowly unhinged his eyes. The sight of a blurry night sky before him was an odd comfort. This was an image he knew. Stars, occasional patches of which were blotted out by clouds, shone down on him. He was gratified to know that flaming-tipped icicles weren't threatening to skewer his body like a pincushion. Perhaps those were saved for later in the frozen-hellfire-initiation process.

A few hard blinks and the image before him came into focus . . . right before his remaining breath left his bruised lungs.

In front of his eyes, a haloed aura outlined the stunning vision of his angel. For that's what she must have been. What other explanation was there?

"Angel." The whispered word was infused with disbelief and awe. Never had he imagined an angel with such piercing blue eyes and sensual dark curls. Hell, he'd never imagined an angel in his proximity period, let alone this one.

His angel.

"Sir, are you hurt?"

Why was she asking that? Was he hurt? Sure. But it was nothing her voice couldn't cure. Her words were a balm to every raw wound that festered within him. Dick's eyes drifted closed as he basked in her song.

He was in heaven.

"Rosetta! No!"

The shrill in his angel's voice twisted his insides. He snapped his eyes open.

And was not prepared for what he saw.

A quick head toss to his right showed the front hooves of an enormous chocolate-brown mare who was about to barrel down right on top of him. No, not on top of him. On top of his balls. Self-preservation kicked in. He barrel-rolled to the right. The hooves narrowly missed his skin but pinched down on the slack of his shirt. The whinnying and neighing told Dick just how pissed off this creature was.

He could relate.

Pinned, he tried to roll again. The sound of fabric ripping filled his good ear. A cold blast assaulted his side. His torn shirt gave him the leeway he needed to crabwalk backward. He managed to scoot his butt along the grass several feet in the dark before the horse caught on. The mare turned her sights on him again. More kicking. More neighing.

"Rosetta! Stop that right now!" His angel's high voice rang out from behind the horse. But what could she do? Surely angels had better things to do than wrangle a spooked horse. And where had the horse come from?

The questions came fast and furious. His chest pumped for air. The damn horse wasn't so inclined to give him a reprieve, though. She reared up again, hooves hovering over Dick's stones.

What was it with this horse and his balls?

Before the horse slammed down, his angel threw her open palms on the horse's side. She ticked out a combination of shhhs, coos, and murmurs. Whatever her horse gibberish meant, the nonsense worked. The mare immediately calmed its jumping. The snorts came hot and heavy out of its flared nostrils, though, as it paced in circles. His angel kept her hands on the animal's coat, never breaking contact. Again with the murmurs and coos.

"Sir! Oh, my gosh. Oh, my gosh. Oh, shoot. Sir, are you all right?"

She was talking now. Definitely talking, he was sure of it. Her lips were moving. At least, he thought so. It was hard to tell given the outline of her massive curly hair. The light had turned sparse, for which he was grateful, but it was just enough for him to catch bits and pieces of her features. Her angelic glow from when he'd first seen her was gone. The dark night and spotty starlight took over. The hair, though, he couldn't ignore that if he tried.

As he attempted to sit up straight, he groaned. His hand flew to his left side where his shirt had been torn. A glance down revealed he hadn't been as lucky as he'd thought. One of the horse's hooves must have nicked him in the ribs. No blood that he could feel, thankfully, but he would definitely have a bruise come morning.

Wait. The dead didn't bruise. Did they? A slight inward wince produced the telltale signs of an injured rib or two, but his full chest expansion was reassuring. Last he'd checked, the dead didn't need to breathe, either. On a great painful inhale—and yes, something was definitely bruised—he tried to mentally take stock of his situation but came up short.

Dick rose to his feet with a barely concealed grimace.

"If you can just stay there a moment, I'll put Rosetta in her stall and be right back."

He tried to call out to her, tried to secure her attention, but the words died on his lips as he watched in silence.

The angel guided the beast back toward a stable building on the other side of the lawn. To his great surprise, the damn animal just listened to her. The mare didn't even have a bridle on. She just followed.

The animal followed the angel . . . to a stable. A *working* stable.

A brief flutter of unease drifted through Dick's stomach. He'd always imagined heaven as a lot of things, chief among them being a place he'd never see, but there was no doubt in his mind that where he was standing wasn't it.

He must still be on Bellamy's farm. Puffs of white vapor jutted out of his mouth in quick exhales. The cold of the night was doing its best to seep into his bones. If he stood there any longer with his mouth hanging open like a dead fish, he'd freeze before he got any answers.

And that was a problem. He needed answers. Namely because Dick wasn't certain, but he was *pretty* sure—no, very damn sure—that Bellamy's property no longer had a working stable. And Bellamy definitely didn't have any staff tending to the animals. His cabin and farm were his alone now.

But then, where did this angel come from? And whose horse was that?

Tension began to creep higher up his throat as he peered around the landscape. White fencing enclosed the grassy area where he stood. Next to the fencing, just inside of it, was a dirt trail. At least he thought it was dirt in the low light of the moon.

Buildings. More buildings than he had seen yesterday outlined the property. What looked like barns and horse stables dotted the perimeter. All the trees he had relied on for cover when he was waiting for Bellamy were gone.

No, this wasn't Bellamy's cabin off Lake Roland. There was no lake, for one.

The cold seeped further into his skin as the angel jogged back his way. A quick glance down at his body told him he was not dressed for the elements. His trench boots, wool trousers, and long-sleeved button-down linen shirt would have to suffice. And he hadn't noticed them before, but rays of light from tall streetlamps were spaced evenly throughout the property. The angel cut through several on her way back to him. The brief yellow beams highlighted the mass of curls bouncing on her head.

"I'm so sorry about that, sir," she said, a bit out of breath. "Rosetta's in heat and is pretty miserable to be around at the moment."

Dick took in her small form. The woman, for she was definitely a woman despite her tiny stature, was unlike any he'd ever seen. She was dressed in light-blue overalls. Her overcoat was, well, the only word he could think to describe it was . . . puffy. Yes, it was puffy. And shiny, even in the scant moonlight.

At a loss for anything more sensible to say, he let fly the first words that came to mind. "You're no angel."

Confusion and indignation painted the woman's features. The sharp wing of her brows, the wrinkle of her nose, the snarl of her upper lip. This was no angel but a woman. And he was an expert in detecting when he'd pissed one off.

"I never claimed to be." She huffed and cocked a hand on her hip. "But I did just keep Rosetta from squishing you into that not-yet-frozen pile of horse poop you're standing in."

A quick glance down confirmed her statement. The ball of his trench boot was thoroughly encased, as promised.

Lovely.

"Our stallion's at the vet right now," she said with a shrug, as if that explained things. It barely touched the surface, as far as he was concerned.

The woman's gaze darted around the field before she held out her hand to him. "I'm Cami. How did you get out here, sir? It's almost eight thirty at night. Are you here to see Mallory?"

Something was very wrong. He couldn't figure out why, but his gut had soured. His brain couldn't make the connections. In the absence of anything else that made sense, he did the only thing available to him.

He reached out and took her hand.

CHAPTER 2

Camilla Foster had no idea what she was looking at. Yes, there was a man standing in front of her, holding her hand, but beyond that, she needed help connecting the dots. She had just begun doing her night checks on the horses in residence when the prone form of a man took up shop in the pasture where Rosetta was penned. That was a problem because Rosetta was one of the most prestigious mares visiting O'Neal's Equine Services, the horse breeding farm Cami lived on, which was owned and operated by her mother's friend, Mallory O'Neal.

And more to the point, the horse had no doubt just entered her heat cycle and was more than raring to go. Heck, Cami was pretty sure that if she squinted at the pasture hard enough, she'd see "time's a-tickin' 'cause this tail's a twitchin'" carved out in hoof prints in the dirt track around the field. So when she heard a man grunting too close to the sexed-up breeding mare, she'd kicked it into high gear.

He hadn't spoken yet. Hadn't introduced himself, hadn't offered an explanation for why he was there or anything. No, the only thing he offered was his hand. And there it sat, a frozen clamp thawing around her much warmer fingers. His hand was a bear claw compared to hers. Rough calluses compressed and bumped against her smooth palm. A tense squeeze ended the connection before his cold grip receded. The touch stayed with her long after his fingers left, adding another element of chills to an already frigid night.

Maybe the skin-to-skin handshake had been a bad idea. She had taken her gloves off when she threw her hand out. Something about personal introductions with physical barriers always felt wrong. Her mother had been a big proponent of the firm handshake. And, well, for a woman like Cami with her five-foot-one-inch frame, it was a pipe dream to try and offer a firm handshake through layers of leather and wool, but she tried to hold her own anyway.

They both stood there, the frozen air around them hardly moving. He kept looking at her, but his gaze was a bit off. His eyes looked almost startled, wary. His sandy blond hair stood up in waves at all angles, evidence of his scuffle with Rosetta. Her memories of the skirmish brought her back to the present. Her eyes danced down the rest of his body . . . his ill-clothed body, she might add.

The white linen shirt he wore was ripped on his left side, a gaping hole exposing smooth skin pulled taut over a ridged abdomen. The fabric was strange to her, though. Baggy and loose fitting where she wasn't used to seeing extra fabric. Perhaps it was another trend some musician was touting on MTV. Regardless, it was in no way weather appropriate. Gosh, he must be freezing. She was just about to say something to that effect when the breadth of his chest expanded, almost as if he was getting ready to answer her. Would he finally speak?

"Dick."

Well, not the response she thought she'd get tonight.

"My name. Dick . . . Um, Richard Stevens," he said, pulling his hand back.

"Right. Well, Mr. Stevens, why don't you come inside with me. I can take a look at your ribs and make sure you're not hurt elsewhere. I'm so sorry about Rosetta, again," she said as she began walking back toward the barn. "How did you say you got onto the property, by the way? I noticed you lying there on the grass. Did you have an earlier run-in with Rosetta?" She was half walking, half talking behind her shoulder. She was cold, but it wasn't so much from the weather. She couldn't put her finger on what was unnerving her. Perhaps she ought to chalk it up to Rosetta's hormones.

"The gate was open," Dick said. The words came out so clipped and deep. His voice resonated, almost grated against her skin. Was he angry? Hurt? Of course he was. Rosetta had almost castrated him.

"I'll have to talk to Mallory about that." She opened the door to the stable and showed him in. "Don't worry. The horses are all penned for the night. Rosetta was my last one. Now, the main office is closed for the evening, but I can call for Mallory. She's expecting you, yes?"

She walked over to the black phone on the wall of the stable. Picking up the receiver, she dialed Mal's number for her apartment above the office and waited for her to pick up. She was probably watching her recorded soaps, so she would be none too happy for the interruption. Oh, well.

As the phone rang on the other end, Cami watched the man out of the corner of her eye. He was circling. Or rather hovering? She wasn't quite sure what to call it, but he definitely seemed out of his element. As she tracked his movements, the phone clicked over.

"This better be good. I just popped in my Y and R for today. You know how I love me some Victor Newman time. He's such a dream-boat. I tell ya, Cami, that man can stoke my coals at any age. Heck, it probably helps matters that I'm drier than seasoned firewood down there."

Yikes.

"I know, Mal. I mean, about the soaps thing, not the . . . well, yeah. And I wouldn't bug you normally." Cami adjusted the receiver on her shoulder so she could keep an eye on Dick as he walked past the stalls. "This guy showed up for you. A Mr. Stevens? Had a bit of a scuffle with Rosetta out in the field, but I got her penned and out of the way. He's here at the stable with me just so I can make sure he's not hurt or anything. Want me to send him over to the office?"

"Stevens? Nah, I'm not expecting anyone. The only man I want in front of me right now, or on top of me for that matter, is Victor. Anyone else can take a hike," Mal said around what sounded like a giant spoon. Most likely her ice cream shovel.

"No? He's not here for you?" She switched the phone to her other ear as her eyes warily tracked the man around the barn.

"Nope. Cut 'im loose so I can get back to my TV time here. Talk to you in the a.m."

"Um, okay."

A deep sigh drifted through the phone. "What is it, Cami?"

"It's just that I'm not so sure he's from around here. Maybe he's one of those veterinary drug reps? You know they always pop up unannounced."

"Fine. Throw him in the bunkhouse for the night, and I'll let him pitch to me in the morning. But he better have some decent samples, and I mean *decent*. I'm talking thirty-day-supply kind of decent. The last fool who strolled up in here left me with a single dose of that camelina oil. Supposed to make the horses' coats all shiny and full. Yeah, well, the only thing that came out shiny was their shit. Slid out shiny as molasses and just as runny. No, thank you. Hopefully, this character's got something better for me. Later."

Before Cami could say anything else, the phone clicked dead. She hung up the receiver and turned back to the man. If Mal didn't have an appointment with him, why the heck was he here?

More uneasiness crept along her spine as she walked up to him. "Sir, Mallory's not available now. You're welcome to come back in the morning, or I can show you to our bunkhouse. It's vacant tonight."

His back was toward her. In that moment, she got an eyeful of what she hadn't been able to see clearly outside. His shoulders were so wide, she wouldn't have been surprised if he had to turn sideways just to fit through doorways. The bulk of him was impressive. He reminded her of those New Zealand rugby players, built for strength, speed, and everything in between. His torso tapered down to a trimmer waist, but nothing dainty or thin. No, his waist was clearly the core foundation for the pillar of granite that was his upper body. Below the belt, though, was the most rounded tush Cami had ever seen.

Yup, it was official: she had definitely been spending too much time around horses and Mal's biker friends. No biker ever had a tush like that. He must definitely play rugby in his spare time. Definitely.

He turned around slowly and met her gaze. This time, it wasn't as wary as before. More intense. More purposeful. It offered Cami hope that she could maybe get some more information out of him. Her guilt over Rosetta's behavior still clawed at her.

"That will be fine, thank you. I'm grateful for the bed," he said.

"Oh, okay. Sure. The bunkhouse is down past the stable, not far from where you were. You can't miss it. It's the only other building in that direction. Key's under the mat. Tomorrow morning, you can just go to the main office. Mal's usually ready to go around eight. It's the smaller building at the end of the drive. Sign's right out front."

"Thank you."

More silence.

The man wasn't moving, and Cami was terrified he'd injured himself but refused to say anything, either out of some BS macho male pride or, worse, out of motivation to hurt Mal's business with an injury lawsuit. Either way, she needed to make sure he was all right before he left the property.

"Well, why don't you come over and have a seat? I'll take a look at your side and see if I can fix you up for tomorrow. I'm so sorry again about Rosetta."

A smile finally crept across his face, and for the first time, she noticed the scarring along his skin. The entire left side of his face was pockmarked. Gosh, what had happened there? His skin reminded her of her acid-washed jeans, all splotchy and tight.

But that was a terrible thought to have. She mentally chastised herself. The man had clearly suffered through some sort of trauma.

"Are you good at fixing things, Cami?"

The question jarred her out of her thoughts. "Excuse me?"

"You said you'd fix me up. I'm inclined to take you up on that offer." The smile she'd found somewhat endearing a moment ago turned almost predatory.

She suddenly understood why Rosetta was spooked.

Old habits die hard, it seemed. The quick open-close number Cami did with her mouth gave Dick the confidence he needed. In the absence of explanations, Dick reverted back to the only thing he knew with certainty: how women responded to him. They loved to hate him and loved to love him. He was the scoundrel who did the dirty things their husbands refused to do, as well as the deformed oddity well-bred ladies were too curious to ignore.

Initially, he had pushed the thought of Cami out of his mind when his senses got overloaded. However, he refused to let her see him falter. If he was alone, he may have allowed himself to panic. Clearly, he was not where he knew himself to be. So, instead of floundering, he leaned into what he knew, what had always worked for him, worked to ground him. He played to people's expectations.

He wasn't called Dick for nothing.

The seat Cami had offered was a small, round stool off the side of the main stalls. Easy enough to just look at it for what it was. A circular bottom with four wooden legs. But as he slowly walked toward it, he was grateful for the distance. As the straw crunched under his boots, he took the walk as an opportunity to appraise his prey further.

He was right in his assessment of her dark curly hair. The mass was only trimmed to her shoulder, but it had the volume of a ballerina's tutu. How very different from the women he'd bedded before. Her uniform, as well, puzzled him. She dressed like a common farmhand, her worn blue overalls covering what little he could see of her petite figure. And petite she was. Her head barely cleared his chest. Honestly, she seemed like more of a toy doll. A raggedy, well-used toy doll.

Her eyes, however, were a different story. The blue that shone brightly from them, even in the dim light of the stable, was arresting. And at that moment, those blue eyes looked at him with trepidation.

That would do nicely.

Dick halted right next to the stool. Without ever breaking eye contact—because he could see her rock from foot to foot and could play off her clear discomfort—he grabbed the hem of his torn shirt and pulled it free of his waistband. A quick shuck over his shoulders and the trampled fabric left his skin. Christ, it was cold, but not as cold as outside. He dismissed a slight shiver and couldn't help but smirk as her eyes traveled down the length of his chest. He was a big man, and the broads always enjoyed looking their fill. But why should it end there?

He balled up his shirt and began rubbing it across his chest and around his neck, wiping away the dust and grime from his lovely tumble with Rosetta. It wasn't lost on him how Cami's eyes widened when he flexed his upper arm as he reached around toward his neck.

Good. He could use that.

"See something that needs fixing?"

A quick shake of her head had the short curls on her forehead landing across her eyes. She huffed them back into order and picked up a red metal box that hung on the wall next to her.

"Sure, yes. I mean, just your side, then, right?" She set the box on the floor, unhinged the lid, and began rummaging through. While she did that, he glanced down at his side. No blood that he saw, but the skin had already started to mottle with a splotchy yellow hue. Lovely.

He did his best to hide his wince when he bent down, but when she quickly appeared at his side, he knew she had seen his discomfort. Damn.

"Rosetta got you pretty good there, huh?"

"A bruised rib at the most." He dismissed the injury. "It'll heal."

"Oh, I'm sure it will. But let me try to help a bit before you head out." She grabbed a pad of thick white cotton and held it to his left side, right over his ribs. Her fingertips brushed against his chilled skin, causing him to shirk away briefly. Hardly his intended reaction, and damn it all if she didn't notice that, too.

"Ticklish a bit?" He stared down at her face and, for the first time, saw her smile. The blush that crept up her olive complexion was hardly noticeable, but, oh, it was there. He couldn't for the life of him understand why his squirming would make her smile or why she continued to stare at him. He was supposed to be making *her* uncomfortable.

Before the thought could leave his mind, her eyes darted back to his side. "Hold this a sec."

She placed his hand over the cotton while she went to retrieve yet more cotton. What was the woman doing? He wasn't bleeding or anything. What wound was there to mend? Did she intend to patch him into a quilt, for God's sake?

When she popped back over to his side, she pushed the thick cotton he had been holding more tightly against his ribs. And that was when the wince turned into a groan. Damn, that hurt.

"Easy, there. If the ribs are bruised or dislocated at all, pushing them back into their normal alignment will help as they heal on their own. Now, you hold still while I wrap them."

"Whatever you say." He gritted his teeth.

She laid the new sheerer cotton over the pad and began walking around him like he was a damn maypole. She kept lapping him, all while unraveling this fabric as he held the cotton pad tightly to his ribs. Though he had every intention of being the predatory insect in the scenario, it wasn't lost on him how quickly he became ensnared in her spider's web.

Fucking figured. His plan wasn't working. None of what he saw made any sense and the more laps she did around his naked chest, the more the urges to hyperventilate and run rose up inside him.

"You done yet, woman?" She had to be done. How much fabric could she fit in that little metal box anyway?

"What's the rush? After all, you came here under the impression you had an appointment with Mal, only to find out you didn't. I'm happy to mend you up since our horse attacked you, but it's no skin off my back if you reinjure yourself." She pulled the fabric taught with a final tug and smoothed over some adhesive bandages to keep it all in place. When she was finished, he did a quick twist to check the movement of everything.

Tight, yet more comfortable. He had no choice but to be grateful.

"Thank you." The words were bitter on his tongue. Her kindness was foreign and jarring.

"You're welcome, and the name's *Cami*. You can save the gender monikers for the horses." Her hands rested on her tiny waist, though he could hardly make anything out under that uniform she wore. The pop of a generous hip, though, was plenty visible.

"I'll see whether there's an extra work shirt you can use before you head out," she said as she stomped over to a side closet. Ah, so he *was* getting under her skin.

Before he could figure out his next course of action, a ball of blue fabric the same color as her attire hit him smack dab in the face. He caught it before it fell to the ground, but when he looked up, all he saw was Cami's backside as she stormed out of the stable. A *harumph* off to his right drew his attention. Turning his good ear toward the sound, he got an eyeful of the lovely Rosetta once more. Her lips were cast back in a snarl, revealing her large white teeth. She swung her head from side to side, flinging saliva every which way. Clearly, she hadn't yet warmed to him. No, that was putting it mildly.

The bitch was pissed.

As Dick stood there, half naked and clutching a shirt that wasn't his, in a building he didn't know, on a property he had never seen before, and with the only two creatures he'd met hating the sight of him, the cold panic finally sank in.

He was well and truly fucked.

CHAPTER 3

Cami fiddled with the trunk latch on her Honda Accord hatchback. The darn car was twelve years old and temperamental at best. Like everything else in her life, she was at its mercy. However, in this particular instance, she was already running fifteen minutes behind her usual fifteen-minute buffer window and was Not. In. The. Mood.

Whether it was her car or the space she called home for the last two years, Cami was a perennial cellar dweller. Every grueling effort had her straining to reach the next rusty rung of a ladder that she hoped would carry her out of her crummy circumstances. Too bad that ladder dangled an inch too high above her head.

Take her living situation. To say she lived in a studio apartment would imply that said apartment would actually be one of many styles to choose from: one bedroom, two bedroom, penthouse. As if she could have chosen the spacious one-bedroom next door with the dining room and galley kitchen but had gone with the studio because she preferred a more open concept. Hardly. Her ceiling consisted of steepled rafters crafted from oak logs, and her entire living space made up the giant cavern between the two bay windows on each side. Her couch, coffee table, bed, dresser, and small armoire were strewn about the narrow expanse of real estate like Tetris blocks vying for a decent fit.

She lived here, in a barely legal apartment above a maintenance barn, because she was broke. She only had a portion of her inheritance money to live off, and as an aspiring opera singer who had been studying the craft for the last eight years, she couldn't fall behind. Most opera singers who landed their first company role already had ten years of training under their belts at least, most of which were from private vocal coaches. Cami had no access to private vocal anything. When Cami's mother died, she'd been left with a meager inheritance, and her mom's good friend Mallory took her in. Mal offered her a barter deal living on her horse-breeding farm to enable her to continue working toward her dream of becoming a professional opera singer.

But, hey, the rent was cheap: free room and board on a farm about twenty minutes from the Sutherland Conservatory of Music in Rochester in exchange for night checks on the horses and a pervasive equine aroma on all her clothes no amount of detergent could remove. And all the manure-caked boots a woman would ever need.

She was well and truly blessed, for sure.

"C'mon, baby. I promise I'll find a way to get you those new tires you need if you just pop your hatch so I can get on the road. Please . . . " She groaned as the tips of her gloved fingers slid underneath the frozen metal handle. Reluctantly, the hatch popped open. "Yes! Finally!"

Cami offered up a silent prayer to the car gods for getting her on the road—and to help her figure out a way to come up with the money for those tires. Tossing her olive-green canvas bag in the back, she slammed the hatch shut and raced around to the driver's seat.

Man, her head was not in the game today. Her encounter with that Dick guy last night had unnerved her to no end. Where the heck had that guy come from anyway? Meeting with Mal, her left foot. Cami could count on one hand the number of times Mal had met with anyone after business hours who *wasn't* the vet. That was one of the many things Cami loved about the woman: her respect for clear and present boundaries. There was never anyone on the property during Cami's night checks.

And yet, this guy had shown up out of nowhere. In Rosetta's paddock. With no appropriate winter attire whatsoever. In February. Jeez, did the man not know about winters in upstate New York, where they got ten months of winter and two months of tough sledding? Hello! His clothes also reminded her of what old newsies with a paper route would wear, except he was much older. And more muscley. With facial stubble on a delicious cleft chin. And a smoking hot backside.

Gah!

She slammed her head back against the headrest. She tried to shake the image of Mr. Dick Stevens, but that had been an exercise in stupidity. Granted, it had been a good long while since she had spent any time with a male who wasn't either an equine or one of Mal's middle-aged biker friends, but still. The girl had standards. And no man who went around spouting "woman" left and right was anyone she wanted a piece of. It didn't matter how tight and right a hiney he had.

The man was a disrespectful jerk, clearly. And the better looking they were, the worse they were because they never had to be anything otherwise.

Her gloved index finger poked around for the ignition keyhole, but her scattered thoughts wouldn't settle on starting the car. Her normally logical, focused brain was not guiding her to put that puppy in park and hurry her late butt to the conservatory. No. Instead, her skin began to warm with thoughts of how heated Dick's torso felt as she wrapped the gauze around him. Circling in his orbit, his chest as hot as the sun . . .

"What the hell are you doing up so early? I thought your classes didn't start until eight thirty?"

Aaaaand just like that, her fiery daydream was doused by a five-foot-tall flannel-clad Mal standing next to the farm's bumper pull horse trailer. Mal's hip was cocked on Cami's driver's-side door, her boots firmly planted in the dirt. With a sigh, Cami let her car key dangle from the ignition and climbed out.

There was no hope of being on time, then. Darn.

"I had an early meeting with one of my professors. Mrs. Katrukova agreed to work with me privately for thirty minutes before her first class. Her son needs tutoring in algebra in order to make honor roll and I offered to help. It's another barter deal," she said, the door creaking in protest against the cold as she slammed it closed.

"Does Mrs. Katro-hoosy know you have a head for numbers the way I have a head for high fashion?"

Cami stared down at Mal's attire, which, sure enough, were layers of Brawny-man flannel on top of full-body long johns wrapped up in a very unpretty package of a thick leather, wool-lined overcoat. The coat had been a hand-me-down from one of her biker buddies, not cut for a short woman at all, and sat solidly at Mal's mid-calf when it should have been mid-thigh on a man. The tube socks sticking out the top of her mud-caked boots completed the lumpy package. But the woman definitely looked warm, to say the least, and that was all Mal cared about.

"Hell, how many times have I had to tell you not to leave so much money on the damn table for a tip when you eat out?" Mal went on, holding up a finger to highlight the example.

"Yes, I know, but—"

"And then there was the time you almost bottomed out your car when you overloaded it with the bags of supplements for the horse feed because you miscalculated how many bags you'd need." She ticked off another finger.

"That wasn't entirely my fault, though. I thought they were sold by the bucket! The clerk on the phone didn't tell me—"

"And just last week, you almost set your stomach on fire because you tried to double your chicken enchilada recipe but quadrupled the jalapenos by mistake." Another finger went up.

"All right, I get it! Simple math may not be my thing, but it's seventh-grade algebra. I think I can handle that," she said, arms crossed.

"If you say so. Why do you need private lessons, anyway? You're paying all that tuition for that fancy music program to begin with. Aren't they already teaching you what you'll need to know?"

"Yes, but that's not enough," Cami said with an exasperated sigh. "I'm in the ensemble for the conservatory's production of *La Sonnambula*, but I think I have a decent shot at the understudy role for the lead. I'm not nearly where I need to be for that, though, training-wise. And I can't get there without private tutoring. My classmates, they've all had private vocal training since they were in utero. The only way I can even hope to compete is to barter for coaching time."

Mal huffed out a snort and shook her head to the side. The white puffs of her breath reminded Cami of Rosetta when the mare was annoyed or bored. The resemblance was both comforting and ironic.

"Why you think those rich snots are better than you, I'll never know. Your mama always said your voice was like a songbird's. Money may grease the wheel of opportunity for some, but talent is talent. Plain and simple. You can't buy that."

"Yeah, well, it was also Mama who left me in the predicament I'm in," Cami grumbled, though Mal caught wind of it. Before Mal started running off at the mouth, Cami interjected. "No, I don't mean it's her fault. I miss her terribly, and not a day goes by that I don't wish she was here with me. Please don't give me that look."

At that, Mal's lips slapped shut, and she settled back against the car.

"I was just talking about that stupid clause in Mama's will, that's all." Cami dropped her chin into her scarf and toed some gravel with the tip of her boot. She hated talking about the loophole in her inheritance, but she also couldn't ignore her frustrations.

When her mother died in a car accident eight years ago, Cami had just graduated from high school. They had been two peas in the proverbial pod. Her mother had Cami on the younger side, at twenty-four, with no father to speak of ever entering the picture. The result? An almost older-sister-like relationship that was a giant mashup of all the authoritative family members in her life but interspersed with the fun and exuberant ones as well.

When she passed, an estate attorney had delivered the news that had even further changed Cami's life. As she sat in his office's pleather armchair a week after her mother's death, with Mal gripping her hand, the balding man had opened a copy of her mother's will and read the words that sealed her fate.

To my dearest Cami,

I have outlined the particulars of your inheritance here. Yes, what you've been told is correct. Upon my death, twenty percent of my worldly assets are yours to do with as you see fit. The other eighty percent will be waiting for you in a trust until you find your gem. Cami, I know you are capable of wondrous and brilliant things. I need you to learn, baby, that there is no shame in needing help to get there. Find your rock, my love. Someone to help you bear the weight so you can soar higher than any dream imaginable. The world is too big for you to carry alone. And when you find your person, there's not a thing on this earth that could stand in your way.

Love,

Mama

Cami recalled the attorney clarifying her mother's request. She'd had to ask a few times because it all sounded so absurd, but, nope, she hadn't gotten it wrong. The remaining 80 percent of her inheritance would only come due to her once she got married to her "gem," whatever the heck that meant.

"Your mama was just looking out for you, Cami. You know that. Now, I don't pretend to know her reasons, but she always had a strong sense of true north. Just hang in there," Mal said.

"Yeah, I know. Hey, maybe I should just find someone who's in a bind like me and offer a bit of my inheritance if they agree to marry me." She chuckled. "That would go a long way in fixing my problems. Heck, I know there are plenty of married couples out there who live separate lives. Gosh, can you imagine?"

No, Cami couldn't imagine. But the idea sure sounded nice. A win all around.

"Either the caffeine hasn't hit your brain yet or your noggin's too overcrowded with dumb shit daydreams to let any common sense sink in. Now, get your car out of the way so I can haul this thing over to the vet and get my stallion back on the farm," Mal said as she trudged over toward the truck's door.

"Love you, too, Mal!" Cami called after her, a smile creeping up her face at the way Mal chose to show her love. Ain't no warm and fuzzies coming from that woman.

Back inside her car, Cami turned the ignition and headed off down the driveway. As she turned out onto the main road, she racked her brain with what she could remember of middle school math. Something about A plus B equaling C.

CHAPTER 4

Exhaustion was a scary thing. It could claim a poor bastard despite his most stubborn wishes. He could throw water on his face, stare at the stun, run laps, and beat his body into the ground until it failed. But eventually, exhaustion would drag him under. The adrenaline coursing through his system would backfire. His body would be too fired up to be productive. His head would pound so fiercely there would be no hope of forming any rational thoughts. His muscles, strained and battered from the exertion, would give out.

Dick resembled all of that as he stared up at the wood beams lining the bunk bed above his head. At some point during the last eight hours, he must have hobbled over to the bunkhouse the lovely Miss Cami had directed him to, though he couldn't remember his legs making the journey. Everything from his toes to his earlobes melted into the thin mattress at his back. The morning sun peeking through the small window opposite his bunk hinted at the new morning, but his brain could hardly register the information. Logic told him he'd slept through the night.

Logic could go to hell. Where the fuck was he?

That thought got his ass moving real quick.

Aside from his boots, he'd slept in his clothes. He didn't need any more surprises sneaking up on him, and he wanted to get out of there right quick. Once his boots were laced, he grabbed his trench knife from under the pillow and tucked it into his sock before heading out the door. The morning was crisp, though thankfully nowhere near as cold as last night. Chilly drops of dew painted his leather boots as he trotted silently over to the stable where Cami had brought him last night.

The bunkhouse had been devoid of any helpful information. It was literally just that: a boarding house with a handful of made beds, a small kitchenette, and a bathroom. It was Army barrack basic, which he appreciated on some level. But the rest of him needed intel.

Huffs and grunts of penned horses rose up as he slowly pried open the barn door and stepped inside. The metal gears of the door groaned against the cold, the mechanisms operating with the same hesitation as Dick.

He had never spent any considerable amount of time in a horse barn before, and most of the things looked unassuming enough. However, there were plenty of things that rattled him to the bone. And that was no easy feat, considering his time in France during the Great War. But there was a difference between seeing a man lying dead on the battlefield, all life drained from his eyes, and seeing something his mind couldn't even comprehend. Death was a universal language: it looked similar across all channels. That barn, his encounter with Cami, all of it was completely foreign.

As in, not possible.

For the longest time, he just stood there, trying to get his bearings. He tried to let his wartime training take over, tried to trick his mind into following a list of orders and commands, but it just wasn't having any of that. The phone on the wall, for starters, was unlike anything he'd ever seen. When he walked over to examine it further, he couldn't make any sense of it. The black corded receiver, the shiny silver buttons with numbers and letters etched on them, the monotonous tone that emanated out of the headpiece when he lifted it off its carriage. On one level, he recognized it as a telephone because he'd seen Cami use it in such a fashion. But there was no waiting for an operator to connect her. And how the hell did she know what buttons to push?

When he finished examining the phone, he quickly backed away from the thing. His heart had started pumping too much blood to his body, he was sure of it. His breaths became quicker. The urge to run and hide took hold, but he tamped it down as best he could. In the light of the new morning, his brain had, thankfully, switched into survival mode.

Yes, he had questions. So many questions. But those had to wait. First, food.

Grateful no one else had come back to the barn yet, he scoured around and thanked whatever God had chosen to keep his sorry ass alive so long for the small barrels of apples and carrots tucked in near the fresh hay. He originally thought lack of food would be the biggest shock to his system . . . until he perused the barn's office near that black telephone.

The sun had barely begun to rise, but there was enough light that Dick could clearly see everything in front of him. There was a solid wood desk, which looked normal enough, but it was what was above the desk that threw the gut punch. Affixed to the wall was a board of cork, with several pieces of paper fastened across its expanse with thumbtacks. As Dick crept closer to the board, the blurry words began to come into focus. Numbers, weights, schedules began to sharpen. Until he recognized the dates.

Mare Breeding Record - Rosetta (February 1988)

2/21/88 - Resistant/Indifferent; palpate

2/22/88 - Interested; speculum

2/23/88 - Winks vulva, urinates; ready to be treated

The lists went on and on. Notes on horse temperament, diet, aggression. But one terrifying thing remained the same: the date.

In a panic, Dick yanked the board off the wall and laid it flat on the desk. His fingers were thick, and true, he wasn't much of a reader, but as his hands shakily drew lines under each entry of text, the pit in his stomach grew. He had to make sure, make absolutely damn sure he wasn't reading things wrong. His index finger settled on the final entry on the record in front of him. The dates were still all the same.

Those records were all dated for the year 1988.

Dick clenched his teeth as he stared at the date stamped across those papers. It mocked him. For no way in hell could it mean he'd traveled sixty-nine years into the future. The idea of time travel was laughable. A cock-and-bull fairy tale. Hell, it was more plausible that Dick would get hitched than magically shot through the decades. But how could he refute what was before him?

And even though he couldn't make heads or tails of any of it, he also couldn't ignore the mess he'd found himself in: no food, no shelter, no money.

He dropped the cork board the remaining half-inch onto the desk and jumped back, as if the thing were red-hot. Deep breaths were his saving grace as he closed his eyes and tried to slow his racing heart. His fingers found a warm home in the pockets of his pants. Such a simple action, tucking one's hands into their pants. It was a calming, casual gesture that both soothed the doer and gave the impression to others that everything would be all right.

If it were only that simple.

The backs of Dick's knuckles bumped against an apple he'd forgotten in his pocket. Content with the knowledge of where more were located, he allowed himself to crunch into it as he backed out of the barn. At least he could eat. He'd take that small saving grace before he turned his task to sorting through the muck that was his situation.

As he walked toward the small building Cami had told him was the main office, voices drifted over to him. He ducked around the building quickly, then peeked his head around so only the tips of his hair and his good ear would be visible, barely.

Cami was standing outside a vehicle, speaking to a short, heavyset woman. Mal, he presumed. As the conversation picked up, words and phrases reached him that weren't quite making sense in the context. Bartering? Marriage? But as their discussion sank in, pieces of the puzzle began to fit together, and Cami's circumstances began to take shape.

Dick hunkered down behind the side of the building as Cami drove away. The gravel cloud under her strange vehicle's tires plumed into a foggy haze. The other woman's massive vehicle and trailer weren't far behind as she exited the property right after.

He slammed his back against the rough brick wall and slid all the way down until his ass hit frozen dirt. His knees crept up close to his torso as he wrapped his legs in the large navy-blue overcoat he'd found in the bunkhouse. It wasn't as cold this morning as it had been last night, but that didn't stop him from rocking to keep warm.

That last thought knocked around Dick's skull for a few more cycles. A spark of an idea began to form as he glanced back down the gravel road where Cami had driven.

Cami.

He'd overheard her tell that woman Mal about how she had some inheritance, but something she'd only be able to touch once she got married. An inconvenience, apparently, but did it have to be? She'd joked about marrying someone to claim the cash, then kicking back some of the earnings to the new man in exchange for living separately.

On a shot, Dick sprang up from the ground so fast his half-frozen feet didn't have time to register the change in position.

Marriage. In exchange for money, shelter, and time to sort out his situation.

As Dick walked back to the bunkhouse, he cupped his hands against his mouth and blew warmth into them. When he rubbed his fingers together and blew again, the chill began to abate. A plan was forming.

He rarely had a problem getting a woman to say yes. And this would be no different. His cold day in hell was just starting to warm up.

CHAPTER 5

The brakes felt like sandbags under her boots as Cami coasted her Honda to a stop in front of Mal's office. She'd probably need to get those looked at, too. Add it to the frickin' list.

She could never catch a break in the money department, and boy, did she need one. Her tutoring lesson with Mrs. Katrukova had cast a bright spotlight on just how far she needed to climb. It was only a thirty-minute session, but it was enough to show Cami where she was and where she desperately needed to go.

During the session, Mrs. Katrukova's fingers glided across the piano keys and Cami kept pace, or so she thought. Her voice danced up and down the scales for her range without effort, and *that* was the problem. The high C was right there, the coveted high note for full-fledged sopranos, but try as she might, she couldn't grab the darn thing. When her voice crept into her upper range, it cracked. Her vocal cords gave up the ghost of a brief wail and sank back down to their underwhelming comfort zone. It was embarrassing, frustrating, and all sorts of defeating. The bored look in Mrs. Katrukova's eyes didn't help the situation.

Cami was wasting everyone's time.

Perhaps she hadn't been as warmed up as she should have been (thanks to Mal for her ill-timed lecture on how Cami sucked at math), but she could get there with the right training. And one or two thirty-minute sessions in exchange for algebra tutoring wasn't going to cut it. She needed cash.

But first, hot chocolate.

Her boots crunched across the frozen strands of straw strewn haphazardly along the path leading up to the main office building. The glass windowpanes of the front door were frosted over along the edges. That left small holes through which she could peer inside, though there wasn't a reason to. She knew what she'd find. This office was her second home.

And just like any good home, she kept it appropriately stocked with packets of instant hot chocolate, bags of mini marshmallows, and cans of whipped cream.

The bell above the door jangled as she walked in, announcing her arrival to all of no one. It was a little after one in the afternoon and Mal usually ate lunch in her apartment around that time.

Cami turned to throw her winter coat on the coatrack. Its massive weight threatened to topple the slim wooden rod, but the rack recovered its balance. She unwound her forest-green scarf from her neck, freeing her previously confined mass of curls from under its weight, and added it to the pile.

"That's a lovely color on you."

Cami whirled around so fast, her shoulder knocked into one of the coatrack's extended arms. The wooden pole went down, coat and all, but not before Cami attempted a rescue mission.

As she leaned forward to catch the neck of the rack, her balance gave out. The toe of her boot caught on the pedestal base. Her knee buckled and slammed into the wooden neck. She clenched her teeth at the crack of the impact. The rack crashed to the floor, its outstretched arm pointing at Cami's face as she tumbled toward it.

She squeezed her eyes shut, but the impact never came. Instead, something strong and solid wrapped around her midsection like a harness. The added protection stopped her forward momentum. Her face hung a few inches above the coatrack's arm, her nose barely kissing the ornately carved wood. As the blood rushed to her face, she glanced down at the supports holding her suspended.

Iron bars in the form of a man's arms trapped her in mid-motion. They were settled just under her breasts, in a way-too-intimate form of protection. The heat at her back seeped through her sweater and crept its way into her senses.

"Easy there, angel. Wouldn't want to wreck that pretty face of yours." The voice's low timbre needled its way into her psyche.

She remembered that voice.

The arms pulled her back and firmly placed her on her feet. The warmth around her receded. Goose bumps pebbled on her skin and every nerve ending nearly cried out at the loss of contact. Her body remembered him while her head tried its hardest to forget. Turning—though much more slowly this time, thank you very much—she came nose to chest with Dick Stevens. The man who was partially—all right, mostly—responsible for her frazzled morning.

"What are you doing here?" she barked out before realizing she should have probably thanked the man. But gratitude didn't have a time limit. She could still say thank you later. Besides, she was a little too consumed with the narrowly-escaping-sudden-death event that had just jump-started her heart. The darn thing was still running its paces as if it were a hamster flying through revolutions on its wheel.

"You told me to come back, remember? For my appointment with Mal." He stood a few feet from her. His presence in the room took over the standard-size no-frills office. The space had become a veritable shoebox. The confidence oozing off the man was infectious . . . and unnerving.

"Ah, yes, well, good. Hope you two had a good chat," she said as she bent over to poke at her knee. Yup, definitely going to be sore tomorrow. But thankfully, her kneecap still felt like a kneecap. No broken pieces or anything.

"Yes, we had a good talk, *thank you*." The words dripped off his tongue in a taunt.

Jerk.

"Oh, Cami! Good. You're back. I see you've met Dick." Mal trotted down the stairs that led from the woman's apartment. In her hand was a half-eaten tuna sandwich. Flecks of breadcrumbs sat on her bottom lip as she chewed.

"Yeah, we've met," Cami grumbled.

"Good. He's going to be our new stable hand for a few weeks. You hear about Gerry?" Mal squished another bite of sandwich into her mouth.

"Wait, what? No. He's still in Florida with his wife visiting her family, right?"

"Yup," she said around a mouthful of food. "And it looks like he'll be there for a while longer. Tami went into labor, so they're staying put. Her parents are over the moon to become grandparents, and I'm not going to be the one to pee in their Cheerios over the ranch being short-staffed due to their little bundle of joy. But luckily, Dick showed up at a perfect time."

At the mention of Dick, Cami's ears perked up, but not in a good way. More of how she would listen to the air slowly leaking out of her tire. She waited for the other shoe to drop.

"Dick mentioned he stopped by last night and had a run-in with Rosetta."

A pause. "Yeah." Waiting, waiting. *Get to the point, Mal.*

"I had just gotten the call from Gerry this morning, and Dick walked into the office right after looking for ranch work. Well, shoot. I don't need to be told twice about one door closing and another opening. Besides, the man's got muscles, don't ya, Dick? Can't argue with that." More munching from Mal. More panicking from Cami.

"Yes, ma'am," Dick said with a smirk, his arms clasped behind his back.

"Hired him on the spot. And the man was happy to deal in cash. Lord knows I hate getting Uncle Sam involved in my damn ranch. And since Dick's not from around here, he'll be staying at the bunkhouse until Gerry comes back. Dick, I know you already met Cami. She lives above the maintenance barn next to the stable and does night checks on the property. Girl knows everything about this place, so, Cami, I'll leave it to you to show Dick the ropes."

Cue screeching brakes.

"I'm sorry, what? Mal, I've got classes, schoolwork . . ."

"Not right now you don't. Go get Dick settled, and I'll check on everyone tomorrow morning. Welcome to O'Neal's Equine Services,

Dick." Mal walked over to the fridge, grabbed a soda, and marched back up the stairs.

As if she hadn't just left a smoldering pile of poop on the floor for Cami to clean up.

Cami darted her eyes over to Dick, who was still standing there with his arms braced behind his back, the corner of his mouth ticked up in that stupid smirk.

Well, her day was about to go from bad to worse.

And she never did get her hot chocolate.

Dick had never held much stock in fortunes. They were a crock of bullshit for naïve hopefuls who lacked the balls to do what it took to get ahead. But he couldn't deny how fortune favored the brave in his case.

He was in. At least, he had a roof over his head, a small stipend coming his way to cover meals, and more time with the lovely Miss Foster. It had been easy enough to meet with Mal. The workman's clothes he'd swiped from the stable passed him off as what he needed her to see. And fortunately, Mal was a talker. A short-staffed talker who had a giant hole in her roster that Dick was happy to fill. He hadn't had to say much. Probably wouldn't have been able to even if he tried.

As he walked out of the office behind Cami, he tried not to let the relief show. Tried to keep up his facade. When Mal first told him what the stipend was for a live-in ranch hand, his chin had nearly hit the floor. Mal was going to give him in one week three times more than the Army paid him in one month! But that thought was jarring, too. Had the value of a dollar changed that much in sixty-nine years? Perhaps he didn't need this marriage plot after all . . .

But he wasn't a fool. He had no idea if he could get back home. How had he even gotten here? And this Gerry person was sure to come back at some point. And then Dick would be out, along with the money. He still had so many questions, and his biggest foe was what he didn't know. What he did know, however, was that he needed a plan beyond the next few weeks. So, yes, a stream of inheritance and an on-paper-only marriage was still on the table.

"So Mal hired you just like that, huh?" Cami's singsong voice floated back to him as he followed behind her into the bunkhouse.

"Yeah."

She snorted as she turned to him, a hand on her hip. "That's all you have to say, then?"

He shrugged a shoulder. "What else is there to say?"

The wrong thing. Apparently, the wrong thing was left to say. And he knew he'd said just that by how she squinted her eyes at him.

"Look, Cami," he said, taking a step closer.

She backed up in equal measure. "Miss Foster is fine."

Dick grinned at the affront. Last night, she was Cami. Today, Miss Foster. He had no idea why getting a rise out of her was so rewarding. But he was good at the game, and he needed to lean heavily on his skills at the moment.

"May I speak frankly, *Miss Foster*?"

Her eyebrow raised at the question. "As long as you can do it quickly. I've got fifteen minutes to show you around before I need to get back to studying."

"What do you study?"

"If you must know, I'm an opera singer. Well, training to be one, anyway."

So, his angel did have a knack for song after all. But it wasn't lost on him how her defenses immediately went down. As if on cue, her body relaxed at the mention of her studies. She no longer forced the arbitrary empty space between them. Her feet shuffled forward a bit. Her shoulders dropped, and she loosely swayed a tad more.

"Is a singer not a singer?"

Her eyes, which had been focused down on her feet, rose to meet his. "Well, yes, I sing. But I'm not ready to sing with the pros yet. I'm training at the Sutherland Conservatory of Music in Rochester. I'm not attached to a touring company or anything yet."

"Professional or not, it sounds to me like you very much are an opera singer. It seems silly to discredit yourself based on semantics." Dick walked away from her and stood next to the rows of bunk beds against the wall. "So, you have aspirations to be part of a larger opera company, then? What's stopping you?"

The weight of the sigh that left Cami and traveled across the room bothered him. What burden was so immense that it weighed her down so much?

"That's easier said than done." Cami followed him over to the bunk beds and took a seat on a bottom mattress.

"Enlighten me, then. I'm curious."

Her head cocked to the side at his further prodding, but she obliged him. "Money. In order to get that good, you need access to extensive private vocal tutoring and begin your training when you're still in your teens. The training is rigorous but vital in the opera world. For most singers, it takes so long to get that good. I've loved opera my whole life, but I've never had the resources to train with the big guns. And don't get me wrong, I love Mal dearly." She raised her hands, palms open. "But this ranch, this gig, it's not my forever home, you know? And those private training sessions? Well, they cost money. Money I don't currently have. Though, hopefully, that'll change one day soon." She dropped her head, resting her elbows on her knees.

And there was his opening.

He grabbed a chair from a nearby desk and positioned it right across from her. "You know, I overheard your conversation with Mal when you were leaving this morning," he said as he claimed his seat, chair turned backward, his legs spread on each side.

Cami slowly raised her head. "What?"

How much should he reveal? Probably not too much. Keep things vague until he could cement his story more. "I was checking out the ranch. I don't mean to pry, but I heard about your circumstances with your inheritance."

There. He'd let that settle a bit. Gauge her reaction.

"What did you hear, exactly?"

"I heard how your mother is deceased—my condolences, by the way—and how there are stipulations in her will that prevent you from claiming your full inheritance. Well, one main stipulation, really: marriage."

Cami sat there, her eyes never leaving his. Her lower lip hung down slightly, and a deliciously cute wrinkle formed between her brows. Several seconds ticked by while they stayed like that, just staring in silence. Dick was a man of action, however. There was only so much doe-eyed shock and awe he could take, as charming as the look was on her.

Pushing off his knees, he rose to his full height and walked two steps closer to her. It would have been easy to intimidate her, scare her with the alternative outcome, threaten her to get his way. But standing there, looking down at the shocked, vulnerable expression on her face, he couldn't believe he was having a change of heart.

No, he didn't want to force her. But he *would* persuade her.

Dick squatted down to the floor so he was at eye level in front of her. His elbows were braced on his knees, his fingers dangling limply toward the floor. "I could help you with that arrangement," he said, the fingers of his right hand drifting slowly forward, an inch away from lightly brushing against the back of her hand.

"Arrangement?" she said with a stutter.

"Yes. A marriage in name only, which would result in you claiming your full inheritance. I would receive a previously agreed-upon portion, of course, and you would finally have the means to pursue your opera training. Become the most sought-after opera singer of your time and all that," he tacked on for good measure, his fingers waving for effect. "No messy talk of cohabitation or having a family needed. Just a strict business transaction. Nothing more."

Cami's eyes cast off about the room. The crease between her brows deepened. Could she seriously be considering it?

Dick stood and walked over to the other side of the bunkhouse, intent to let her stew over his offer while he inspected the rest of his lodgings. The toe of his boot barely crossed the threshold to the kitchen area when she finally spoke.

"But I don't like you."

Ouch. Not surprising, but it didn't matter. "You don't have to, angel. Just think about it."

"To be clear," Cami said, the quiver in her voice betraying her outward show of confidence. "You want me to think about . . ."

"Marrying me," he said, turning his neck to the side but never looking at her. Without giving her an opportunity to respond, he walked into the kitchen to examine the space.

If— No, *when* she said yes, it would be the easiest money he'd ever made.

If only getting back home would be so easy.

CHAPTER 6

Christmas trees. Definitely Christmas trees.

But not those beautiful Irving Berlin "White Christmas" Christmas trees. No, Sandy's earrings looked more like the sad Charlie Brown Christmas tree, with its lackluster foliage and underwhelming colors. As the soprano sang Amina's opening aria of *La Sonnambula*, pretending to gaze adoringly at her beloved Elvino, Cami couldn't take her eyes off Sandy's earrings. It was like a jewelry flashbang. Solid gold hoops the size of a baseball, with the gaudiest tree embellishments she'd ever seen dangling inside the hoops. But even from where Cami sat, the branches were lanky and sparse, not lush and jubilant.

The woman wore gold tree jewelry, for crying out loud. And *this* was the woman who would draw crowds to the theater and have patrons fawn over her voice.

Cami tried very hard to stifle her sigh from where she sat in the theater's third row with the rest of the students. She was in a foul mood. No, that wasn't quite right. Lions whose prey got away were in foul moods. An Upper West Side divorcée having a crystal chandelier delivered, only to have it drop and shatter by the deliverers, was in a foul mood.

Cami was fire-spitting pissed. George Patton had nothing on her and the vulgar vitriol that floated through her head. And that was saying something since Cami abhorred foul language. Her conversation with Dick from yesterday—did it even constitute a conversation when one just dropped a bomb and walked away without checking for casualties?—grated on her nerves. Try as she might, she couldn't shake the lingering temptation of his offer, as foolish as it was.

And then there was Sandy to deal with.

Sandy Projansky—yes, that was her real name—was the complete opposite of everything Cami admired in a leading soprano. Maria Callas, she was not. Sure, Sandy planned to go by her stage name, Sondra Progini, but that hardly did anything to gussy up the woman's attitude or class.

Sandy had been a thorn in Cami's side since Cami first enrolled in the program. Straight from jump, Cami's goal was clear: improve her range from a mezzo-soprano to a full soprano. The leading soprano sold tickets. The leading soprano got sponsorship deals.

The mezzo-soprano often played the best friend whose role occurred in the first scene and was not heard from again until the final bow. Yes, there were, of course, exceptions: *Carmen*, for one. But more often than not, the law of averages applied.

The mezzo-soprano got bupkis.

So, for reasons Cami was never able to comprehend, Sandy homed in on Cami's goal and, like a true diva, countered with a goal of her own: keep Cami in her place and make sure she didn't tread on the soprano's turf.

Which was why sitting there was such a torture session. Cami should be studying, practicing, not watching the conservatory's future Amina soar to new heights. It should be *her* up on that stage, darnit.

Anger and, yeah, jealousy, bubbled up something fierce. If she had to stay put in that tiny theater seat for another moment, she was liable to kick out like a mad donkey and destroy the furniture in front of her.

That would hardly be a way to make friends and influence people. *Mrs. Katrukova, can you please consider me for a soprano role? And, yes, I'll have those theater seats I destroyed promptly repaired.*

Ha.

Thankfully, the blessed aria ended a beat later. Muted claps from her classmates echoed around her. Sandy— *Sondra* did an obnoxious curtsy lower than was needed. Really, did her crotch need to be three inches from the floor to show her gratitude?

Cami scoffed as she began packing up her bag. She jammed her water bottle into the bag's side pocket and rushed like hell out of her row. Of course, her efforts were stifled by the bottleneck of classmates at the end of the row gabbing up a storm. The metaphor wasn't lost on her.

She was stuck, placed exactly where everyone wanted her to be. It didn't matter what *she* wanted or where *she* saw herself. She fit nicely into their little row, and it was up to the powers that be to move her this way and that as they saw fit.

As if on cue, the bodies cleared out, and Cami made her move.

"Oh, Cami! Are you running out so soon? What did you think of the aria?"

Crap.

As Cami turned, hiking the shoulder strap of her bag higher, she grinned her fakest, kill-'em-with-kindness smile she could at Sandy. The woman had her hair piled high and tied off with a pale purple scrunchie. Her black denim pants were formfitting, accented by her gold belt buckle, and the violet of her tucked-in button-down shirt brought out the blue in her eyes. Every long leg, smooth curve, and pink-painted lip on this woman stood out in stark contrast to Cami's smaller, flat-as-a-board, wild-haired mess.

And yeah, though she hated to admit it, the witch could sing.

"Hi, Sandy. Great job up there," Cami said and quickly turned around to head for the exit at the back of the theater.

"You know, I think Melanie is doing a great job playing Lisa. Did you not also try out for that mezzo role? I mean," Sandy said, leaning closer, "it's more *appropriate* for you, don't you think?" She smiled as she unscrewed the top of a plastic bottle filled with her yellow turmeric-infused water and tipped it back to her lips.

"I wasn't aware there were any inappropriate roles in this production," Cami said, trying her darndest to keep the venom out of her voice. She needed to leave. *Now.*

"Of course not. No, Vincenzo Bellini was a genius. Incredible how he had the forethought a hundred and fifty years ago to cast a mezzo as the betrayer and backstabber of the production. How Lisa tries to steal Elvino away from poor Amina." Sandy shook her head and tsked.

If Cami pulled her arm back just right, she'd have the perfect angle to clock Sandy in her perfect nose. The thought of *Sondra Progini* trying to hit those high notes with a broken septum was soothing, albeit temporarily so.

As the daydream began to clear, Cami registered Sandy stepping closer a second too late.

"Oh, my goodness! How clumsy of me!"

Cold, wet liquid splashed across Cami's long-sleeved beige sweater. Her chin dropped. Sandy's bright, yellow drink blossomed out into a pattern across Cami's chest. The water seeped beneath her sweater, then into and under her cotton bra. Droplets pooled under her breasts and trickled down her stomach to the waistband of her pants.

The wet sensation shocked her at first, but the sound of giggles and snorts delivered the second punch. As Cami slowly raised her head, Sandy had her dainty hand up over her mouth, doing her best to fake stifle a belly laugh. Others, as well, laughed and snorted before quickly averting their eyes and leaving the theater.

Cami took her bag, draped her coat in the crook of her arm, and raced out of the room. The frigid winter air hit her sweater, and the wet spots quickly turned to flash-frozen fibers against her skin. That was all it took for her conviction to cement itself.

She was done playing second fiddle. She wasn't going to lie around and live off the scraps of the Sandy Projanskys of the world.

Screw that. She'd blaze her own trail. She just needed the money. It was there. It was always *right there*. What was she so afraid of?

Heck, she'd buried her own mother when she was only eighteen and had been busting her butt working for Mal while studying opera ever since. She could certainly handle a marriage of convenience if doing so would make all her dreams come true. It was just a scrap of paper, anyway. A marriage in name only. A marriage that could give her the money she needed to soar.

But could she really do that, though? Honestly consider marrying a stranger for money?

Yes. Yes, she could. But this Dick Stevens character? With a voice that grated over her like gravel and melted her insides like butter over a hot biscuit? Who she'd only met two days ago? Jeez, the man gave her whiplash, rubbing her raw one minute while soothing the sting the next. No, the jury was still out on him. If she was going to do this, cooler heads needed to prevail. No decision worth making wouldn't benefit from a few nights of mulling things over.

Five days. She'd give herself five more days to weigh the pros and cons. By then, she'd have been around Dick for a full week. Surely, after that amount of time, her course would be clear and she'd have a better sense of things.

She walked to her Honda, content with her decisionless decision.

The yellow trigger in his hand was hardly the type of trigger he was used to. It was a long, curved piece of plastic that formed into the shape of his palm. The trigger had a neck, too, which snaked down into the belly of a wide cylindrical green bottle. The adhesive label on the bottle had bright yellow letters claiming "Natural Horse Fly Repellent." What *natural* meant was beyond him. He had no idea why Mal wanted him to spray the stuff on the horses, but he wasn't about to argue. Though, the smell of the beasts alone would certainly be enough to repel any kind of fly, horse or otherwise.

As Dick squeezed the yellow trigger, a fine spray misted over Martin, the stallion most recently returned from the veterinarian. The farrier would be paying him a visit later today, so Dick was to get the male bathed, dried, and sprayed with whatever this stuff was that Mal had instructed him to use in preparation for the visit. As he spritzed more of the solution on the horse's coat, a loud snort drew Dick's eyes upward.

Martin's white nose was a few inches away from Dick. The stallion tossed his head from side to side, almost throwing the reins from Dick's hand.

"Easy there, Marty boy," Dick said as he petted the white horse's long nose. He leaned forward, as if in private conversation. "I don't like the smell of this shit any more than you do. And between us boys, I don't think you need it. You're ripe enough on your own. But orders are orders. Now, this won't take long. Just a few more sprays and you can run around all you'd like."

A loud bang rang out across the field behind Dick. He turned with his right ear toward the noise but kept his hands firmly on the reins so Marty wouldn't spook. Dick hated surprises.

Though the surprise running across the field was certainly a welcome one. Cami had just slammed the door on her vehicle and was jogging toward him.

The last week of Dick's life had been nothing if not surprising. He never shied away from manual labor, and in truth, his muscles appreciated the exertion. The tasks on the ranch hadn't been too different or difficult from what he knew from back home. But the surprise he looked the most forward to every day was Cami. He worked starting right after sunrise, feeding and tending to the horses. At seven a.m. each morning, he had learned to make sure he was out watering down the dust in front of the stable. From where the garden hose was positioned at the side of the stable, it gave him a clear view of the front of the maintenance barn—and Cami as she ran down the steps of the barn each morning and straight to her car, always in a hurry.

He tried to tell himself he was just eager for her answer to his proposition. But if he was being even the slightest bit truthful with himself, and boy, did he hate any kind of inner-reflection, she was the only real tether he had to this world at the moment. As confused as he was, seeing her every day, in her routine, had begun to ground him. Something he could rely on each day when nothing of his new life was reliable.

"All right, Marty. Seems like you got off easy with the spray nonsense. Go have a run," Dick said to the horse as he removed the halter from around the beast's head. He gave him a light tap on its flank before Martin ran off into the paddock.

"Dick!" Cami yelled out across the way. Even from that distance, he could make out her light pants of breath.

He liked the sound of his name on her lips. Liked all her sounds, really.

"Dick," she said as she reached him, slowing to a light trot before stopping.

"I see you've got a handle on my name then, Miss Foster." He smiled.

"Oh, cut it out. Listen, I thought about what you said. About . . . the arrangement you proposed."

Dick didn't say a word. Just folded his arms across his chest, with the halter looped around his wrist. He needed to draw her out a bit more. As desperate as he was, he mustn't show it.

Thankfully, Cami noticed his silence and took the bait. "I'm in," she said, her chin jutted out in determination.

Dick's lip quirked up slightly, but he rubbed his nose and faked a sniffle to hopefully hide his tell. On the inside, though, his relief was immense. He would relish every win that came his way.

"Just so there's no room for misinterpretation, Miss Foster. *What are you in on?*"

Her eyes shifted to Martin trotting through the pasture, unbridled and unharnessed. Did she envy his freedom in that moment?

"Marriage," she said, turning her eyes back to him. "A business agreement where you and I enter into a marriage for the mutual benefit of my inheritance. I'll give you twenty percent in exchange—"

"Thirty percent."

"What?" Cami scoffed, her neck shirking back. "No. It's *my* inheritance."

"It's not yours at all unless you enter into a marriage agreement with me. Unless, of course, you've found another way to pay for your opera lessons." Dick was twisting the dagger a bit, but he needed to. He couldn't take a risk that the money wouldn't be enough. And he had yet to sort out the value of money in this time. He couldn't afford to sell himself short. Literally.

"Fine. Twenty-five percent," Cami said through tight lips. "And that's as high as I'll go. This money is all I have left of my mother, and even though I'm willing to give a portion of it over to you, I can't risk more foolishness beyond what I'm already agreeing to. God, and I can't even believe I'm doing that much." She rested her palm on her forehead, shaking her head slightly.

"Deal."

At his abrupt acceptance, Cami raised her head and nodded her approval. "But we live completely separate lives. As you said, a marriage in name only. Understood?"

He smiled as she threw his own words back at him. The tête-à-tête was thrilling. He admired how she stood up to him, especially given her stature. He was wrong to have judged her based on her size.

"Agreed," he said as he removed his thick leather glove and extended his palm toward her. Cami did the same, pinching the knitted fabric at the tip of each finger to reveal her hand. It was clear that both of their gloves did a poor job of thorough insulation because when she placed her smaller hand in his, there wasn't much warmth to share between them.

But there was something more.

As they both squeezed each other's fingers firmly in a handshake, Dick had somehow become rooted to this woman. But he couldn't stay. No, this was only a temporary arrangement, something to see him through this inexplicable circumstance he'd found himself in. And once he found his way back home, back to his time, he would be comforted in knowing their deal had enabled her to pursue what she loved. For once, his snide needling and coercion would benefit someone other than himself.

All that was left to do was marry a beautiful woman solely for her money.

CHAPTER 7

"What do you mean, we can't claim the inheritance?"

Cami hit another roadblock in her grand scheme to marry a stranger. Turned out, they had laws on the books that would prevent someone from marrying a stranger, as it were.

When Cami went to the city's Bureau of Vital Statistics a few days later to apply for a marriage license, the first snag she'd hit was Dick's surprising lack of knowing his social security number. For crying out loud. Who didn't know their social security number? But leave it to her to pick the one man who didn't.

Figured.

Dick had assured her he'd find the information. But to say she didn't really trust him to do so was on par with saying she didn't really trust a three-year-old to file her taxes. It was something about the questioning look on his face when she asked about it. The application for a marriage license was very straightforward: bride's name, groom's name, bride's place of birth, groom's place of birth, etc. When it came to the social security numbers, however, Dick had this curious look on his face. As if he had been caught off guard.

She had seen the man nearly get trampled to death by a wild in-heat Rosetta and he hadn't looked half as stunned as he had when she started going through the paperwork.

Something wasn't quite right, but she couldn't put her finger on it.

So she settled on plan B. She'd try to see if an engagement alone would be enough to satisfy the terms of the will. As if she could ever forget the wording, the exact language in the will rose up in her mind: *Upon my death, twenty percent of my worldly assets are yours to do with as you see fit. The other eighty percent will be waiting for you in trust until you find your gem.*

Cami latched onto the gray area in the wording. Surely "gem" was subjective, right? Yes, she recalled the stipulation of marriage, but what about an *intended* marriage? Would that be enough? It had to be enough. And Cami was prepared to argue her heart out to make it so. Until Mr. Donnelly, her mother's estate lawyer, took said heart and wrung all the hope out of it like a wet mop.

"Your mother's last will and testament clearly states that the remainder of your eighty percent inheritance shall be paid in full once you are married. And by law, Miss Foster, the only way one can prove marriage is by procuring a legal marriage license. Legal, mind you, as in signed by the bride, groom, two witnesses, and the officiant." Mr. Donnelly peered down over his glasses directly at Dick, who had been sitting silently in the cushy chair next to Cami.

Why, oh why, couldn't Dick have changed out of his work clothes? Cami stole a glance at Dick and sized up the standard farm-issued spare work duds he was currently sporting. It irked Cami to no end that the man only wore what the farm had on hand. Did he know those spares were in case his regular clothes became ruined or torn? Gerry never went through that many pairs of Mal's work overalls. Heck, his wife would have killed him to see him take advantage of Mal's resources in that way.

Yet the genius here didn't get it. God, would it have killed him to put on a pair of dress pants and a tie? Or, you know, at least clean the horse manure off his boots before he came in and stomped all over Mr. Donnelly's carpet?

As she continued to give Dick the sideways stink eye, some of the venom left her when she noticed how his broad shoulders filled out the flannel shirt he wore underneath the overalls. The straps barely seemed to fit over his chest, the metal clasps holding fast on a wing and a prayer.

She blinked the thoughts away and turned back to Mr. Donnelly. "Yes, I know the language. But I'd like to argue that my mother's little 'gem' line wasn't entirely clear. Might an engagement, a coming together of two people with the intent to marry, suffice? Isn't it just a game of semantics? Surely, my mother's intent is met. Dick and I would like to get married, but the delay in acquiring a license puts us at a disadvantage." Cami leaned forward in her seat and put on the best puppy dog eyes she knew how to wear. "We'd be able to have the wedding of our dreams, the wedding my mother would have always imagined for us, if access to my inheritance was granted *before* the nuptials. Please?"

Oh, she was laying it on thick. But the girl was desperate. If she wasn't supposed to be marrying the man next to her, she wouldn't have put it past herself to jump up on the table and flash some leg.

No, she'd never actually do that, but in her mind, she would resort to all sorts of Jessica Rabbit moments.

"Miss Foster, I'm afraid there's nothing I can do." Mr. Donnelly removed his glasses, rubbed the bridge of his nose, and closed the file folder in front of him. A stronger cased-closed message Cami had never seen.

She couldn't believe it. After all the internal back and forth, the abuse from Sandy, heck, even the vocal criticism from her four-legged friends, she had arrived at yes. Dick, by some miracle, had arrived at yes. And this man, who had all the intimidation of Mr. Rogers, said no?

She was fuming. Furious. Depressed. Exhausted. Defeated. She had ridden this roller coaster of emotions ever since Dick threw that ball toward her strike zone. She had sized it up, was so certain she could hit it out of the park. And when it was right in front of her, she swung with everything she had . . . and missed.

The floodgates Cami had held in check so tightly quickly opened. She dropped her head in her hands and let go.

———

Defeat was never something that sat well with Dick. Despite his injuries in the war, he was grateful he had at least earned them while his country came out on top. There were some wars, however, he couldn't win. Such as convincing Mr. Donnelly that Dick was worth bending the rules for in this case.

It wasn't lost on him how the man sized him up. The look of disgust, it seemed, transcended time. The man's eyes raked over Dick's appearance, his disapproval clear as he took in Dick's muddy boots (sure, let him think it was mud), his dusty hair, and, as always, his disfigured face.

Under normal circumstances, Dick would drink it in. In a past life, he would live off the judgment as if it was life-giving nectar. Eat it up to fuel his own vengeful appetites that always simmered below the surface.

But something had changed.

To his left, a crown of dark curls bobbed lightly as Cami tried to fight an onslaught of sobs. She had tried so hard. The dress she wore for the occasion was a bright red number speckled with tiny white flowers. It had clear buttons going down the front, a stark contrast to the brass ones he was used to, and delicate capped sleeves. A pair of white slip-on high heels finished off the ensemble. All of it was completely ridiculous to wear in February, but it was obviously important to her that she dress to impress. It showed her commitment to their mission. Showed her commitment to *him*. A hollow pang thrummed in his chest at the thought. The feeling was there, though he barely recognized it anymore. Commitment, loyalty, those were all sentiments he'd crushed long ago, relegated to the depths of his emotional catalog. The disturbance was uncomfortable, but in a good way. The same as when he'd work his muscles after a long period of inactivity. A welcome change of pace.

Like hell he'd let a paper pusher derail their train.

Dick pushed off the armrests of the chair and stood to his full height. What did he plan to say? Hell if he knew, but whatever his dim-witted mind would come up with would no doubt be more menacing if delivered from a position of height. Maybe he'd even flex a biceps or two if it would help the little toad behind the desk take a hint. Before he could even roll his sleeves up, said toad began croaking.

"All right, all right, Miss Foster. Please, none of that, now," Mr. Donnelly said, a previously undetected stammer making itself known between syllables. His eyes locked on Dick's stature, and yup, that stammering got a whole lot worse. Mr. Donnelly's Adam's apple bobbed on a gulp before his eyes shifted back to Cami.

"Look, I knew your mother. She was a lovely woman, and it was an absolute tragedy when she died, with the car accident and all. I wouldn't wish that on my worst enemy." His eyes landed back on Dick. He hunched back farther in his chair, as if bracing for impact.

Good.

"I'm sure Miss Foster would appreciate what you have to say, Mr. Donnelly. Like she said, this would mean a great deal toward honoring her mother's memory," Dick said.

A great sigh left Mr. Donnelly's chest. Dick knew a sign of defeat when he saw one, though he kept his mouth shut on the subject. He was never one to hold out for hope.

"Miss Foster, here's what I can do," he said in hushed tones. "I am willing to offer you an extension of good faith."

At that, Cami's head slowly rose. "What do you mean?"

The tip of her nose had turned pale pink. The phrase "cute as a button" came unbidden to Dick's mind. He quickly brushed it off and turned his attention back to the lawyer.

"What I mean, Miss Foster, is a show of trust. I will take the steps required to settle your inheritance and expedite the funds to you. But," he said, his finger raised, "you *must* produce a legal application for a marriage license no later than thirty days from now."

The scraping of the chair legs next to him jarred Dick out of his daze. Had the man really just said yes? Beside him, Cami was already on her feet, a bouncing ball of energy. Christ, her mood swings would give him whiplash at this rate.

"Oh, thank you thank you thank you, Mr. Donnelly! You won't regret this, I promise." Her hands were clenched in front of her in a combined fist pressed so tightly Dick thought she intended to crack all of her knuckles at once.

"*Thirty days*, Miss Foster. After that, it all goes back into the vault, so to speak. I mean it. I'm risking a good amount of my professional reputation on this gamble," he said, pulling out a piece of paper from his desk drawer.

"You won't be sorry, I promise. Yup, in thirty days, we'll have that marriage license application. Don't worry. Right, Dick?"

Her bony little elbow to his ribcage brought him back to the conversation.

"I'm sorry, what?"

"I *said*, in thirty days, we'll have that marriage license application, and Mr. Donnelly shouldn't worry. Right?" she said through gritted teeth.

"Oh, yes, right. Of course." Dick nodded.

"Please fill out this form with your banking information, Miss Foster, so I can expedite the bank draft to your account. It will take seven business days for the money to be deposited."

As Cami took the lawyer's pen and scribbled away, the stone in Dick's gut began to settle. A big reason for their application's original delay had been his lack of preparedness to provide certain details about himself. His date of birth, for one, would be a massive red flag. He doubted a court clerk would overlook the fact that he was nearly over seventy years older than his bride-to-be.

What would he list for a residence? The farm, he supposed, but that was temporary. How accurate did the recorded information need to be? Would they easily detect falsehoods? Christ, if he were back in 1919, he would have no trouble with this at all. He knew at least a dozen forgers who, for the right amount of money in their palm, would provide any documentation or credentials Dick would need. And they were highly convincing copies, too. Here? He had nothing. Not even one of those social security numbers Cami was asking him about.

Cami shook Mr. Donnelly's hand in both of hers as she took a stack of papers and walked toward the door. He mindlessly followed, acutely aware of the giant predicament he'd found himself in.

He had just become married, so to speak, and the money coming their way would safeguard both of them for the immediate future.

The only snag being that he didn't actually exist in this future. And how long would it be before the cards holding up his delicate house came crashing down?

CHAPTER 8

The shade of red Cami picked out for her toes was perfect. It reminded her of the red dress Carmen would wear when she was ensnaring the young infantry officer Don José. As Cami blew on her toes, the crumpled-up tissue spacers protecting against smudges, she reflected on the most iconic operatic work ever written for a leading mezzo.

And she hated it.

Yes, the melodies were entrancing. Yes, there was the Habanera, *the* song that became so ingrained in popular culture, the younger generation recognized it more for its appearance in commercials than on stage. But it was so . . . expected for someone like her, with a vocal range like hers. She yearned to do the unexpected, to command the stage with the same authority and prowess previously reserved for the leading soprano.

Well, screw that. Not anymore, thanks to her mother's inheritance. And, well, she supposed she should thank Dick also. Though that was a bitter pill to swallow. Twice now she owed him a thank-you. Yet, the words couldn't come. And she couldn't put her finger on why.

Cami stood and, toes up, hobbled over to her boom box. She plucked out the cassette tape in there, replaced it with *La Boheme*, and plopped back on the couch. When Mimi's lyric soprano notes wafted over her, Cami gave into the moment and sang.

She didn't worry about her perfect form, or lack thereof. Lying on her back with her feet up and her eyes closed, she opened her mouth and let the aria take over. In those precious private moments, she was on stage. Behind her own eyelids, she commanded the music. Her diaphragm contracted at the right moments, her lungs filled with breath. The melody floated through her apartment, the soft warbles of her voice accenting the perfect places in the more-than-a-century-old Italian libretto. Her lips quivered and her eyebrows crinkled as she sang *adagio*. A brief pause for the orchestra to enliven the moment, then she opened up and soared.

Mimi's love for Rodolfo.

Amina's love for Elvino.

Cami's love for—

A loud banging sliced through her aria. Cami cut off her singing and popped up, hobbling over to the boom box. She jammed her finger on the stop button.

"I'll be down in a minute!" she hollered, annoyed beyond belief that her smooth lacquer might get smudged. Was she a dolt for painting her toes in February? Well, she hadn't planned on going anywhere else that evening. Cami had managed to bang out her night checks early, and with her radio clock reading 8:32, she was supposed to be in in in. Not hop hop hopping over to her bed under which she stored her summer sandals.

"Well, that wasn't what I expected to see when I got up here."

Cami was on her hands and knees, head tucked under her bed, tush in the air, and toes suspended precariously above the rug. At the sound of Dick's voice, she yanked her neck to the side and got a forehead full of bed frame.

"Ow!" A dull pounding took up residence behind her eyes as she flung her hand over her head. "Ugh, what the heck are you doing up here? I said I'd be down in a minute. And that's a private entrance downstairs, mind you. You don't see me hoofing it over to the bunkhouse at all hours of the night just to sit on your couch and watch TV, do you?"

Cami stood up, flip-flops in hand. She carefully removed the tissues from between her toes and nudged on the sandals.

"I didn't want to wait." Dick shrugged. "And I'm glad for the choice. I very much enjoyed your little hands and knees number. What's on your toes?" He jutted his chin toward her feet.

"I painted them."

"Why?"

"Why does anyone paint their nails? Because I wanted to. What's it to you, anyway?" Cami popped her hands on her hips.

"Seems odd, but I'm not up to date with the latest beauty trends." Dick walked farther into her apartment.

"Oh, no, you don't! You take those boots off right there, buster. I just cleaned these floors. And I don't recall saying you can make yourself at home, but since you're just going to do it anyway, go ahead."

"Thank you, angel." Dick smiled as he kicked off his boots, shucked his coat, and threw it on top of the pile by the door.

"What's with the nickname all of a sudden? Last I checked, nicknames are hardly needed for the marriage application," she said, crashing down onto her couch. Dick occupied the love seat to her left, though with him sitting on it, there was definitely no room for two. "And why don't you ever wear your own clothes? You've been shacking up in the bunkhouse almost a week and a half at this point. I can't believe you'd be such a moocher to only wear Mal's spare work clothes. Don't you have any of your own?"

Again, he wore another plaid flannel button-down shirt. Though at least he was out of the overalls. He was in regular denim jeans today.

She hated how good he looked in them.

Dick sat there, his left leg crossed with his ankle resting on his right knee. His elbow draped casually against the armrest, and it was infuriating. His presence in her tiny loft seemed to suck all the air out of the space.

He refused to answer a single one of her questions. The man was made of Teflon. Anything she fired at him just slid off and settled at his feet. She sat there, fuming, and waited for answers.

Nothing.

"Say something!" Cami sprang off the couch, her arms flung wide. When the smirk on his face remained, she gave up and stormed over to her kitchen area—for she didn't actually have a kitchen. No way in hell she'd let this man ruin her evening ice cream plans. He'd already intruded on that sacred ritual once before.

"What were you singing?"

That stopped her mid-scoop. "Oh, so he can speak. Lovely." Back to scooping. "If you must know, it was Puccini's *La Boheme*. It's one of my favorite operas." She lifted the scoop to her mouth and licked off an errant chocolate chip before putting the lid back on the tub.

"So, you booked those lessons then?"

"Yeah, I did. Beginning next week, I have daily afternoon sessions at the conservatory. Two hours a pop."

Again, she needed to thank him. Crap. She hated feeling guilty.

"Look," Cami said with a sigh, still staring down at her slowly melting bowl of mint chocolate chip. She couldn't face him. Not yet. "I know I don't always show it, but I'm grateful for, well, I'm grateful to . . ." The words were there, but she just couldn't get them out. She took a deep breath. "I'm just grateful. That's all."

Once the words left her, she felt lighter. No, they weren't sappy (thank God), and they didn't make her vulnerable. They were simply the truth. Why had the truth been so hard with Dick?

She turned around, ice cream bowl in hand, and was met with the press of warm, soft lips against hers.

What's with the nickname all of a sudden?

Why don't you ever wear your own clothes?

Dick was sure the thrumming inside his chest was so loud, it could be heard clear across the field. With every question Cami fired at him, every accusation he couldn't combat, his defenses were chipped away. She was peeling back layers he wasn't prepared to reveal.

His head—well, both of them, he supposed—fought back in the only way he (they?) knew how.

When she was at the counter, with her back turned to him, his body took over. Amazing how everything about her drew him in. He had been outside in the field, heading back to the bunkhouse, when he heard her singing through the window. It was arresting, harrowing. Being near that voice, knowing who was commanding it, well, he couldn't have passed by it if he'd tried.

Then, when she got her back up, she was stunning. Breathtaking. All fire and fury in a delectable little package.

Dick was already waiting when she turned around. Like a viper, he bent down and snatched those delicious lips in an instant. Cold, minty lushness assaulted his senses. Gently, which was an exercise in patience as he was not a gentle man by nature, he massaged her mouth with his own. Soft kisses fluttered between them, him trying his damnedest to do no more than peck and lightly prod. No, he would not be a beast with her. He just needed to take her mind off her attack-dog line of questioning.

But, oh, he wanted more. How would she respond to the slight slip of his tongue along the seam of her lips?

Before he got the chance, she pulled away. "What are you doing?" she panted.

But Dick could clearly tell the fight had gone out of her. Their foreheads still touched, and his fingers rested softly on the sides of her hips.

"Again with the questions, Cami. Can you not just live in the moment?"

"Not when the moment is melting my ice cream."

He chuckled, taking the cold bowl out of her hands and placing it on the counter behind her. "I owe you a bowl of ice cream, then," he said, smiling.

Cami stared up into his face, that crinkle appearing in her brow again. He knew the sign: more questions were coming. Before she could fire more his way, he interceded.

"Cami," he said, putting his finger over her lips. "I know you have questions, and you're right to have them." He removed his finger once he was content she'd remain silent for a moment. "We're in this together now. Trust me to get you what we need to secure the marriage license application. That's all you need from me. The rest is not relevant to our arrangement."

"And what about that kiss? That wasn't part of the arrangement."

"No." He raised his hand up to rub his thumb along her jawline. His eyes traced his hand's movements, the curve of her lips, the slope of her nose, the ice blue of her eyes. "But contracts often have bonus addendums."

He lowered his mouth to her neck. The soft spot behind the lobe was a particular favorite nibbling location for Dick. But on Cami, she all but melted when he kissed her there.

He snaked his arm around her slight waist and pressed her flush against his body. As if the protest office had closed for the day, Cami gave in to his ministrations. She slackened a bit in his arms, and her head lolled back slightly. Her eyes fluttered closed, and her mouth parted on the next exhale.

"I like bonuses," she said on her next breath, "but I still have questions . . . Oh . . ."

He smiled against the slender column of her neck as he kissed his way down and over to the hollow of her throat. He fought back his urges tooth and nail. What he wanted was to strip her bare and bend her over the back of the couch. What he wanted was to wrap her hair around his fist and pull at the same time as he pushed into her. What he wanted was . . .

Not to be that animal with her. With Cami. His angel.

In his own time, he'd been a barbarian with women. He'd given no qualms about abusing them, defiling them. Hell, many of them loved it. Loved him. Sought him out for what he could do, *would* do.

But he didn't want that anymore. Didn't want to be seen as that hellish beast in this time. By some miracle, he had been given an opportunity to start over. And while he worked to figure out the whys and hows of it, he wouldn't look the gift horse in the mouth.

The urges were still there, though. The temptation. Being this close to Cami's skin, his fingertips mere inches away from the edges of her clothing, the urge called to him. Just a bit higher and he could tear her shirt to shreds. A firm tug and he'd have her open to him and unable to move. It was all so close, so easy.

He jerked back from her, dropping his hands to his sides. He couldn't do this. Couldn't be that man with her. Shaking, he ran to where he'd thrown his boots and coat.

"Dick? What's going on?" Cami watched him scramble for the door as he threw his feet in his boots like the floor was lava.

"I have to go," Dick rushed out. He hadn't even bothered to lace up his boots before he flew down the stairs, ran through the maintenance barn, and made it to the fresh open air beyond. Once outside, he bent over, braced his hands on his knees, and sucked in great gulps of frigid winter air.

Quickly, the chill of the night began to seep into his body. He never bothered to put on his coat. The poor thing sat tossed aside on the grass, a sad shell of denied warmth. Dick's skin began to prickle from the cold. Tingles raced up and down his spine. His lungs hurt from the effort to breathe deeply.

He needed the pain, needed the distraction.

Because with that single kiss, Camilla Foster had just cracked his soul wide open . . . and he had been found wanting.

CHAPTER 9

Baltimore, MD - 1896

"He's yours now, Archie."

The thud of the valise hitting the worn wooden floorboards of his father's apartment was so loud, it rattled Dick's teeth. He couldn't imagine why it made such a heavy sound. All his mother had allowed him to pack were a few clothes, his tin soldiers, and his jacks. Was there something else in there his mother had managed to sneak in? Some sweets, perhaps?

"What are you on about, Ada? I spend my time with the boy just as we agreed." His father, who he saw about once a month, leered over at him.

Dick's mop of blond hair went every which way on his head, and his suspenders barely held up his pants. At five years old, he was growing so fast, his mother always commented he'd shoot through the ceiling if he didn't slow down. Perhaps his father didn't like him so tall? Dick looked back and forth between his mother and father. Yes, he was nearly up to his father's chest now. He nibbled his lip, unsure whether he should be proud of his growth.

"I've had an offer from a man who's been calling on me. He went to speak with my father earlier this week to ask for my hand. I'm sweet on him, Archie, and he doesn't know about little Ritchie. Father thought it best to keep him a secret. It would only scare away the suit-ors," Dick's mother said, her eyes cast down toward the floor.

Archie grunted as he walked toward the coffee table where a small glass with amber liquid sat. He lifted it to his lips. The glass left a wet ring behind on the wood. "Your father thinks he can hide the truth forever, does he? That others will never find out his innocent little Ada enjoyed herself too much with a scoundrel like me and became a mother at sixteen? So, what? You'll just abandon him, then? Is that the answer?"

Dick feared to look up at his father. He hated when the man drank the amber liquid. A few times, his father would drink milk with him at breakfast and cut Dick's toast into funny shapes. He always loved that. Maybe there was some milk in the kitchen Dick could find. Would that make his father happier?

"Oh, enough," his mother said, her gaze rising to meet his father's. Her voice got louder, the way it did when Dick left his toys out. Dick always got upset when she yelled like that. "My parents have taken me and Ritchie in. Cared for us, despite my foolishness and your lack of interest in making me an honest woman. So when Louis made an offer to my father, what was he to say? 'No, you can't marry my young, compromised daughter whose bastard son the family is rais-ing'? Oh, please," she said, crossing her arms as she rolled her eyes.

"I'm not fit to raise a boy. You damn well know that," his father growled out.

"Well, I wasn't fit to become a mother when I wasn't even out of my adolescence, was I?" She fumbled around in the pockets of her skirts. Did she have peppermint sticks tucked away in there again?

"So, that's it, then? You're just going to up and leave? What'll the arrangement be? Hmm? Are you so callous a mother you'd abandon your own son for the sake of bettering your own damn life, woman?"

Father was using swear words again. Gosh, how he hated when his father drank those drinks. Dick wondered if he should walk over to his father and give him a hug, try to make him feel better. He hated it so much when they argued like this. He was about to walk over when his mother threw an envelope on the floor at his father's feet.

"There's your arrangement, Archie. You should have enough to provide for Ritchie for some time . . . clothes, food, and the like. Provided you don't piss it away on whiskey and women."

His father kneeled down to pick up the envelope with the paper money inside. He never looked back up, just stayed crouched on the floor, his eyes on the envelope in his hands. "You're really leaving."

"Yes, I am." Dick thought he heard his mother sniffle like Dick did sometimes when he was trying to be brave but didn't really want to be. "I know you'll care for him, in your own way. And when enough time has passed, I'll come find him again. This is hard on me, too, you know. But my choices were taken away from me the moment I let you get under my skirts."

Before Dick could ask why his mama might be crying—because when Dick sniffled, it was usually because he was crying a lot, too— she turned and walked out the door.

———

"Nooo!" A guttural scream tore through Dick's throat. The sound shocked him awake. His eyes sprang open. His chest heaved in great gulps of air. A sheen of sweat coated his bare chest, and the sheets beneath him were damp and sticky. After a few more deep breaths, he registered his surroundings.

He was in bed at the bunkhouse, not his father's apartment. His legs were tangled in his bedsheets, not poking out the bottom of too-short trousers. Pressing his chin to his chest, he took in the expanse of his upper body, the strength of his arms, the hair speckled across his torso. He was not a five-year-old boy anymore, but a twenty-eight-year-old man.

Who no longer resided in Baltimore, Maryland, in 1919, but in Rochester, New York, in 1988.

It was just a dream . . . No, a nightmare, then.

Content that the horror show had passed, he swung his legs out of bed. He bent his elbows on his knees and let his hands catch his heavy skull. His fingertips tried to massage away the pounding in his head. Christ, why was there so much knocking around up there?

He hadn't thought of his mother in years. Yes, once he reached manhood, she had reconnected with him. Hell, he'd even spent the occasional days with her, and for what it was worth, he got on moderately well with some of his step-siblings; Helen, for example, he adored. Though his mother's rejection and betrayal still cut deep. Sure, the wounds had scarred over, but the affliction below the surface was always ripe for reinfection. What was it about him that allowed a mother to so easily cast aside her son? It gnawed at him to this day how he hadn't been enough for her. Even still, he could never bring himself to do what she did to him. He couldn't cut her out completely. So why would his brain pick the worst day of his boyhood to invade his dreams?

On shaky legs, he rose out of his bunk. He needed to clear his head. Plus, if he was being a little honest with himself, a part of him was afraid to go back to sleep. Would he return to where he'd left off in his dream? He was a man now. Had half his face blown off in a damn war, for Christ's sake. He was well past childish hurt feelings.

He grabbed a flannel shirt draped over the back of a chair and threw it around his shoulders, but couldn't be bothered with the buttons. He padded toward the front door, the sweat from the bottoms of his bare feet leaving light footprints across the wood. The bracing cold metal doorknob in his palm was a welcome tincture, promise that the frigid air outside would go far to revive him.

The front porch of the bunkhouse ran from edge to edge along the building's face. A traditional white ranch fence with three rails encased the worn porch. Dick rested his weight on his elbows as he leaned over the fence, looking out into the pasture.

The cold air was biting but welcome. His feet and bare chest took the brunt of the elements, but that was just fine with him. He welcomed the feeling, any feeling that wasn't shame and betrayal. As he mulled over what few childhood memories he had of his mother, a flash of light off to his left caught his eye. Funny because he almost never noticed anything coming from his left side . . . his deformed side. Yes, while his vision in that eye was fine, his left ear's severely diminished hearing still gave him a handicap. Though it'd be a cold day in hell before he ever admitted it to anyone.

The horses were penned for the night, so there shouldn't have been any movement across the field.

Unless you're a jackass falling through time and you land in a horse pasture where a bitch-in-heat mare almost makes you a eunuch.

A chill tingled down his spine as he shook off the memory of Rosetta's advances.

His eyes skated across the dark landscape, scanning for the light he thought he'd just seen. The moon was high, so perhaps its beams reflected off something. But, no, there was nothing nearby except the stout trunk of an oak tree, and certainly nothing metallic off which a beam of light could be reflected. As Dick eyed the tree's massive expanse of branches, another movement drew his eyes back down to the trunk.

The air around the tree's base began to ripple, dancing like summer's heat radiating off asphalt. The tree's trunk became blurry, as if it stood behind an Army convoy and was engulfed in fuel exhaust heat. As Dick squinted harder, his brows furrowed in uncertainty, a slight figure stepped out from behind the tree.

There. That was the light he saw a moment ago. But it was coming from a woman.

And he recognized her. Well, aspects of her.

Streaks of silver in a mass of otherwise honeyed curls reflected the moonlight back at him. They were long, past her shoulders, but not unruly. More controlled chaos. He leaned farther over the railing, his breath coming out in pants of white mist. Paint chips began to dig under his fingernails as he gripped the wood more tightly.

The distance between them prevented his detection of distinct facial features, but from the shape of her face and the build of her body, he knew.

God, the woman looked like Cami. But not quite. The hair color was off, and this woman clearly had some years on her. But he couldn't ignore the resemblance.

So he ran.

Dick turned around inside the front door to throw his feet into his boots kept by the entrance. Fuck the laces. Whirling around, he leaped off the three porch steps in one stride and bolted across the field. If he felt the cold before, he sure as shit didn't feel a thing now. Cold air assaulted him every which way, but he was on fire.

"Hey! Wait!" he screamed, pumping his arms as the woman's image blurred more in the distance. But with how hard he was running, anything would look blurry. He was about a hundred paces out when he noticed her hand resting on the trunk of the tree next to her. The hand didn't look solid, though, but rather had wisps of white mist dancing around it, licking at her fingers.

When he began to slow down, those same white wisps engulfed her entire body, as if every pore of her skin were exhaling into the cold night.

Well, didn't that make him slow the fuck down right quick.

Before he could register what he was looking at, the woman turned her head toward the maintenance barn. Confused, he glanced back to where she was looking. The lights in the barn were dark, except for the safety lights Cami had told him about. Above the barn, equally as dark, was Cami's apartment. A total lights-out situation with nothing to see there.

"Lady, if you need something, tell me what . . . " he said, turning his head back to address her. But she was gone. The only remnants of anything were barely visible puffs of breath floating in front of him.

"What the . . . ?"

Dick stumbled forward, entering the space where the woman had just stood. Spinning in a circle, he looked at the ground for clues to how she could have vanished. Because that was what happened, right? A quick jog around the tree turned up nothing.

She wasn't there. But, Christ, Dick *knew* he'd seen her. Why the hell else would he have run out of the bunkhouse in the middle of the night with hardly any proper clothes on?

Frustrated, he clenched his fingers in his hair and squeezed his eyes shut. After a moment of trying to level out his breathing, he opened his eyes . . . and his stomach nearly bottomed out.

There, directly on the tree trunk in front of him, was a smattering of light-green dust.

A niggling memory tickled the back of his mind. Hesitant yet curious, he walked closer to the trunk. The green dust was like a homing beacon, something he was called to regardless of the why. Cold wind whipped at his bare skin as he squatted down to the ground. The smudge on the tree was mere inches in front of him. Of its own accord, his index finger floated up and hovered above the smattered dust.

The memories came back to him in a rush. Fear and confusion had clogged his senses the moment Jacob Bellamy had tossed him into that well. The hollowed-out pit in his stomach returned as he recalled the helplessness of falling to his death. The claustrophobia of the well's walls around him, choking his breath and his life.

His finger hovered closer to the tree as jarring tremors snaked up his body. Though they weren't from the cold.

The healing abrasions on his legs still throbbed at the memory of having been rubbed raw, almost sanded down, when Bellamy tossed Dick into the well, headfirst. The entire front of his body, though clothed, had been brutally scraped along the frozen surface of the well's outer stones as he was upended into the cavern. All manner of muck and grime had coated his pants when he fell.

But when he had looked back up at the surface, marveling and pining for his final view of the moonlight before darkness descended on him, a hint of green on his pants caught his eye.

Pale. Shimmering.

He had brushed his fingers through it.

Right before he'd passed out and woken up sixty-nine years in the future.

CHAPTER 10

The heat of his fingertips had seeped through her T-shirt. It'd been barely a touch, but she was surprised the pads of his fingers hadn't incinerated the fabric clean in two. Every near-contact point was an inferno. And her lips and neck, the places on her body where he'd *actually* touched her?

Super-bloody-nova.

She should have been paying attention to James's performance as Elvino. Should have been waiting for her cue to sing with the rest of the ensemble assembled at the back of the stage. It was creeping toward the end of the opera. Normally, she liked it when they did the full opera rehearsals. Breaking it up into sections just killed the momentum and music for her. But this time, she couldn't give a fig about the music.

The only melodies floating through her head were the moans she recalled herself making under the onslaught of Dick's searing kiss.

But it wasn't supposed to be like that. They had agreed. *Agreed* that their marriage arrangement was an on-paper-only objective. They weren't a real couple with real feelings, real intimacies, or real physical inclinations that happened because they lived on the same property. And saw each other every night as she was doing night checks and he was cleaning tack. Or each morning when he was feeding the horses and she was leaving for her tutoring sessions.

Nope. This was a marriage of convenience. Nothing more. And besides, he was an absolute bear. Yes, she needed to remind herself of that little factoid. Keep that little gem front and center. He was crass, arrogant, and didn't care a whit about anyone else's feelings. And he was extorting her out of her inheritance! Well, no, not really because she'd agreed to it and it was a mutually beneficial arrangement. But still! It was a miracle the horses even tolerated him. Didn't animals have a sense for nasty people?

But Mal loved him. Probably because his mouth was just as foul as hers, so they spoke the same language in that regard. And Gerry was still firmly situated in Florida with no official return date, but hopefully, that would change soon. So, Dick was sticking around for a little while longer.

These thirty days were going to be a monumental test of willpower, for sure. No way would she let the cad get near her again.

This was business. Strictly business.

The shuffling of footsteps around her brought her attention back to the production.

Crap, she'd missed her cue! The ensemble had already formed their semi-circle around the grieving Elvino. A sleepwalking Amina was due to walk out any second, but Cami wasn't where she was supposed to be.

Scrambling, Cami quick-stepped toward her fellow ensemble singers. She hoped like heck the instructor didn't see her. She didn't need another strike against her.

The body to her left caught her off guard. Cami turned and slammed her shoulder into someone. Loud grunts resounded from both parties. Cami gained her composure, though her shoulder throbbed beneath her cupped hand. To her great horror, the other person she had knocked into was Sandy, who had been cued to float on stage for the start of Amina's sleepwalking sequence.

It all happened so fast. Sandy, whose arms were outstretched as part of Amina's trance, had taken Cami's shoulder directly to the back of her right shoulder. She never saw Cami there. And why should she? Cami wasn't supposed to *be* there.

Like a spinning top, Sandy lost her balance and whirled around in a complete circle. Her wide arms only bolstered the imagery. A crack rang out. Sandy lost her footing. Her slipper-clad foot turned in on itself, and she went down fast. Her nose and mouth connected with the stage, where Sandy landed with a thud. Why Cami had expected her to bounce up like Sandy was made of rubber, she had no idea. The woman definitely didn't bounce.

"Sandy! Oh my gosh, Sandy! I'm so sorry!" Cami ran over and hovered her hands over the poor woman's back. She was both unsure how and afraid to touch her. She didn't want to cause any more damage. But a side-eye toward Sandy's deformed ankle told her she had caused quite enough damage already.

A groan from Sandy drew Cami's concern back to the more vital parts of Sandy's body. The soprano raised her head up. Blood spilled out of her nose like water escaping through a crack in a dam. And speaking of crack, Sandy had a wide gap in her teeth, accentuated by all her other straight teeth, which were now painted red. Looking down, Cami saw two red almost-rectangles with points on the end lying on the stage.

Sandy's two front teeth.

"Honey! Oh, shit. Are you all right? Move!" Cami was shoved out of the way by James, who, in addition to being the company's Elvino, was Sandy's fiancé. "Mrs. Katrukova, call for an ambulance! Oh, God. Oh, God . . ."

"You . . . *bitch!*" Sandy spat at Cami. Literally spat. Small drops of blood speckled Cami's shirt and neck with the accusation. But the "tch" of the word didn't land. Instead, it came out like a lisped S. The image of a viper immediately came to mind. "You did that on purposssse! She chhhripped me!"

Eyes from all around landed on Cami.

"No, it was an accident. I was late to my mark. I swear I didn't do anything on purpose!" Cami held her hands out in front of her.

"Cami, let's get Sandy to the hospital. Everyone, class is over for the day. We'll resume tomorrow," Mrs. Katrukova said. "Cami, a word, please." The woman draped her hand around Cami's shoulder.

Cami walked over to the piano's bench seat on the floor of the theater. Her neck was craned back so she could watch James help Sandy off the stage. Blood was still dripping everywhere, trailing in Sandy's wake. Her slippers left smudgy half-footprints in the stuff. She was like a wounded gladiator being carted out of the arena.

"I know this wasn't your fault, my dear." Her instructor's dulcet tones invited Cami back to the present and gave her the attention Cami didn't feel focused enough to return. Gosh, her hands were still shaking. She quickly sat on them.

"My, oh my, what a mess," Mrs. Katrukova said, grabbing a theater seat across from Cami.

"I'm . . . so sorry." Cami's bottom lip trembled through the apology.

"Oh, I wasn't implying anything about you, Cami. It was clearly an accident. But this does leave me in a bit of a bind."

Was Mrs. Katrukova going to the police? Had Cami just assaulted someone? Her ears flooded with her pounding pulse. A light dizziness threatened to crack through the surface and take her down. What would she do if she went to jail? Maybe one of Mal's biker friends had a connection—

" . . . you'll have to sing Amina."

The lights above were too bright. Her senses all around were starting to go because Cami could have sworn Mrs. Katrukova had just said something about her singing Amina.

"I'm sorry. What did you say?"

"Yes, well, Stacey is away this week," Mrs. Katrukova said, wringing her hands. Stacey was the understudy for Amina.

"Oh, but she'll be back soon, right? She can take over Amina for sure."

"It's not that simple. The production is in a few weeks. Yes, she can resume the role when she returns, but do you have any idea who the conservatory has invited to attend? Representatives from the Metropolitan Opera House, the Los Angeles Opera, the Canadian Opera Company, and even several national tours. My goodness, the director has even extended an invitation to the Royal Opera House.

This conservatory has an opportunity to launch careers here, Cami. That is what our students pay for, not to mention our very wealthy and generous benefactors. And that will not happen if we simply decide to wait on a lead-worthy soprano to 'come back soon.' No, we must continue our rehearsals straight through until opening night."

Cami shook her head through the whole thing. Disbelief weighed her down and prevented her from forming sentences. Could she really be offering what Cami thought she was offering?

"But I'm not ready," Cami whispered. "Not yet, at least. I only just started my private tutoring a week or so ago. And that's Sandy's role, Mrs. K. I can't do that to her after what just happened."

"We are out of options. Yes, I agree you've still got quite a bit of growth ahead of you. But there isn't anyone else in the company who knows the part and has studied it as closely already. No one except Sandy and Stacey. And Sandy will be fine on her own, believe me. Her family has so many darn connections, I'm still amazed she chooses to study here instead of a music program with a higher pedigree," she said carefully.

Mrs. Katrukova rose to her feet. Her palms smoothed down her skirt, though there was hardly a wrinkle there. "Tomorrow, you shall sing Amina. And we will go from there. One day at a time. But," she leaned down lower so no stragglers in the theater could hear them, "an opportunity like this doesn't happen often, especially for a mezzo. I suggest you not squander it. There are no second chances in this business."

The faraway look in Mrs. Katrukova's eyes hinted at something, like the woman had more to add. She stared at the floor in silence, as if she'd forgotten to finish speaking. Then, her eyes found Cami's again and nailed home the one thing Cami needed to hear.

"It would make your mother proud."

And just like that, Cami was Amina.

CHAPTER 11

Holy frickin' smokes!

Cami still couldn't believe what had happened. Her gloved fingers tightened around the steering wheel as her beater Honda bounced down the property's driveway. She couldn't tell if the car was as excited as she was or if that was just its overinflated tires talking. The temperature was cold, but it hadn't yet dipped below freezing. It surely would in a few hours, but for the time being, her buzzing excitement had done a fine job of keeping her warm and energized.

Tomorrow, in front of her entire student opera company, she, an ensemble mezzo-soprano, would be singing the lead soprano role. And it wasn't a joke or a trick. There wasn't some stipulation she had to abide by, like, yes, she could sing it, but she'd have to do free math tutoring for the rest of the school year. Or, yes, she could sing it, but only while the lead soprano was off getting costume fittings and just so the orchestra could keep up with their own rehearsals. No, she was really going to sing Amina. For a whole week.

And she would sing the heck out of that role.

Cami threw the Honda in park and bolted down the path toward the maintenance barn. She could hardly get up to her apartment fast enough. Her mind was so scattered, she didn't even know what she needed to do first. Call Mal to tell her the good news? Run to her cassette player, pop that puppy in, and practice right away?

Mal. Definitely Mal first. Then practice.

The lights were on in the stable next door as she sauntered up to the maintenance barn. Low voices reached her ears, so she figured Mal was probably in there. Martin had finally gotten his go at Rosetta today, so he was no doubt a very happy camper. Mal usually let him have at least two or three goes at the mare, if she'd have him, and liked to check in on him before she called it quits for the evening. Cami thought back to Rosetta's temperament of late. Yeah, there was no way that mare wouldn't have him.

Cami slowed her pace as she neared the stable. She had been wrong. Only one voice carried out to where she was standing. A male's voice.

Dick's voice.

He was not the person she needed to speak to at that moment. Nope. No siree Bob. As far as she was concerned, it was that man's fault she'd gotten herself into this mess. Well, not a mess, really, as it'd now turned into an immense opportunity to show her stuff. But if he hadn't kissed her, she wouldn't have been distracted with all manner of lusty thoughts. Lusty thoughts of his lips and his end-of-day stubble that lit up her skin. Lusty thoughts of her being caged against the kitchen counter, trapped by his wide-as-a-mountain-and-just-as-hard chest.

No. No no no. *Shake it off, girl.*

" . . . Cami needs that number if this marriage thing will work."

Her ears perked up at the mention of her name. Definitely Dick, but who was he talking to? She didn't hear Mal respond back, and no one else was supposed to be on the property at that hour. It was almost seven in the evening.

"You have any idea where I can get one of those magic numbers? Do you, girl?"

Girl?

Cami tiptoed to the front door of the stable, which was still open a crack. The large barn doors were otherwise closed for the horses. She wanted to hear more, but an uneasy chill creeping up her spine told her to stay out of sight. She slid her back flat against the door and angled her right ear close to the opening. When she inched forward slightly, she saw Dick brushing out Rosetta, talking to her.

"Between you and me, I don't know how I'm going to make this thing work. I haven't come up with a plan yet, to be honest. This whole thing is beginning to scare the shit out of me."

Dick had Rosetta out of her stall and standing on some fresh hay. She didn't seem as interested in what he had to say, though, judging by the way she kept bending down to nibble in between pats.

Dick didn't seem phased in the least. No, but something else looked to be bothering him. He had his coat and gloves off, as he always did when he was working in the stall. His sleeves were rolled up to his elbows. Even from where Cami stood, and with only one eye on him, she could see every tendon and sinew in his forearms as he brushed out Rosetta's coat. And since Rosetta was on his right side, his left side faced her. His injured side.

"I've got another three weeks just about until Cami and I need to apply for that damn marriage license. And I ain't got no fucking clue what a social security number is. Nor how to go about finding one. Any ideas?" he said, looking up at Rosetta. The mare just snorted and resumed her munching. Dick took her cue and resumed his brushing.

"Nah, didn't think you'd know either," he said, the quirk of his lips lifting his mouth in a half-smile. In the muted stable light, with his tousled blond hair and that grin on his face, Cami was assaulted with a new image of Dick: charming.

"Then there was that woman last night."

Nope. Definitely not charming. Still an ass.

Another woman? Really? Cami's stomach bottomed out a bit at that. No, they were never exclusive, specifically. And, yeah, the marriage was a sham, but she thought he'd at least . . . well, she didn't know what she'd thought.

"That woman out by the oak tree, she was the spitting image of Cami, I tell ya. Hair was a bit longer and a different color and stuff, but that was Cami staring back at me, for sure."

What the heck was he talking about? The other woman looked like Cami? Did he have a thing for short, broke girls with curly hair and aspirations to excel in an art form that was dying out along with its AARP audience?

"She was older, though. A good twenty or twenty-five years older than Cami, I'd say. And you want to know what really gives me the willies? I know Cami's mother passed on some years back. This woman looks exactly like what I'd imagine her mother to look like. And then . . . she was gone."

Cami had lost the battle against being discrete. Her whole head had peeked around the door opening. How could . . . ?

"She was real, I swear it." Dick reached into the bag at his hip and offered Rosetta a carrot. "But then, maybe she wasn't. When I got close—and, yes, I may have still been half asleep—she was standing next to that tree, and it was almost like she was on fire but without the flames. No, that's not right. She looked like anybody else, but there was this white smoke about her. The way you see your breath in the cold, but all over her body, you get my meaning?"

Another snort from Rosetta, followed by more munching.

"Then there was that green dust on the tree right after she vanished," he continued, gazing off as he mindlessly brushed out the same spot of Rosetta's coat again. "That was when I knew. That dust, that woman, Cami. It's all connected. Maybe she sent me forward in time by putting that green dust on my pants to begin with. How the hell else can I explain why I was about to die one minute back in nineteen nineteen, only to wake up—alive—sixty-nine years in the future? I haven't the foggiest. But one thing's for sure. It's all connected. And until I can figure out how to get back to my own time, like hell I'm letting Cami out of my sight. She's got to be my ticket back home. Or if I get stuck here, my ticket to surviving in this time."

Cami couldn't feel her toes, her legs, or any other extremity. She was solidly numb. But it wasn't from the cold. No, every word she had just overheard from Dick's casual one-sided conversation with a horse settled beneath her skin. Tiny daggers prickled all over her body.

There was no way she'd heard things correctly. No way. Because if she did, she would have heard Dick telling Rosetta that he'd traveled through time sixty-nine years to land himself here. Quick math put him just at the end of World War I.

No, uh-uh. Nope.

And her mother? He'd somehow seen her mother? As what? Some kind of ghost? No, this made absolutely no sense. None of it.

But what did make sense was his intention to never let her out of his sight.

Yeah, fat chance, buddy. She wasn't anyone's prisoner. Certainly not some psycho mental case who thought he'd traveled here from the past and Cami was somehow the key to that little journey.

The panic she fought off made her jittery. Her arm inadvertently leaned against the door. The old wood creaked open, revealing more of Cami standing in its wake. Dick had previously adjusted Rosetta, turning her around to brush her other side. When he did that, his right side faced the barn door.

The groan of the wood immediately drew his attention. The color in his face drained away as he met Cami's eyes. A crunchy thud was the only sound between them as the horse brush he was holding dropped to the floor.

Without a logical thought ready to go upon being discovered, she did the only thing she could.

She ran.

CHAPTER 12

Twenty-six seconds.

That was how fast Dick could run one hundred and fifty yards. He could measure the exact distance with just a glance. His whole body would thrum with a charge to execute that shuttle every single time. When he was a runner in his infantry regiment in the war, the average distance between the trenches on the front line had routinely been one hundred and fifty yards. His training drills, for months, had consisted of nothing other than markers upon markers upon markers of one-hundred-and-fifty-yard shuttle runs. Always, he could make it in twenty-six seconds. Without fail.

Cami was about that distance away from him now, barreling out onto the field. Like hell he was letting her get away without allowing him to explain things. He had no idea how he'd work his magic mouth to spin a tale that wasn't utter bullshit, but he would. He'd figure it out.

Too many pieces had fallen into place for him lately. He had been too fortunate. If there was any doubt in his pea brain that someone up there had gifted him with nine lives, he could just lay that to rest right then and there. Because his luck had just run out. No more having his cake and eating it, too.

Good. He hated cake. Made him too doughy.

"Cami, wait!" The abrupt tone of his voice nearly spooked Rosetta, but like he gave a shit. The mare couldn't get out through the barn door's slight opening anyway, but Cami could. And so could he. His legs were sluggish in the cold, but they quickly warmed up as he pumped his arms. This run was nothing. Hell, there wasn't even any enemy fire coming at him.

No, just the daggers Cami shot his way whenever she looked behind her.

"Cami, wait! I can explain!" The power he sent to his thighs and calves made his legs eat up the distance between them. She ran, but it was scattered and unorganized. She ran to flee, clearly, but didn't have a destination. While all he had to do was home in on his target.

"Someone help me! Help—"

Dick barreled into her from behind. The force knocked the air from her lungs. He took advantage of her stunned state and nabbed her around her waist, tackling her to the ground. They went down in a heap of tangled legs and arms. Cami, warm and flushed with exertion, lay on her back, a prisoner between the frozen ground and his overheated body. She writhed beneath him, trying to crawl free. Her damn screaming didn't let up either, so he pressed his weight into her body and covered her mouth with his right hand.

"Stop your screaming, woman, and listen to me. Just *listen*," Dick pleaded. The moonlight was minimal, and he prayed she'd be able to see in his eyes that he wasn't going to hurt her, wasn't going to do anything beyond talk.

But the fear reflected back in her panicked eyes knocked something loose.

How many times had he been in a similar situation? Where he aggressed on a woman? Where that fear fed the buzz, for either one or both parties? It didn't matter whether it was asked of him because some women got off on the thrill of bedding a monster. Or whether his darker nature floated to the surface in the heat of the moment. He was a brute, a beast.

And looking down into Cami's face, with the skin around her eyes stretched taut in fear and tears pooling at the rims, he knew the truth of the situation. She saw what they all saw, what they expected to see.

A brawler. Thief. Murderer. Worse.

Well, he was done.

Disgusted with himself, he quickly pushed off Cami and stumbled several feet away to give her a wide berth, his limbs shaking. "Please, I won't hurt you, Cami. Fucking Christ, I'll swear on whatever you'd like me to swear on that I won't hurt you."

Cami just lay there, back still ramrod straight on the frozen grass. She peered up at him underneath her long lashes. The tears hadn't fallen yet, but they would. They always did.

"Are you hurt? I mean, can I help you up? I'd very much like to help you up. I won't touch you, though, if you don't want . . . " he hedged. His boots took him a few steps forward before he lost his nerve and retreated back to where he was. God, he was losing it.

Slowly, Cami sat up, bent her knees, and stood. Her eyes never left his. She just stood there, slack-jawed. Thankfully, she'd stopped screaming.

"I don't know what to say," he said, his arms wide at either side. "I obviously didn't expect anyone to be standing there listening to my one-sided conversation with a horse. But . . . yes. The conversations we have with ourselves are always the most truthful, aren't they? Something about having a captive audience of like-minded individuals, I guess." He rubbed the back of his neck and looked down, half afraid to look in those piercing blue eyes that had yet to ease up. But he'd come this far already, so he swallowed the lump in his throat, looked up, and held her gaze.

And for the first time since he'd arrived here, he challenged her to meet his gaze and see a glimpse of the real him. Not the thug who dreamed up a marriage scheme to take her money. Not the womanizer who tempted her out of more than her ice cream. Not the bastard who'd just chased her down and tackled her to the ground. But the *real* him.

"The truth, Cami, is as you overheard it back in that barn. My name is Richard Stevens, and I was born in Baltimore, Maryland, in eighteen ninety-one."

Fate had carried him this far. He had to trust it could carry him a bit further.

When Cami was in second grade, Mrs. Langholtz had all the students make a kaleidoscope out of paper towel tubes, reflective paper, and some colorful beads. It was simple enough, yet Cami distinctly recalled how dizzying the silly craft was. The movement, the colors, the onslaught of light and angles. While stimulating, the darn thing gave her a headache.

Dick was that kaleidoscope now.

Cami sat on a four-legged stool in front of the stable's office while Dick paced the length of the barn in front of her. The blanket around her shoulders offered little warmth or comfort. Some of the low-hanging barn lights, which were no more than single light bulbs decked out in fancy lantern fixtures, swayed with the wind Dick kicked up on each pass. Heck, he was pacing so fast, and she was sitting so low compared to his height, that every time he walked past a light fixture, he'd block it out completely. The effect was like a strobe, only slower and more deliberate.

And then there was the silence.

Against her better judgment, she'd allowed him to walk her back to the barn. To explain things, he'd said.

Oh, please. As if anyone could explain away something as major as time travel.

Hey, Cami. I know I said I'd marry you for your money, but there's a little snag. You see, I'm actually ninety-eight years old, but I swear I don't look a day over sixty-five. Still want to get hitched?

And, no, she was absolutely *not* seriously considering for even a hot second that this man was sane.

Uh-uh.

The scratchy crunch of hay under boots paused her nervous musings. Dick halted in front of her, his shoulders and biceps bunched, hands fisted. His eyes were cast down at the ground. Great puffs of breath left his lungs. He was a bull penned up for too long.

And the sight kicked at her heart.

She knew all the signs of an animal in captivity. She didn't need to examine the tension in his muscles more closely or check him over for signs of physical abuse. It was clear as day.

This man had seen his fair share of the insides of cages. Maybe not literally, but no liar would fight back the torrent with such an ironclad will. Dick stood there as if he was trying to do his best to put the pin *back* in the grenade. A liar wouldn't hold back the floodwaters. No, they would just come up with another fabrication, an additional layer of deceit to keep their head above water. But Dick wasn't doing that. He was actively changing his course before her eyes.

Abruptly, he jerked his head up. His eyes widened, and an unspoken idea registered across his face. "Stay here." He whipped his arms straight out in front of her and held his palms wide. "Give me five—no, three minutes. I need to show you something."

Then he was gone. The only disturbance left in his wake was the slight puff of dust kicked up by his boots on the floor of the barn.

Well, that and the alleged time-travel puzzle her mind was left trying to unravel.

A moment later, he returned to the barn. His chest pumped with exertion, and his skin was slightly flushed from the cold, but he didn't seem to care. In his arms was a pile of clothes. Cami squinted at the balled-up fabrics before he fell to his knees in front of her and rifled through them.

"Here." He pulled out a set of pants and began searching for something along the back of the waistband. The pants had seen better days, for sure. Cami couldn't tell if the drab brown was the original color or if it was from the caked-on dirt and mud. But the sight of them sparked a memory.

"Those are yours."

"Yes. These are the clothes I was wearing when you first saw me in the paddock. Look, here." Dick's thumbnail pointed to a red heart-shaped tag sewn into the inside of the garment as he held it up to her. She squinted at the tiny letters, barely making out the words.

"It says 'Hamilton Carhartt Cotton Mills.' You probably know it by 'Carhartt,' though. It's the same brand of work pants Mal keeps in the bunkhouse and stable," Dick clarified.

"Right." Cami sat back and shrugged after examining the tag.

"What does that have to do with anything? It's a popular brand of outerwear for the labor industries."

"Look again. More closely this time."

The plea in his eyes and the desperation in his voice tugged at her heart. Confused, she leaned down again and tried for a closer look.

The lettering of the logo was different than she was used to seeing. Before her, fancy cursive slanted across a white label. Not the lowercase block letters she expected to see. And the company's name had been printed inside a gold train car plastered on top of a red heart. "From Mill to Millions" bordered the outline of the heart's two lobes while "Union Made" was printed prominently at the bottom of the patch.

A patch. Not a tag as she'd first thought. And though the patch was an unusual shape, worn white stitches crossed its planes in a square shape, leaving the edges of the heart and overhangs of the train not sewn down.

The whole presentation looked careless, unfinished. She'd never seen a clothing manufacturer not take more care to secure their brand on their garments before. At the very least, why wasn't the outline of the patch stitched down completely?

"Because when you're tasked with clothing and outfitting America's soldiers for a new war while having little-to-no resources, you cut corners," Dick replied.

Had she asked that out loud?

More questions rose but stalled out on the tip of her tongue as Dick moved his finger down farther, drawing her attention to another patch. This one was a solid white rectangle, sloppily stitched around the border in navy-blue thread.

Hamilton Carhartt Cotton Mills
Contractors to the United States Army
1605 Michigan Ave.
Detroit, Michigan
1917

Cami's tongue rasped against her teeth like sandpaper. The cold air in the barn flew through her lungs, frigid and fast as her quickening heart demanded she suck down more oxygen. Because staring at the date at the bottom of that tag was sending all sorts of confusion her way.

Then she took a closer look at the pants. Squinting past the dirt, her eyes finally absorbed what they couldn't before. The uneven stitching across the seams, the lack of holes or obvious threadbare patches that should accompany any clothing manufactured in 1917, the brass buttons and fasteners she'd only ever seen in pictures.

Oh, my God. It's true, then. He's really from the past. Holy cannoli!

When the cogs finally clicked into place, Cami raised her head to study him some more.

Despite the chill in the barn, courtesy of leaving the barn door cracked open, his tan skin was flushed red. The pockmarks on his left side became more pronounced, the deeper red of his complexion highlighting the shadows in his uneven scarring. His mouth opened and closed so often, he reminded her of a goldfish waiting for food to be sprinkled down into its tank.

He needed help.

"Cami, I . . . uh, I'm trying to find—"

"I believe you." The words rushed out before she could second-guess them.

"Thank you," Dick said softly, slightly bowing his head. She didn't miss the exhale of relief that rushed out of him.

"You're welcome."

"I hardly know where to start with it all," he said with a sigh.

"It's always best to start at the beginning, I find. But that can wait until you feel ready." Cami pulled away slightly so she could glance up at him.

A soft chuckle vibrated through his chest as he took in her smug expression. "How the hell could you possibly believe me?"

"Well, because you believe it, I guess. Besides, the more I mull over the idea of it, the more it makes sense to me. The clothes, the lack of personal details, not having a job or place to live. It all just clicks, as crazy as that sounds."

"Again, thank you. I will find the words, I promise. I just need . . . "

"Time," Cami said as she stood and lifted the blanket off her shoulders. "Take all the time you need. A good night's sleep will help, too.

And in the morning, we can sort it all out." She walked to the door of the stable to head back to her apartment above the maintenance barn. When she was four steps away from him, she turned to Dick. "I'm not saying I like you, because I don't, but I am saying I'm willing to listen to your story."

Dick looked up at her and nodded once. The harsh lines of his chin told her he understood his marching orders.

Good.

But as she walked out, her own walls began to show cracks in the facade. Her stomach soured at what Dick's revelation ultimately meant for Cami.

If he'd really traveled from 1919, then he wouldn't have a social security number. Which they both needed to apply for the marriage license.

Without that information, her opera career had no hope of ever getting off the ground.

CHAPTER 13

"Y ou are officially my captive for the next thirty minutes. Talk."

Of all the scenarios where Dick could imagine himself being open to conversation, this was the bottom of the barrel. How chatty could one be, after all, when crammed into a sardine can and your knees punched you in the chin at every bump? This hatchback, as Cami called it, was like no vehicle he'd ever ridden in. He was largely used to open-back Army trucks that ran in the convoys. Plenty of room back there. One could sit comfortably and still had room to set their rifle down.

"And buckle up, mister. I'm not having you spiderweb my windshield because you're too macho to click it, thank you very much," Cami said as she fiddled with some knobs and buttons on the front console. Immediately, cold air rushed out of the slats facing him. As if the coating of ice on the vehicle's exterior hadn't been enough of a pain to chip through just to get in the damn car. Now she expected to freeze him from within as well?

Hunched over his knees with his shoulders curled in, Dick managed to twist his head to the left just enough to glare at his chauffeur. "I'm sorry, but were any of those words spoken in English? I'd be happy to answer you if I knew what the hell you were saying."

He tried to twist his hip bone away from the vehicle's center console. He was too wide for this tin can, dammit, and the rigid material in the middle was poking his hip. His latest adjustment had him partially facing Cami. His left hip, instead of his butt, rested on the bulk of the seat.

Christ. Was this how women felt when they tried to cross their legs under a low table?

"Now, now, that's no way to start the day. And your seat belt needs to be on. It's that black fabric belt to your right. Just pull it across your lap and buckle it in. And hey, be grateful this little gem doesn't have those new fancy automatic seat belts. I wouldn't want to blow your mind on only your second outing."

"So this is not a newer vehicle. I'm not surprised."

"And just what the heck is that supposed to mean, buddy?" Cami raised her hand toward the windshield, almost in an accusatory manner. Her eyes never left front and center, even though she was clearly addressing him.

A model citizen, then, not taking her eyes from the road. How annoying.

"I merely meant that, judging by the accumulation of, shall we say *character* built up around the car's body, this thing has seen some years. Hell, woman. Your rust stains have rust stains." Another sharp bump in the road caused Dick to nearly bite through his tongue.

"You've now wasted five minutes of our thirty-minute drive. Best get to yapping, Mr. Time Traveler. What's your story? And it better be a good one, or I won't take you to the mall after class for some new clothes." The smug grin on her face told it all. She had him over a barrel, and they both knew it. If he was to fit in here, he needed a proper wardrobe.

Dick knocked his left temple against the headrest. He had promised her words, and it was time to deliver. But how much to tell? It burned him to admit it, but he still needed her. Though Cami had found out about his circumstances, it didn't change his need for funds and security. He still needed to see this marriage thing through. And Cami, for all that had happened, was being generous with her time. She'd offered to take him to her music conservatory and show him where she studied, and most importantly, it would be an opportunity to be introduced as an intended couple. He had a part to play in this, and he needed to remember that.

"I fell down a well and woke up here."

The only sound that followed was the road gravel crunching under the vehicle's tires.

"Nuh-uh, I need more than that, and quit fidgeting, will you? You'll make me crash."

"I can't help it. This heap on wheels—for I refuse to believe this is any sort of daily-use vehicle—is squeezing me tighter than a damn virgin." Dick twisted again, this time all the way to his left so his right hip was facing front entirely. Cami's profile became his new head-on view.

"Hey, watch it with the language. My baby's sensitive." She patted the steering wheel almost lovingly. "And so am I."

"What, angel? Does my mouth bother you?"

Cami's eyes darted his way. Her pert nose turned up in disgust before she resumed her focus on the road. God, did he love getting under her skin. "Twenty minutes. Time's a tickin'."

Dick rolled his eyes and settled in as much as he could. His eyes slid shut as he prepared to dig up what he wanted to stay good and buried. "I was a runner in the Great War, part of the 313th Infantry Regiment. 'Baltimore's Own,' we were called because most of us hailed from there."

"The Great War. World War I, you mean?"

"World War I? You mean there have been other wars? How many have there been in the last sixty-nine years?" He didn't have the words to articulate why that reality bothered him. Or perhaps he didn't want to share them. The deaths of fellow soldiers, the crippling explosions, losing his hearing, learning to fucking walk again, months of rehabilitation. All for what? More war? Haunted memories threatened to rise to the surface, but he fought to tamp them down.

"A few," Cami whispered.

Her silence told him to continue. He had many questions, but those could come later. This was his time to say his piece.

"I had a friend in my regiment, a fellow runner. Jacob Bellamy. The fucking golden boy of the company. Well, we started out as friends, at any rate. But he's the one I have to thank for my lovely mug and hearing loss."

Cami's hands gripped the steering wheel more tightly. Ah, so his face made her uncomfortable.

"Well, I had an opportunity to . . . reconnect with Bellamy on his family's farm outside Baltimore." No way in hell would he tell her the whole story, but a piece of truth would satisfy her and get the spotlight off him. "We fought."

"What did you fight about?"

"A woman." Not true, necessarily, but it was real enough.

"Really?" She groaned. "That's so immature."

"Jealous?" A reddish tint rose in her cheeks. Dick loved how easy she was making this. She looked damned delicious when she was all flushed and angry.

"Hardly. Just not surprised by your pigheadedness, I guess." There was no venom in the taunt, however.

"Anyway, our fight occurred on Bellamy's old family farm. We got too close to the well. I fell in."

"You fell into a well," Cami deadpanned. "How are you not dead?"

"That is the magical question, isn't it? When I tumbled over, I fell for what seemed like an eternity. The farther down I fell, the more paralyzing the darkness became. However, before I hit the surface of the water, my stomach turned in on itself, and I was hit with the worst vertigo of my life. I passed out, only to awaken under the lovely Rosetta's heels."

"And what was all that about seeing a woman? You said you thought she was my mother?"

"I don't know. I must have been seeing things," he rushed out.

They rode in silence the rest of the way. Saying the words out loud solidified his plight. He had no choice but to trust her, having been backed into a corner. But the retelling surprised him, actually. Yes, he was forced to play his hand, but a part of him was relieved at having done so. Not only that, but the thought of opening up to her, at least partly (for he wasn't yet ready to fully reveal the whole green-dust-and-seeing-ghosts thing to her) felt comfortable. Natural.

Ten minutes later, Cami's car turned onto a long paved driveway.

Giant buildings of various stones and facades dotted the landscape. Several more cars sat stopped on a large black expanse of pavement nearby one of the buildings.

"Here we are. The Sutherland Conservatory of Music. My home away from home." Cami shifted a control in between the two of them. She turned the key and everything shut off, but she hadn't yet moved to exit. Cami faced him. "Thank you, Dick."

After the thirty-minute drive, it was clear she had warmed up nicely. It took some time, but that cold air from the vents had turned to heat. And her complexion benefited. Her nose was no longer red. Her lips, previously tight and slightly purple, were flushed a healthy pink.

While he stared at those lips, Cami leaned over and brushed them against his cheek, leaving him with a warm kiss.

On his left cheek. His ruined cheek.

Dick froze, uncertain how to react. His first inclination was to pull away, hide his left side, apologize to her in some way for no longer being a whole man. Because she had kissed him where most women were horrified to even look. Before he could even address it, Cami moved on as if it hadn't mattered. As if his face wasn't the stuff of nightmares.

"Now, let me introduce you to my world," she said with a smile so wide, it was infectious.

He was quickly realizing he'd follow her anywhere. He never stood a chance.

Of all the days to have stage fright, this was one hell of a day. It was Cami's first rehearsal as Amina. She knew the role, knew the arias. She was as prepared as she'd ever be. What she wasn't prepared for, however?

Performing in front of Dick.

They were wrapping up the last number of the day on the practice schedule. It was Amina's sleepwalking scene and featured the most prominent (and most challenging) aria. The blocking for *Ah! non credea mirarti!* called for Cami to float across the stage in a pensive dreamlike state. In the song, Amina laments the loss of a flower's beauty as it dies, how she cannot bring it back to life even with her tears. An ultimate pining for her lover, Elvino, who left her.

But as Cami moved across the stage, she had the rarest opportunity to look at Dick. *Really* look at him, head-on, under the guise of a sleepwalking dreamer. He had parked himself several rows back, right under where the balcony overhang began. It wasn't lost on her that the lighting on those seats was diminished.

So she stared at him. No, she did more than that. She searched his face for any sign, again, that he was untruthful. She had been granted this opportunity, hidden as Amina, to assess his features undetected, and she wouldn't squander it.

Not once since she'd met him had she thought him ugly. Yes, she imagined an injury, for his face was heavily pockmarked and marred with scarring. But it never stood out as anything that detracted from his presence. On the contrary, it added vibrancy to him, in a way.

He was not perfect. But there was a life lived, in whatever capacity that meant.

Man, did she envy that.

As she wrapped up her song, she noticed how Dick sat with his elbow bent on the armrest. His mouth was resting on three of his curled-in fingers while his pointer finger and thumb supported his left cheek and chin, respectively. His eyes had tracked her every movement. It was both unnerving and exhilarating. To be looked at in that way by a man. Especially a man as dominating, tempting, infuriatingly alluring . . .

And soon-to-be married to her.

Crap.

"All right, well done. That's a wrap for now, everyone. I'll see you all tomorrow," Mrs. Katrukova said, closing the lid of her piano.

When the instructor ended the class, Cami grabbed her bag, leaped down off the front of the stage, and walked up the aisle toward Dick. He hadn't moved a muscle.

"So, what'd you think?" she said, way too eager to hear what he had to say.

His gaze fixed on her, but he said nothing. Disappointment settled like a shroud around her, but she brushed it off. Jeez, if he didn't like it, couldn't he at least be polite and lie like everyone else?

"Well, I know opera's not for everyone. No matter." She hiked her bag higher on her shoulder. "You've earned yourself a new wardrobe for enduring it anyway. C'mon, let's go."

When she was ten paces ahead of him up the aisle, she finally heard the squeaking bottom of his theater seat spring back into place. An indication he was following her. Good. The jerk probably realized she held the upper hand—and car keys—in this scenario.

By the time they walked out of the theater and across the parking lot, Dick was solidly on her heels. The pain in the pooper still hadn't said a word. God, if he hated opera that much, how would this stupid marriage even work? She just had to remind herself that they weren't going to live together or anything. They'd go their separate ways after the papers were signed. As she fumbled for her car keys in her bag, she chanted her newly formed mantra in her head.

On paper only . . . On paper only . . .

Key in hand, she unlocked *his* door first. Because she was such a frickin' gentleman, apparently. As she fiddled with the key in the lock, her nose twitched slightly. An unusual metallic and charred scent wafted her way when a strong breeze came through. Her eyes stung a bit from the smell, but a few strong squints to clear the field fixed the annoyance. She was beyond grateful when she opened the door and started trotting around to her side, eager to get in and escape the wind.

Cami had just rounded the back of her car when her feet left the ground. The air whooshed out of her lungs. Upended, her pelvis was assaulted by Dick's hard shoulder as he hoisted her over his body. Her head, previously upright, banged against Dick's lower back as he ran.

"Dick! Put me down! What the heck is going on?" Furious, she tried to kick out, but he had her knees in a vice grip in the crook of his arm. The scene behind her blurred with each bounce of Dick's stride. He was running so fast, his legs consumed the pavement. Her bag slipped from her shoulder and dropped halfway through the parking lot.

"My bag! Dick, put me—"

The explosion engulfed Cami's Honda. The fireball ate up the car and spewed molten pieces of wreckage everywhere. The force of the blast knocked Cami and Dick to the ground. Every ounce of air in her lungs was eaten up by the elements around her. Her head connected with the concrete as hot air reached her skin. A great heavy weight smothered her. A massive hand clutched her head to a warm chest.

Dick's chest. And his heart beat so fast next to her that it threatened to burst out of its rib cage. His muscles tensed around her, in sync with painful grunts. Metal clanged as it hit the nearby pavement.

"I've got you, angel. I've got you," Dick panted through strained breaths.

In the protective cocoon of Dick's body, Cami finally put the pieces together.

Someone had put a bomb in her car.

<h1 style="text-align:center">CHAPTER 14</h1>

"Holy shitskies! Are you two okay? Are your asses singed or just spooked?"

Dick raised his head, the effort of which was more of a task than his neck had been up for. Why he bothered, he didn't know. There was only one person he knew of, in this time or otherwise, who had a fouler mouth than he did.

And Cami had called her.

Mal stormed up to the two of them, ducking under the yellow ribbon sprawled across the parking lot. Just what the police thought that would keep out, Dick hadn't a clue. But he hardly cared. His senses were so overloaded he was liable to burst apart and go up in smoke as fast as Cami's car. Harsh blue and red lights on top of police vehicles assaulted his vision, only worsening his growing tension headache. They swirled around in dizzying circles, lighting up the conservatory's property like sunlight through stained glass.

He tried to compartmentalize it all, push the obnoxious stimuli down so he could focus on what was currently twisting his insides into a knot. Cami, draped in an institutional-gray wool blanket, was a catatonic bundle in his arms. Though the initial body quakes of hysterical crying had subsided, her shoulders still hitched on the occasional sob. Now, she just lay against his chest, unmoving as the dead.

He knew shell shock when he saw it, and the battle one needed to fight to come through the other side. He clutched her to his chest more tightly.

Thank God he'd been there.

After the EM-something-or-others offered their medical aid to Cami and him, Dick refused outright. For both of them. He knew jack shit about medical care here and figured it had to be better than what he was used to.

Because someone had just tried to kill his soon-to-be wife with a gunpowder firebomb.

But like hell he was about to trust anyone he didn't know to care for her. He didn't give a shit about their shiny tools, newfangled gadgets, and elaborate ambulances. So he took care of things his way. When those fancy field medics gave him an out in the form of his signature on a Refused Medical Attention form, he took it. And, hey now, after a few polite yet damn insistent glares, they even let him sign off for Cami on her behalf.

In Dick's experience, it was always so much more productive to be feared than loved. Sure, that had been the root of many of his problems, but he'd lean on whatever skills he needed to in that moment.

"Hi to you, too, Mal," Dick said. "Thanks for coming to get us."

Dick leaned down and glanced at Cami. She sat next to him on the bench outside the main performing hall's front door. Her left thigh was flush against his, and her hunched body lay compressed against his chest. His arms hadn't let go of her. Hell, his palm cupping the back of her head and cradling it into his shoulder was at his insistence. He'd block out the sun if it meant she'd be shielded from any more harm.

Cami hadn't spoken since he'd settled her down on the bench. Now that Mal had arrived, he'd hoped she would come up a bit for air. And she had to have known Mal was standing a few feet away.

Still, she wouldn't move.

"Angel, Mal's here," he whispered into her ear, hooking a few errant curls behind the shell of her ear. His voice was like gravel. A combination of him screaming and inhaling the kicked-up dust was no doubt the culprit of the irritation. Maybe that was why she stayed quiet as well. Was her throat on fire? Did she need water? Had he missed something when he'd checked her over initially?

Concern mixed with his remaining adrenaline. He snaked his left hand under her thighs and leaned her back on his right arm. Lifting, he settled her on top of his lap, with her legs hanging over his left side. He forced his fingers through her hair and gently raised her head until he could see her face clearly.

Her blue eyes had dimmed from when she had been vibrant and happy singing on stage. Thankfully, though, they still locked on his own. Aside from the dirt and grime coating her olive skin, she was flawless.

Thank fuck.

He had taken the brunt of the hits when the car debris went flying. Had aimed to shield her as best he could. Thank God it worked. His too-big body, with his too-foul mouth and his too-stupid brain, had finally done something right.

He'd saved his angel.

Content with what he saw, he'd let her keep her silence for a little while longer. Some trauma couldn't be worked through in a group setting. Leaning forward, he brushed his lips against her forehead and settled a kiss between her brows. Without waiting or looking for a reaction, he snaked his hand around the back of her neck and urged her back to the sanctuary of his chest.

"Mal, just drive us back and let me get her home," he said as he repositioned his arm under her knees. In one fluid motion, he rose to his full height. Cami's slight weight in his arms was nothing compared to the heaviness he felt in his chest over her silence.

"Of course. You need to talk to anyone else here before we turn tail?"

"No. I already cleared us with the field medics," Dick said, his eyes never leaving the top of Cami's head.

"Field medics, eh? That's kind of a fancy term. Well, call them what you'd like, but I call them a pain in my ass most of the time. I spoke to Greg Peters before I left, by the way. He was the one who called me, you know. Peters is a detective at the Rochester Police Department, and he'll get to the bottom of this. He and I go way back. He's been in my motorcycle club for years. His wife, Nancy, makes a mean tiramisu, too, with those coffee-soaked cookie things in it," Mal said, moving her fingers to demonstrate the placement of whatever cookies she was trying to describe. "Anyway, when he saw Cami was involved, he called me. Cami's call to me came in right after his. And I still can't believe—"

"The truck, Mal. Please. I need to get Cami home."

Mal stared at him while chewing the inside of her cheek. Her eyes raked over him, no doubt taking in the same work jeans he'd been wearing every day, one of the two different flannel shirts he'd found in the bunkhouse, and the boots he'd arrived here with. He was also covered in dust and peppered with bloody gashes he was too stubborn to have properly patched up. Cami, still silent, was huddled under the blanket in his arms. Her body had relaxed immensely, and her breathing had evened out. Judging by the slow rise and fall of her shoulders, exhaustion had finally won out. Cami was asleep.

"You're not married yet, you know," Mal said in a whisper, clearly aware of Cami's dozing state. That caught him off guard. She knew, then. "Look, I know the stipulation in her mama's will. I know about the cockamamy plan you two are putting together, fixing to get married so she can cash in and pursue her dream."

Dick raised his chin at the comment.

"I like you, Dick," she said, shaking her head. "You're a good worker, the animals have taken well to you, and heck, you're not hard on the eyes either. But I know you're not stickin' around, and you've got secrets painted all over you. There ain't enough spit shine in the world to shine you bright as a new penny, or me either for that matter, and that doesn't bother me one lick. But that girl there," she said, pointing at Cami. "Her mama never would have wanted her to settle, you get my drift?"

Mal held Dick's gaze before she turned and led the way to her truck. It was as clear a statement as any.

He wasn't good enough for the woman in his arms, and he never would be.

Warmth had finally seeped into Cami's core, and the gentle rocking motion soothed the tension from her bones. The hollow sound of boot heels on hardwood was comforting. Familiar.

Stairs. She was being carried upstairs. And not just any stairs, but the stairs to her apartment.

The back of her knees and the side of her cheek were sweaty, as if they'd been stuck against the same surface for some time. What started out as warmth was quickly morphing into discomfort. She tried to stretch her legs out, but whatever was holding them pushed back.

"Easy, angel. We're almost to your apartment." Dick's baritone voice, though barely above a whisper, echoed in the stairwell. He was the one carrying her upstairs. But why?

As the question entered her head, the movement stopped. She opened her eyes for the first time and saw the red door to her apartment. She remembered when she first moved in and had convinced Mal to let her paint it. There was only so much brown a girl could take before she felt like she lived inside a tree trunk.

"Hold tight. I'm going to set you down on the top step for a moment."

Her stomach dropped on a flutter as he lowered her. The hard right angle of the top step was harsh against her bottom after having grown used to the cushion of Dick's arms. She lolled her head against the wall, all the while still cradled in the nook of Dick's shoulder as he supported her with one arm. With his other hand, he skimmed his fingers under her purple shag welcome mat and came away with her spare key.

"How did you know . . . ?" she asked with a wince, her throat quickly shutting down the whole talking thing. Her tongue was as dry as a cotton pad.

"I hate to say it, but you're not that original. Another thing that hasn't changed much in sixty-nine years? Putting spare keys under doormats, apparently," Dick said as he rose to unlock the door.

Ah, still a jerk, then. Glad to hear not everything had changed.

A scratch and a click later, and the door swung open. Dick pocketed the key and lifted her again.

"Not . . . your . . . key," Cami forced out through the discomfort in her throat.

"Listen, you can yell at me all you want when you have a voice with which to yell. And, believe me, with pipes like yours, I could listen to you scream and holler at me all day. But first, we need to get you clean, watered, and rested."

Why did she need to get clean? She'd already showered this morning. And she hadn't spent any time around the horses yet. Her night checks weren't for a few more hours.

Mustering way more effort than she thought she'd need to, she raised her right arm, the one not still tucked against Dick's chest, in front of her line of sight. Her eyes squinted as confusion took root in her mind.

A coating of black grime and gray dust was smeared across her skin. Her nails, which she had painted a vibrant red just a few days prior, had crusted splatters of deep crimson marring the shellac. Was that . . . blood?

All at once, the protective bubble her mind had erected around itself popped. Everything flooded back to her in a deluge of memories.

Singing Amina in front of Dick.

Walking back to her car to take him shopping.

An acrid smell that bothered her.

The explosion.

"Oh, my God! My car!" She tried to sit up but forgot she was still midair against Dick's chest. Her legs kicked out as her torso sprang up. The sudden jolt knocked her head directly into Dick's chin.

"Fuck!" he hollered as he shuffled over to her couch and plopped her unceremoniously into the cushions so hard she bounced. His hand flew to his chin. He worked his jaw back and forth while walking back to kick the door closed.

"Sorry!" Cami said with her hands held up toward him. She swung her legs over the side of the couch in an effort to get up and go check on him. But the moment she rose, her legs revolted and refused to support her weight. Her butt sank back down into the cracked leather cushion. Her limbs were as weak as a newborn calf.

"Is that any way to thank me?" Dick ran his tongue along his bottom row of teeth.

"Thank you?"

His hand dropped to his side, and he just stared at her. That was when she finally got a good look at him.

He was a mess. His blond hair was caked with a gray coating of dust. The red-and-dark-green flannel work shirt he wore had a line of dark crimson straight down the front. It didn't move with the fabric, though, as if it had dried where it landed.

Blood.

Cami followed the trail of red up to Dick's face. The column of his neck had crusted slashes trickling down, but no active bleeding that she saw. The origins, it seemed, must have been hidden gashes behind his ears and on the back of his neck. Her eyes went farther up to his mouth, nose, and other facial features. A few deep cuts and scrapes were scattered about, but nothing as bad as what she suspected he was hiding behind his neck. Charcoal gray smears deepened his complexion and made the ice blue of his eyes stand out as if peeking through a storm cloud.

Then she remembered.

Dick flinging her over his shoulders and beating feet across the parking lot.

The force of the explosion knocking them to the ground.

Dick's grunts and muted yells as his back was pummeled with debris . . . while she lay on the ground, protected in the cage of his body.

"Oh, my God," Cami whispered as she settled back into the couch cushions. "You did save me."

Dick stood next to her secondhand coffee table and just stared at her. It was hard to notice at first, but his whole body seemed to shake. The tightness around his lips forced his exhales through his nose, his nostrils flaring with each breath. His fingers had curled into fists at his sides. Repressed power resonated through his bunched shoulders and arms. Cami had never seen him so tense, so silently fuming. His whole body was humming like an apex predator about to pounce.

As soon as the thought entered her mind, he noticeably relaxed.

His gaze, still focused on her, traveled around the rest of her body. He took in her arms, chest, thighs, feet, and back up again. Did it give him comfort to see that she was still whole? Or did she look as bad as he did?

His hands unclenched as he walked over to her on the couch. The low coffee table bumped against the back of his calves as he stood before her. The strain of his jeans protested as he squatted down to her eye level.

"From the moment I smelled that gunpowder, I knew what was about to happen. It's true that my hearing is shit. But in exchange, my smell is as sharp as a tack. And one doesn't come through a war without being able to smell the enemy at the slightest whiff." He held out his hand to Cami. His eyes never left hers. "I was always going to get you out of there. But for now, let's get you cleaned up."

Cami stared down at his upturned palm, unsure what she was agreeing to if she accepted his invitation. This wasn't part of their arrangement. His presence in her apartment was too close, too over-powering. She hadn't asked for a savior. Didn't need one. But then, recent events had just done a lot to prove her wrong in that regard.

"Why a bomb? Why me?" she said, her lips trembling at the thought of what those answers meant for her.

"All questions for tomorrow. But right now, you need to get clean and get some rest. One step at a time, angel."

His logic was sound, he had her there. But there was still one more question she needed an answer to. She raised her eyes to him. "Why 'angel?'"

The brightest sunniest smile broke through the storm cloud cover of his face. She hadn't seen it before, and it was all the more beautiful perhaps because of its scarcity. She got the feeling he didn't smile often, and that saddened her to a degree.

"Salvation comes in many forms, I suppose," he said with a shrug. "Now, c'mon." He tucked his arms behind her back and under her knees. "If I have to keep smelling this crap, my vomit added to the mix will only make it worse."

With Cami held high on his chest, he marched them off to her bathroom.

CHAPTER 15

Dick fiddled with the silver nobs of Cami's shower. While he had seen a few of these at the various hospitals he'd stayed at in his time, or at the upscale hotels where he'd bed a woman here and there, the whole thing was some new kind of fancy for him. Still, the functionality was simple enough.

Cami's bathroom was small. Nothing more than a water closet tucked into the corner of her expansive loft. A basic pedestal sink sat below a plain mirror, and a toilet was affixed perpendicular to the sink next to the shower. On a small shelf above the toilet sat a folded lavender towel. Overall, the apartment took up the whole length of the maintenance barn, but the bathroom was the only closed-in room to speak of. He suspected that a bathroom such as this hadn't been part of the original design. The tiny space seemed like an afterthought.

The shower tucked in the corner had no privacy curtain, which was peculiar. Instead, the showerhead and tiled floor were encased in a glass box, with one of the panes operating on sliding rails to allow for entry. Why anyone would want to get naked and lather up in a see-through box was beyond him. But following the common theme of his time here, it was not his place to question. And he had an urgent task at hand.

Peeking over his shoulder, he watched Cami slump on the lid of the toilet. Though she had come alive for a few moments when they were out in the living room, the steam rising from the shower had obviously relaxed her body again.

Maybe a little too much.

"Nope . . . No, you don't." Dick sprang to his feet and righted Cami before she managed to relax into a puddle on the floor. "Time to get you clean, angel. I hope you don't feel strongly about these clothes. I'm burning them tomorrow."

"No, that's fine," Cami murmured. "Wait, what are you doing?" Dick raised her shirt up over her head, freeing her curls from the tight collar. "You can't just take my clothes off!" Cami quickly crossed an arm over her chest and pointed the other at the door. "Out! Right now. I can wash myself."

"That's cute." Dick unbuttoned his flannel shirt and kicked off his boots. "But in case you hadn't noticed, doll, you were just about to fall over and start kissing your porcelain sink, you're so drowsy."

Cami swiped her arm back over her chest so she had double the coverage and looked down. The tips of her sneakers began toying with the fibers of her bath mat. "No, I wasn't," she said softly, but all the fight had gone out of her.

"Look, you don't have anything I haven't seen before. And I'm not about to save your ass from a bomb only to let you drown in a quarter-inch of water because you were too damn modest to let me help you. No, I'm calling the shots here. I'll keep my pants on the whole time, but I'm going in there with you." Dick tossed his dirty clothes in the corner.

"We're not married, you know. You can't just throw those threats around like I'm some piece of property. I can take care of myself," Cami said, though she couldn't raise her eyes to adequately deliver the threat. Dick's heart squeezed a bit tighter at how hard she was trying to preserve herself.

And he thought *he* was stubborn.

But she'd just been through a trauma, and not that he would ever minimize the pain she must have felt when her mother died, but war was different. She had no experience with how a person changed on the other side. He wished like fuck he didn't either, but he could at least offer his wisdom in that regard.

With the shower steaming up the small bathroom, he walked over to her and stood her up, bracing most of her weight between his arm and the toilet. Without ceremony or exploring things for more than they were, he unfastened the button on her jeans and slid them down her legs. Once they were off, he rolled her socks free and tossed everything in the corner with his clothes. Her white cotton undergarments he left on. He gave her that much, as they weren't soiled from the explosion.

"I know you can," he said, helping her into the shower.

"I mean it. I can. Take care of myself, I mean," she said as Dick's hands guided her head under the hot shower spray. The water beaded on top of her curls at first, and then, with Dick's hand massaging her head, began to slowly absorb into her hair. His other arm was firmly wrapped around her midsection. As the water sheeted off his forearm, he tried not to think about how perfectly her waist fit in the crook of his elbow.

"Of course. You're one strong woman. Not many women I know can survive a bomb explosion." He kept bantering because it seemed to keep her awake. Focused. If she was fighting him, she wasn't knocking herself unconscious against a glass shower door.

"Just call me Wonder Woman," she murmured, her eyelids drifting closed and her weight mostly supported by Dick.

"I have no idea who that is, but you are definitely a wonder. I'll give you that." No way was she going to be upright for much longer, so he had to make this quick. He reached over to the built-in soap dish on the wall and grabbed the white oval bar of soap. Massaging his fingers around the soap under the water, he did his best to work up a lather with one hand. Once he was satisfied with the amount, he put the soap back in the dish and used his fingers and palm to wipe away the dirt and grime from Cami's face.

Her eyes were still closed, and the water had started to carry away the remnants of the explosion. Blood and ash mixed in the water, tinting its color gray and copper before trickling down the silver drain in the center of the shower. Cami's hair had been completely saturated, so he worked his soapy hand through her curls. Each coil wrapped around his fingers in a tantalizing come-hither motion. Some part of him knew he probably should have been using one of those fancy-smelling bottles of whatever on her hair. A few were sitting in a plastic holder hanging from the showerhead. But this was supposed to be a quick and dirty job. Get in, get her clean, and get her to bed.

And that was exactly what he would do.

Once the water at their feet ran clean, he turned off the taps and reached for the lavender towel nearby. Cami was beyond logy and barely able to hold her body upright. It made for a heck of a time buffing her dry, but at least she wouldn't have a problem falling asleep. After he ran the towel over his wet hair and body, doing his best despite the circumstances, he wrapped it around her, scooped her up in his arms, and walked out to her room.

It wasn't hard to figure out where he was going. Her apartment was one giant open space, except for the bathroom. Her bed, draped in a red comforter, took up the corner. He made a beeline over there and gently laid her down on top. Cami's blue eyes fought to stay open, but as soon as she hit the mattress, her small frame immediately curled in on itself.

Under heavy, hooded eyes, Cami struggled to track Dick's movements as he walked toward her small dresser. He wasn't about to let her sleep in soaking undergarments, but he wasn't sure he was man enough to remove them either. When he opened the dresser drawer, he rifled through his options for a moment, having no clue what passed for sleepwear in this time. Oddly enough, he chose a shirt with a man's face on it. Though when he turned it around, the words on the back brought a wry smile to his face

He would never understand the clothing of this time.

When he turned around to head back toward Cami, her soggy underwear, bra, and towel lay in a pile on the floor next to her bed while Cami remained cocooned under the covers. Dick swallowed down his nerves as he walked over to her. Dark brown tendrils fanned out across her pillow. Her delicate shoulder peeked out under the comforter and reminded him of the lack of barriers beneath.

But for the first time in a long time, he wasn't tempted. Oh, he was enthralled by her, certainly, but no other thoughts ran through his mind except keeping her safe. And in that moment, sleep was her safety.

"Dick?" Her soft voice broke through his thoughts as he stared down at her exhausted face. How she was still awake was beyond him.

"Yeah, doll?" He laid the clean shirt on the nightstand next to her, making sure her eyes tracked it so she knew she had clothing nearby.

"Stay with me tonight."

It wasn't a question or a request. It was a command, an order from someone who held a higher power than him, and it was given without hesitation or reserve.

A grin, unforced and unbidden, surfaced on his face as he tucked the comforter in tight around her. Content with her warmth, he grabbed the towel from the floor and walked around to the other side of the bed. On top of the comforter, he laid the towel out. He still only wore his pants, which were no longer soaking, but still damp. His hip hit the mattress first, then his legs as he raised them over the lip of the bed and settled in. When he glanced over, Cami was still facing the nightstand. The steady rise and fall of her left shoulder signaled she'd finally fallen asleep for good. Lying flat on his back, next to an angel, was more salvation than he deserved.

Because she needed him, despite all the cards stacked against him, and he'd be a damn fool to defy orders.

CHAPTER 16

"**W**as fire too hard of an invention? Ow, god*dammit!*"

An abrupt clang jarred Cami out of a dead sleep. Her eyelids sprang open at the auditory invasion. She was still cocooned in her bed, burrowed under her red comforter, when the ruckus snapped her neurons to attention. Too bad her brain also took that moment to bring all her pain receptors online.

Man, did her face hurt. Her eyes still stung as she tried to blink away the sleep threatening to pull her back under. And the back of her head throbbed like a jackhammer. The skin along her hairline and cheekbones was tight, like when a new scrape began the scabbing process.

Then she remembered the explosion. But it wasn't the car explosion that sat front and center in her mind. Oh, no.

It was her time in the shower. With Dick.

Embarrassment flooded her, and she quickly nabbed the edge of the comforter and ducked underneath it. Like a frickin' child hiding from the Boogie Man.

God, what had she done? Well, technically, not anything. He'd just helped her get clean. Yes, that was all. It was an act of kindness. A sweet gesture by a man who'd saved her life. But then why was her body still thrumming with the tingles?

And lest she forget, Dick was a royal class jerk. A mooch with terrible manners, a domineering butt munch, and a stupid . . . heroic . . . savior who rescued her from a car bomb, washed away all manner of blood and gore, and was still hanging around her apartment the morning after one of the most traumatizing moments of her life.

Crap.

And if she were being completely honest with herself, she hadn't really thought so terribly of him in a while. He had gone from a threatening con artist she had to endure to a daily comfort around the farm that her senses would seek out, without her even realizing it.

Another clang from her kitchen area brought her back to the situation at hand.

Dick was still there. In her apartment.

Cautiously, she lowered the lip of the comforter and peered over the edge toward the bull in a china shop. The sight nearly knocked her out of bed.

Dick was standing over by the long table she used to house her hot plate, microwave, and other kitchen items. He was facing her, though looking down. And he was piiisssed. His brows were cast in angry slants over hyper-focused eyes. But his snarl—for she couldn't imagine what else to call it when a grown man curled his upper lip back like a pit bull about to fight—stopped her dead. Her eyes glanced down to locate the source of his aggravation.

In one hand was her white electric kettle nestled in its heating base on the table. He had gotten the water in it just fine, but the lit match in his other hand set off alarm bells.

"Where do you light the damn thing? Hot water. That's all I want is some goddamn hot water," he growled out, clearly trying to keep his voice low but knowing full well his patience wasn't having any of it. He lifted the hot pot off its base and raised it above his head as he ducked and looked under it. He brought the match underneath and tried to catch a flame on plastic. Frustrated, he nestled the kettle back on its base and lifted up the cord instead. Grabbing the plug end, he scrutinized it for a moment and then brought the flame toward the metal prongs.

"Whoa, that's enough! Nope, not that. Blow the match out. You're done, bucko." Cami tossed the comforter aside, sprang out of bed, and two-timed it over to the kettle. She rested her hands protectively over the top of the hot pot and sighed, grateful he hadn't burned the barn down. "If you needed help, you could have just asked, you know."

She took the cord and plugged it into the surge protector on the floor underneath the table. The maintenance barn's top floor hadn't been originally wired for a residence, so she was limited with how many things she could safely plug in at one time. As such, she had fallen into the habit of only plugging in what she needed when she needed it.

"Sorry. I was just trying to make some coffee. Is it always this hard to get hot water? Why can't you just light a fire and be done with it?" He threw his arm out toward the kettle.

A pang of sympathy hit Cami as she realized how hard his circumstances must be. In that same vein, she also noticed he had changed into different clothes, though they were the same pair of jeans and dark green flannel shirt as Mal's other spare pair of work clothes Cami had seen Dick wear before. The image brought her back to how they were supposed to go shopping yesterday before . . .

Then the circumstances sank in.

"Did you stay all night?" Cami asked, the kettle beside her beginning to percolate. Grateful for the distraction, she squatted down to her storage bin on the floor and grabbed her red pour-over coffee dripper. The cool air against her exposed thighs made her realize she wasn't wearing any pants.

She shot up like a rocket and tried to pull down her shirt. A shirt she didn't remember putting on. Glancing down, she got an eyeful of an upside-down Jon Bon Jovi with his wild dirty blond-tipped hair, black leather jacket, sexy smirk, and wolf fang necklace.

"I don't know who that guy is or how you got his face on your clothes, but the back of that shirt appealed to me very much, so I grabbed it for you last night. Helped you put it on in the middle of the night when you needed to use the bathroom. I appreciated the sentiment on the back very much." Dick's lopsided grin was wolfish in its own right.

As she twisted back to look over her shoulder, her field of vision just barely took in the light-blue lettering that spelled out "Slippery When Wet."

Great. Of all the concert tour T-shirts she had in her drawer, he had to pick that one.

"Uh, thanks for everything," she said under her breath, yanking down the bottom hem of the shirt and shuffling over to her wardrobe.

Pants. She needed some frickin' pants, like, *yesterday*. And a bra. No, make that two bras. Should she grab a sweatshirt, too? God, why was she so embarrassed? He was hardly the first guy who'd spent the night.

But he is the first guy who saved your life and watched over you all night.

Cami squinted her eyes shut. Nope, she couldn't focus on that now. Pants first.

She grabbed an armful of clothes from the bottom drawer, kicked it closed with her foot, and scurried across the floor to her bathroom. Safe behind a closed door, she dropped the clothes on the toilet lid and began to strip . . . but not before she got an eyeful of the bra and underwear she'd worn yesterday hanging over the shower door. Her breath caught in her lungs as she slowly reached for it.

It was dry. A quick sniff and her nose came away with the same clean scent of her soap. The pads of her fingers brushed against the fabric. It was soft and pliant, as if it had been washed. Not stiff from a quick soak, ring out, and air dry.

Had that man washed her *unmentionables*?

Mortified. She was utterly mortified.

"And yes, I stayed."

The muffled sound of Dick's words through the bathroom door reminded her that she wasn't alone. The man who had been pummeled with car debris, almost burned down her home, and, apparently, had a knack for handwashing delicates was still in her apartment.

A minute later, Cami cracked the door and slid out of the bathroom, comforted by her protective baggy sweatpants and Bon Jovi. It was the best kind of armor a girl like her could have at that moment.

Dick stood facing her, leaning against the back of the couch. His arms were supported by the old furniture's rigid back. The flannel-shirt-and-jeans combo she had grown used to was still there, but his feet were bare and the shirt was unbuttoned in the front, revealing a center column of golden skin and a dusting of honey chest hair. His shirtsleeves were rolled up to his elbows, highlighting the strength of every curved tendon and muscle. They were vivid reminders of the last time Cami had seen those muscles. When they were cradling her in the shower, supporting her as hot water sluiced off his skin . . .

"Sorry, did you say you stayed the night?" Cami asked, the significance finally sinking in.

"Don't worry. I slept on your sofa. I snuck out around dawn to grab some fresh clothes. And before you ask, yes, I did your night checks. Everyone's present and accounted for," he said with a little mock salute in her direction.

"Oh, gosh. I forgot all about the horses!" she said, running her hands over her forehead and smoothing back her hair.

"Those are the least of your concerns, angel. Why don't you get some coffee brewing and we'll talk about yesterday?"

"Um, about yesterday . . . "

"When someone planted an explosive in your vehicle, which was planned to detonate right as you were leaving for the day."

Oh, *that* part of yesterday. Right.

With a nod, Cami walked over to her abandoned coffee setup and turned on the poor abused kettle. She pulled out her can of Folgers and grabbed two mugs. "That was unbelievable. I remember smelling something off, something metallic, when I got to the car. But I've never been in a situation like that before. I couldn't even process what was happening, what my senses were telling me, and there you were. You just rushed right in and . . . " The memories of the explosion paused her in mid-scoop. "How did you even know so fast?"

"Smelling gunpowder is like breathing in horse shit. You know it instantly, you can't mistake it for anything else, and when you've been around it for so long, it's more familiar to you than the aroma of apple pie. From the second the sulfur hit my nose, I knew to run like hell. I'm just glad I decided to grab you in the process."

The softness in his last remark caused Cami to turn around and lean against the table. Dick was still standing there, staring at her, but the way the corner of his lips rose ever so slightly did melty things to her insides.

Settle down, dangit. At least get some coffee in you before you start thinking with the wrong body parts. Heck, the man's only dressed like that because your little shopping trip got blown up.

Oh, clothes!

"It won't be a problem for Mal to let me borrow her truck, you know. I have to check in with Mrs. Katrukova and the conservatory. If they're still holding classes today, we can try going shopping for you again." Cami leveled off the scoop of grounds, emptied it in the coffee dripper's filter, and tucked it back in the coffee can before she poured the hot water into the funnel.

"What? No. There's no way on God's green earth you're going back there," Dick said, his arms folded over his chest.

"But I'm fine. And I need to rehearse. I'm singing Amina this week. It's my one opportunity to show my abilities as a lead soprano. Like I'd miss out on that," she said, her hands cocked on her hips.

"Did someone not just try to blow that pretty little head off your neck, doll? Are you crazy?"

"The police are taking care of it," she said, her arms spread wide at her sides. "Every sleepy detective and law enforcement official in Rochester was crawling over that place yesterday. Someone would be completely stupid to try that same stunt again. As far as I'm concerned, the conservatory is the safest place in the city."

"I'll remember that when I have to help Mal bury your remains. Besides, aren't you the least bit curious to know who might have tried to kill you? And judging by the fact that *that* little kernel of self-preservation hadn't yet entered your mind shows me you're not in your right headspace yet. So, no, you're not going. End of story." He pushed off the couch and walked over to her, eyeing the coffee's progress.

"Like hell I'm not! Now *you* listen to me, buster," she said, poking her index finger into his chest. "This is my one shot. My *one* shot to prove myself. This doesn't come along *ever* for a mezzo and certainly not one as poor as I am. How many opera singers do you know who tend horses at night in exchange for a roof over her head, i.e., the *barest* of human needs? None! Because every other one of them has the money and resources to go after what they want. Well, I'm through with waiting! Through with wishing! And I'll be *fucking* damned if I run and hide now."

Cami saw red. Breath huffed out of her like she'd just run a marathon, but she didn't care. She'd recently checked in with the estate attorney about when she could expect to receive the money from her mother's will. He'd said that even though he'd begun the process of expediting the settlement, he wouldn't authorize the actual transaction until their thirty-day deadline.

When she and Dick had to produce their valid marriage license application.

So, she had been funding her private tutoring on credit, which she hadn't told Dick about. Borrowing from Peter to pay Paul. And it sucked.

Dick hadn't looked at her, never even brought his eyes up from the red coffee funnel holding the wet grounds. He just stood there as she verbally assaulted him with barrage after barrage of her deepest inse-curities come to light. And while she let her emotions fly, he simply lifted the funnel, emptied the grounds into her garbage can, laid it on the table, and brought the mug to his lips. After a few more sips, he finally spoke.

"Together. We do everything together, got me? That means when you go in to rehearse, buy clothes, or even go for a walk around the horse pen, we go together." Dick finally turned to her. His expression brooked no argument. "Until this asshole is caught, I'm your fucking shadow, understood?"

Her bottom lip trembled as she slowly nodded. She hadn't been prepared for his reaction in the slightest . . . and she didn't entirely hate it, despite his macho bullcrap.

He stepped closer to her, his lips a hair's breadth away from hers, the tension between them a crackling cluster of electricity. "I'm going to be so close to you, angel, I'll be able to taste you just by breathing in your scent."

Cami stood there, her skin tingling from the nearness of the almost contact, her body remembering everything about their previous proximity in the shower. He was challenging her, tempting her.

And she knew it.

Before she could collect herself, Dick downed the hot coffee in a few more gulps, slammed the mug down on the table, and walked off toward his boots in the corner by the door. Once he was geared up, he grabbed the doorknob to leave, but not before turning back to her.

"Consider this a small taste of what it'll be like to be married to me, doll."

The door slammed shut behind him before she was able to throw the mug at his head.

CHAPTER 17

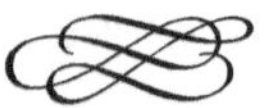

Leanne could see the impressions of Dick's boots in the frost-kissed grass as he stomped across the pasture. The front of his flannel shirt hadn't even been buttoned up, but the cold didn't seem to bother him. No, it was clear the man was ready to spit fire. His fists were clenched so tightly, she wouldn't have put it past him to take his anger out on a barn door or tractor tire.

As she leaned back against the oak tree, the vapor-like tendrils of her curly hair threatened to catch on the roughness of the bark like when she had been alive, but they never would. It was yet another stark reminder of the situation at hand. Reflecting on the past, she began to second-guess herself. She brought her right hand up to her temple and attempted to massage away her frustration. It was a force of habit only. Headaches were, blessedly, not afflictions spirits had to concern themselves with.

But she kneaded her temples anyway, her thumb and middle finger applying pressure of their own accord. Tendrils of white vapor danced around her hand, undulating with the back-and-forth movement of her fingers. Even though Leanne was a spirit and didn't have the worries that came with a corporeal body anymore, sometimes she just wished for the satisfaction of a good old-fashioned head rub.

Had she made the wrong decision in saving Dick's life back in his own time? By bringing him here to meet her darling Camilla, had she done more harm than good?

As she turned to face the bark and raised her hand to the trunk of the tree, the gossamer pallor of her essence floated around her fingers. If she squinted hard enough, she could almost remember what the bark felt like. The rasp of the uneven surface, the knots of the wood, and the occasional indentation where some insect had begun to carve out a home. Such a rough, unwelcoming exterior for such a beautiful, vibrant specimen of life and growth. Her eyes trailed up and down the trunk's body, examining each grain of wood and callused scar.

No, she hadn't made the wrong decision. She had never been more certain. They just needed more time to learn, to find their own potential for growth on the inside. For one didn't get to be a hundred-year-old oak tree without internal scarring. But by adding those layers, those rings of experience, well . . . as she reminded herself, those kids weren't there yet.

Her Camilla had only been eighteen years old when Leanne died in that car accident. When Leanne's cognizance reformed and memories of her life surfaced despite her body dying, she had been welcomed into the spirit world. Immediately, her despair was immense. Her precious daughter and only child was left behind. It had to have been a cruel joke. But it wasn't.

She recalled screaming at Camilla as Mal hugged her on the couch in Mal's office. Leanne had kicked, punched, and threw anything she could. Camilla had never looked up, never saw her there. And after a week of hovering, starved for attention and affection, a voice addressed her for the first time since she'd died.

"Leanne."

Turning around, Leanne looked upon the face of someone she hadn't seen since she was eighteen. Her older sister, Roberta, who was two years older than Leanne and had died in a boating accident.

And that was when Leanne had learned what her new existence would look like. She, like her sister, was a spirit, an afterlifer. Without a corporeal body, she was given this second chance to exist, though differently if she chose to. Some spirits traveled on, content with their earthly lives enough to settle down in the land of creation. Others, however, were restless, turbulent. An abrupt or unexpected death did not make for a comfortable skin, and for some, that skin needed to be stretched and molded before it fit better. Those souls were granted more time to grow accustomed to the afterlife, but in spirit form.

Of course, there were rules to follow. No human should know of their existence, and in exchange for ensuring that ignorance, Leanne and others like her were free to explore. And not just to check in on loved ones but really *explore*. She had been shortchanged the full span of her years, and the recourse for that as a spirit was the gift of time travel.

So she traveled. And it was glorious. After a year or so of watching Camilla move on from Leanne's death and being beyond grateful for the trust and care her friend Mallory had bestowed upon her daughter, she changed her course. With Roberta in tow, Leanne had been afforded an opportunity to see the world like no other.

She marveled as the great pyramids were constructed, each stone hand-chiseled and then lifted using an elaborate system of ramps and levers. She gawked over hordes of men erecting twenty-five-ton sarsen stones—without the benefit of the wheel's invention, which would come later—into Stonehenge. As she traveled, a fly on the wall of mankind's greatest creations, her curiosity was never satisfied.

Her love of history and architecture eventually led her to the Mid-Atlantic, to the creation of the breathtaking Northern Hotel in Baltimore. Construction began on the hotel in 1917, and following the end of the war in 1919, it was at its peak of opulence. Marble lobby floor, indoor plumbing, and the most breathtaking curved bifurcated staircases leading to the upper floors. Leanne, along with her sister, had sat perched on one of those staircases one day when a young woman named Sarah Johansson walked in front of her . . . carrying the essence of another spirit.

Leanne hadn't yet known much about essences or what it would mean to leave behind a newfound part of her spirit self on a living person. So she sat there quietly and observed. Through the conversation Miss Johansson had with a man over breakfast, Leanne learned that Miss Johansson wasn't from 1919 at all, but 2021. Well, her ears perked right up after that.

"Roberta, can we really make someone travel through time?" she asked her sister in a rush, her hands hanging on Roberta's arm but without the weight to pull her down.

"Technically, yes, but it's not looked upon highly," Roberta said, casting a sly eye toward Miss Johansson's blonde head. "We're supposed to be invisible. But yes, if you leave your essence behind for a mortal to touch, they get to go on a lovely one-way ride of your choosing. Now," Robert said with a raised finger, "if a mortal accidentally, or on purpose, *inhales* your essence, that is, takes a part of you into their mortal body, well, it's a rough ride all around."

"What do you mean?"

Roberta nodded her chin toward Miss Johansson. "That woman over there? She may not know it yet, or maybe she does and she's hiding it, but the fact that we can sense another spirit's essence on her isn't a good sign."

"Why not?"

"Because that poor dear is going to be consumed by the essence very soon. I've seen it before a time or two, and it's not pretty. Her skin will slowly begin to turn green as the essence spreads. Once it takes over her heart, she'll be yanked back to her time faster than a yo-yo."

"Gosh, I wonder if Camilla—"

"No," Roberta said, whipping her head around to face Leanne. Roberta's wavy hair was dark brown, but those blue eyes hadn't lost an ounce of their harshness when directed at Leanne. "You leave that baby alone, you hear me? I watched you crumble under the weight of grief after I died, Leanne, and you never really recovered. My baby niece, though," Roberta said with a slight shake of her head, "Mal's got her, all right, Lee? Cami will always miss you, but she's doing her honest best to move on and doing it well. Don't go fiddling with her life thinking you can send her back to some magic time when everything's lollipops and rainbows. Just leave her, Lee. She's got to carve her own path now."

Roberta's old words knocked around inside Leanne's head as she stared back at the bunkhouse. A smile crept across her face unbidden, her thoughts wandering to the first time she saw Dick.

He'd been in that same Northern Hotel lobby she and her sister were admiring when Miss Johansson crossed their paths. Oh, he was anything but a catch in that instance. More like the dregs of the haul you wanted to throw back. She recalled him introducing himself to Miss Johansson, eyeing her up like a prime T-bone steak for Sunday supper. And all in front of that nice man she was with, too. Dick was a lecher and a womanizer if she'd ever seen one. No doubt his insides were just as damaged as his outsides were. Harsh to think a thing like that, but what did she care? She was dead, and he was a first-rate ass.

Until he wasn't.

After Miss Johansson and her companion had left the lobby—her date fuming mad at Dick over more than what Leanne suspected was surface competition—Dick stood there by himself for a time. Oh, he wasn't alone to start with. Like clockwork, he had waltzed down that grand staircase earlier with a hot blonde clicking down right on his heels. The look exchanged between the two told Leanne all she needed to know. Well, that and the woman's mussed hair, lack of lipstick, and tits as perky and up-and-at-'em as a rooster crowing at the sun.

Leanne eyed the woman as she left the lobby, grateful her spirit form let her be a fly on the wall, but only tracked her briefly. She'd seen enough, and the splendor of the hotel had suddenly lost its charm for her. She and Roberta were about to leave when Dick abruptly rushed away from the lobby desk to run outside. Leanne followed, her curiosity getting the better of her. Outside, she was not prepared at all for what she saw.

"Louise, wait!" Dick shouted as he lightly jogged down the sidewalk after the blonde woman who faltered in her step at the sound of her name.

"Shhh," she hissed as she whipped around to face him. "Someone might see you."

"I know, I know," he said, slowing his jog as he approached her while pulling out a billfold from his pocket. "Listen, just take some money for Pete, all right? You said he's been eyeing that toy airplane from Krinsky's Toy Shoppe for weeks now." He handed her a folded wad of bills. The expression on his face was stern and harried, almost as if the act of kindness was as unnatural to him as a toy airplane trying to take flight.

Desperation. That was what it was, between his pinched lips and uneasy fidgeting, the sharp exhales through his nose, and his lack of eye contact. He was desperate, but he didn't want her to pick up on that, Leanne sensed. For the life of her, she couldn't imagine why. Ever the avid jigsaw puzzler in her living days, she decided to stick around and observe more of the young corporal.

The woman on the sidewalk just looked down at the bills, her brow creased with uncertainty. "I'm not a whore," she said, tight-lipped. "I can take care of Pete just fine when my husband's not around."

"Of course you can, and no one's calling you that, doll. I'm just saying it's freezing, your boy's birthday is next week, and your husband hasn't shown his face in at least that long."

Louise stood there, stunned. Her eyes focused on the cash before flicking back up at him.

"Here." Dick grabbed her hand and shoved the money against her gloved palm, curling her fingers around it. "Just . . . just take it."

And then he ran. Just completely turned tail down the street in the opposite direction.

Leanne stood there in disbelief.

So she followed him. Watched him over weeks and witnessed the curious angel/devil existence he insisted on living. Leanne watched, unobserved, when he instigated attacks on men as payment for his debts. She was horrified when he even attempted to brutalize Miss Johansson in retaliation against that officer she was with. Retaliating against what, Leanne hadn't yet learned. That should have been enough to turn her away, chalk him up to the lowest of the low, and move on.

But she couldn't. Because for every outward show of vileness, there was always a competing act of kindness and compassion, though diminished in its presence. She recalled witnessing such a moment of humanity shine through amid his attack on Miss Johansson. Dick had that poor woman slammed up against a boulder, doing his damnedest to play the brute. He tore at her clothes, gripped her throat, but the moves were disjointed. Almost like he was playing the part of an attacker, rather than drawing upon the wealth of his own experience.

And then Leanne saw the second the fight left him. The glassiness that coated his eyes, made more apparent in the moonlight. The tremors in his arms and hands. His grip no longer solid but uncertain. The sharp clench of his jaw had relaxed as well. Soft wisps of breath panted through his lips instead of the deep dragging inhales of a moment ago.

Miss Johansson had noticed the changes, too, and attacked. Fingernails gouged so deeply into Dick's eyes that blood trickled down the sides. The woman bolted across the plaza, and every feminist bone in Leanne's spiritual body screamed for her to follow, to ensure that woman would be found and cared for.

But she couldn't help but look back down at Dick. His hands covered his eyes and screams rumbled deep from his chest as he lay curled up on the frozen ground next to the boulder.

Then the whimpering began.

In the silence of the night, under a moon bright enough to illuminate the darkest of corners, Dick cried. He brought his arm down in front of his mouth and bit down hard on his coat. With his forearm held tightly as a gag, he erupted into it. Full-body wails left the man. His body vibrated with the efforts and shook from the adrenaline. After a minute or so, when his lungs had given all they could, Dick slowly flopped onto his back and stared up at the moon. Leanne recalled gazing down at him, at the red rivulets of blood mixed with tears that dripped down the side of his face like a plagued Nile Delta.

This man wasn't a brute. He was a fake who felt compelled to act the part for some reason. Who on earth would willingly behave as a vile bastard when that wasn't who they genuinely were on the inside? Why put up such a facade? Leanne couldn't fathom, but that man carried a burden like no other.

Well, maybe except for her Camilla.

And that was when the dots connected. Leanne continued to follow Dick, all the while speaking to Roberta about her plan. Eventually, Leanne saw her opening. In the heat of a fight between Dick and that man of Miss Johansson's, Dick lost his footing and was tipped into a nearby well. Acting quickly, she dusted the rim of the well with her spirit's essence right as he fell in. His pants scraped through the green dust as his legs upended fully, sending him falling down the well headfirst. Right before he would have broken through the water's surface, Leanne exhaled a breath she no longer needed.

There hadn't been a splash. Her plan had worked.

Most operas didn't have happy endings. But her favorite, Bellini's *La Sonnambula*, did. All it took was for the poor tenor, Elvino, to uncover his own truth, and for the sad soprano, Amina, to wake up knowing she had never really been alone to begin with.

CHAPTER 18

Orange.

The sweater he was wearing was orange. But not out-of-the-fruit-bowl orange. Because that would have been too straightforward. No, this was called something else. He glanced down at the white paper tag hanging off his sleeve. "Pastel peach cable gauge sweater - men's L."

Apparently, he was a fuzzy peach. Lovely.

"How's it going in there, sir? I brought you over some more sweaters, shirts, and slacks. Here you go."

Before Dick could turn around and answer the department store's fitting room attendant, bright colors he had only ever seen in oil paintings cascaded down over his door. Baggy silk pants hung on the same hanger as a matching blazer, both made of more fabric than parachutes. Long-sleeve shirts followed next, adorned with every obnoxious pattern and zigzag he could imagine. Yellow polka dots, green stripes, even something called red buffalo plaid assaulted every otherwise mundane base color. The patterns were dizzying.

"That lagoon blue suit would look stunning on you!" the attendant hollered on the other side of the door. "It would match your eyes perfectly, especially with that black long-sleeve shirt underneath the blazer."

His gaze darted over to the peg on the wall with yet more hangers. That stack held shirts that were blessedly simple, but still more color than he was up for. Swiping through the garish-colored ones, he landed on the simple black shirt.

"Got it, thanks." Dick put that one on top of his take-home pile, which was pitifully small compared to the wads of fabrics adorning the rest of the wall pegs. Ten minutes in this room, and he was itching to get out. He had never been waited on in his life, and he wasn't about to start with that doe-eyed redhead throwing silk slacks his way.

Dick glanced down at his pile of keepers. The clothes were enough to get him by: two pairs of light denim jeans, six white undershirts, two long-sleeve shirts (both black), two long-sleeve button-down shirts (both in a color called charcoal because they regrettably didn't come in black), a dark-green thick gauge sweater (as far away from pastel peach as he could get), and a plaid fleece pullover in black-and-white buffalo plaid (he had conceded to the pattern, as it was the least garish).

Arms full, he opened the fitting room door. The redhead stood before him, her arms laden with yet more clothes in various colors. God, were those pants *yellow?* Her blue eyes were so big, so enamored of the situation, he sighed a deep breath and soldiered forward to put her out of her misery.

"You've been a big help," Dick said, raising the stack of clothes in front of him as a pseudo peace offering. "I'll just go find my friend and pay for these. Thanks."

The attendant looked down at the clothes in his hands with a frown. "But you don't have nearly enough variety! If it's darker colors you prefer, I have that same sweater you chose in a lush eggplant purple," she said, turning to go look for it.

"Dick, are you ready yet? Oh, good. You've found some things."

Relieved, Dick walked over to Cami while keeping a side-eye out for the terror holding a purple sweater. "Thanks for this, again. I promise I'll pay you back," he said as they approached the cashier.

"Happy to help." She handed over the clerk a plastic card that Dick had never seen before. She appeared to be using it to pay for the items.

"What is that?" he asked, marveling as the woman behind the counter took out a rectangular device with multiple pieces of paper on it and placed the card underneath the paper. In one swift motion, the woman took the black handle to the left of the paper and slid it all the way to the right before swiping it again back to the left.

The woman looked up at Dick with an eyebrow raised. "It's our credit card imprinter, sir," she said as she took the slips of paper and separated them out before handing one copy to Cami.

"Time to go, bucko." Cami looped her hand through his arm and took the bag of merchandise from the woman. "Thanks again," she said with a quick wave as she ushered Dick swiftly out of the store.

"You used that card to pay for those items, didn't you? How?"

"It's a credit card. Basically, it's a line of credit given to me by the bank. I can use the card as payment, and any charges I place on that credit card I reimburse to the bank at the end of the month."

Dick stayed silent as he fell in step beside her. "So you didn't have the money for those items." Not a question.

"Not today, but I will," she reminded him, smiling sweetly.

"You shouldn't have done that, Cami. I can get by with what I have for now. I don't ever want you to put yourself out for me."

"Oh, stop." Cami waved her hand in front of him. "Soon, thanks to you, I will have the money, so it's a nonissue, and I don't want to hear any more about it because I am starving. Heck, my stomach gurgles will likely drown out anything you want to complain to me about anyway. So come, let me introduce you to one of my absolute favorite things about a shopping mall: the food court."

***

Grease and mustard dribbled down the side of Cami's hand as she took a bite of her hot dog. The snap as she bit into it was one of the most satisfying things about the experience. The way the bun folded around the hot dog under the pressure of her fingertips offered a perfect pillow for her favorite mall treat. Two hot dogs, slathered in spicy brown mustard, and a side of waffle fries just made everything better. It had been her favorite treat in high school when she and her mother would go shopping for new school clothes.

Cami allowed herself the brief respite of sinking back into her old comforting memories of her mother. She always picked out a similar version of the same denim skirt each August, and her mother always scolded her for not adding color and variety to her wardrobe. Or when her mother wanted Cami to get her ears pierced, but the sight of needles made Cami's stomach sour. She laughed to herself, thinking back on how she'd been the only girl freshman year still wearing stick-on earrings. She had sucked it up and gotten them pierced that first weekend in September.

A slight movement on the food tray in front of her caught her eye. Before she could say anything, Dick brought the hot dog to his lips.

"What do you think you're doing?" Cami whisper-shouted, reaching out to try and knock his hot dog down to the tray.

"Hey, I'm eating here," Dick said around the mouthful of the half-bite Cami couldn't save from going in. "What? Do you see a bug or something?"

"No, but, gosh, you just put *ketchup* on your hot dog."

Dick stared at her, dog in hand, and blinked once. "Yeah . . ."

"Ketchup is for fries, not hot dogs. We are in New York State, for crying out loud. Do you know how many Coney Island and Manhattan transplants live in Rochester? Tons! Trust me, every one of those shore-loving parents twenty years ago sent their kids to college upstate and you know what? Those kids all decided to stay here. So brats, dogs, and any other kind of German wiener on a bun get the hot stuff. It's nonnegotiable."

Cami sat back and took a huge bite of her hot dog *with mustard* for emphasis before nabbing her napkin to blot at her mouth. The area didn't get many out-of-towners beyond the college crowd, but that was all right. Dick could easily learn the ropes. Because there was no way she'd be seen with someone who put *ketchup* on their hot dog. Especially not someone she was supposed to be married to (but not really, she reminded herself).

A slight smile crept up the corner of Dick's lips. His eyes became hooded, and the whites of his teeth were slowly revealed. His gaze was locked on hers, like a sniper zeroing in. Cami swallowed down the remnants of her hot dog and watched, a knot forming in her stomach, as he slowly brought the offending hot dog closer to his lips. Once in range, his teeth parted and tore into the thing like a shark to a baby seal. Grease popped free of its casing, coating his lips in a sheen of fat. His tongue darted out and made a slow lap around his mouth's perimeter. His gaze never broke free of hers.

Cami watched, shocked, as he sat back and shut his eyes, balancing precariously on the chair's hind legs. She was infuriated and, at the same time, riveted and, crap, was she getting turned on while sitting across from the Chinese food takeout place and the cinnamon roll bakery at *the mall?* A tight pull formed deep in her pelvis, causing her to inch forward a bit and squeeze her thighs together. The pressure helped, but despite the embarrassment, she couldn't look away.

"Delicious," he said, plopping the chair's front legs back down.

The shock of the chair's noise and his words startled her. The soft drink to her right shook slightly as she gripped the table.

"Oh, crap!" Cami reached for the soda as it tipped over the edge, but she was too late. The ice and cola plummeted out of the cup and painted the white denim jeans of the woman who happened to be walking by.

"What the hell? Ugh, I *just* got these. Jamie-babe, help! It's soaking in! Hurry, hurry! Wait, Cami? *You* did this?"

While Cami's hands began to freeze, her fingers holding melting ice cubes and cola, goose bumps prickled along her skin . . . and not from the ice.

Cami slowly raised her head to the voice she had been listening to on repeat since the start of her music program. The voice that had only recently been silenced by Cami's other recent humiliating blunder during rehearsal.

Sandy Projansky stood before Cami. The pointed shoulder pads of Sandy's designer fuchsia blazer were no match for the harsh lines of her eyebrows as she stared down at Cami. Bright purple splotches dotted the bridge of her nose, which had flattened out significantly and was less defined due to the swelling. Her teeth had been fixed as well. Her fiancé, James, was all over her, grabbing napkins off Cami and Dick's table to blot at the cola stains.

What are the odds she'll believe this was also an accident? Slim to none, most likely.

"Enough!" Sandy screamed, swatting James away. A woman toting her two young children near the cinnamon roll bakery looked over and hurried her family away from the commotion.

Cami reached for more napkins. "Sandy, I'm so sorry. It was an accident. I didn't see you there."

"Like hell you didn't. I'll believe that horse shit the moment you stop smelling like it."

Cami plopped back into her seat, her chin nearly hitting the floor at the dig.

"I know about your little tutoring arrangement with Mrs. K.," Sandy said, her hands on her hips. "The whole ensemble knows about it. Did you honestly think your little lessons at this stage of the game would catch you up to the rest of us? Hell, look at you. You're no opera singer. I wouldn't even pay you to sing happy birthday at a five-year-old's party. Well, maybe if you were the clown, I would." She smirked.

Loud clangs resounded around them as Dick shot to his feet. His metal chair had toppled over behind him, as if it inherently knew to skedaddle out of his warpath. Fury, clear and present, radiated off Dick's frame. His arms hung low at his hips, his fists clenched in tight restraint as he glared down at Sandy.

"Ma'am, do watch your tone." The words were short, concise, and spoken so slowly it would have been impossible for Sandy to have missed his message. Or the threat implied in his warning.

Sandy stood there stock still and gaped at Dick. It was subtle, but Cami managed to make out the slight tremble to Sandy's fingers as they clutched the straps to her purse at her shoulder.

"I'm sorry. Who are you?" James asked, stepping in front of Sandy.

"Miss Foster's fiancé." The corner of Dick's lips ticked up at the mention. "You'll be seeing me around."

As flabbergasted as Cami was by Dick's reaction, her stupid mind couldn't get Sandy's words out of her head.

Cami took a discreet look at her outfit. She wore her mother's old college sweatshirt, the collar of which was frayed and the letters on the front faded. Her acid-wash jeans, likewise, were worn thin, with gaping holes in the knees, and not by choice or fashion. Every pair of pants she owned had either holes or patches on the knees from working night checks. So much of the supplemental feed and equipment for the horses were so heavy for her to lift, she had found it easier to just fill tubs and clean tack down on the floor. And her cotton white sneakers hadn't been white since the day she'd bought them. The dusty coat of gray and brown grime was a permanent fixture.

Whether or not Dick was around to come to her rescue, it wouldn't change the way the world saw her.

Sandy stepped closer into Cami's space. Her dark-brown penny loafers crunched on the ice cubes melting into the linoleum. She squatted down and got her face good and close so Cami had no choice but to look at her. Sandy's words were so quiet, Cami almost didn't hear them over the din of the food court.

"Let me make something perfectly clear. This," Sandy said with a subtle circle of her index finger between them, "is not for you. Even if you managed to hit the notes you need for Amina, your presence is shit, and I'm not going to let some wannabe tweety bird flutter around on stage just because her poor mommy told her she had a nice voice. This opera, this production, is huge for all our careers and the conservatory. You need a high level of detail, of focus, to portray the emotional range of the role that's needed to impress the opera house scouts. And, honey, you ain't got it. And lest you think I'm out for the count, I've got one more week of rest and then my doctor's giving me the green light to resume rehearsals. So enjoy your little jaunts on stage for the next week. Just try not to stink up the costumes too badly."

Sandy stood straight up, flicked an ice cube at Cami's leg, and snaked her hand through James's bent arm.

Cami didn't know what was louder: the footfalls of Sandy's loafers as she stomped away, the scraping of the table as Dick moved it to the side, or the pounding heart in her chest.

"Who the hell was that?" Dick asked, anger furrowing his brow as he watched the couple walk away. "And what did she say to you? Cami?"

Her head was down in her hands, and blessedly, her hair fell over her fingers just enough so her face would stay hidden. God, how she hated to show weakness, hated when the tears flowed and there was no holding them back. Aside from when her mother died, she had only ever allowed herself to full-blown bawl her eyes out in front of Mal. No way could she continue to let Dick see her like this. Her meltdown in Mr. Donnelly's office had been bad enough. She resigned herself to two huge sniffles to suck back the sobs and started to stand up, but two firm, warm hands encircled her wrists and gently pulled her hands away from her face.

Dick was crouched in front of her, in the same position Sandy had just been in, yet she was met with an entirely different expression. Concern and curiosity were etched on his face. His lips were pinched together tightly, but the force of breaths puffing from his nose was intense. The lightness of his touch was gentle and soothing, but Cami bet that if she let him, he'd be more than willing to curl those gentle fingers into powerful fists and go to town on whatever was upsetting her. The strain in his shoulders looked unnatural, as if he was trying to be calm for her benefit.

And why was she thinking of Dick as her own personal hero?

"That was Sandy Projansky. The lead soprano in the company at the conservatory, and up until I accidentally took out her perfect nose and two front teeth on the stage floor during rehearsals, she was singing Amina. Our instructor assigned me to take over performing Sandy's role in rehearsals because the regular under-study is out of town. And apparently, Sandy is less than thrilled at the idea."

She stopped short of expanding on Sandy's other criticisms: that she smelled like horse poop, was slumming down the ensemble's pedi-gree, and didn't have the vocal or acting talent to pull off the role. No need to rehash all that to the man she was supposed to marry to claim her inheritance and, oh, yeah, pursue her dreams of being a profes-sional opera singer.

With a glowing review like that from one of her peers, what could go wrong?

While Cami continued to mentally chastise herself, Dick hadn't said a word. Braving the silence, she looked up at him.

"Come with me. I have something I want to show you," Dick said, still holding Cami's hands and guiding her to her feet.

"What?"

He didn't answer, just continued to guide her away from the food court and down the corridor to their right. At the end of the hall, they came to another concourse. He never let go of her hand as he led them to the business in the far right corner. Cami squinted as she looked up. The bright lights declaring "Kilkenny's Fine Jewelry" brought a curious smile to her face.

Dick's palm had begun to sweat a bit as the heat seeped through to Cami's skin, but she didn't say anything. She just followed him as he brought her in front of an illuminated glass case with an assortment of rings laid out on black velvet holders.

Engagement rings. Wedding rings.

"When I first heard you sing that song during your rehearsal, I didn't know what to make of it."

Cami thought back to the rehearsal. "I thought you didn't like it. Your face was so stoic, like someone was driving nails into your feet and all you had to do was grin and bear my performance for the pain to end. You looked miserable." Cami snorted and looked at Dick. He was staring straight into the case of rings.

"I loved your singing, Cami. And that song, that melody, well . . . I remember it from when I was a child." He squinted slightly, as if trying to recall old memories. "My mother, she would hum that melody. The one where you were sleepwalking. I never knew the words, and I left my mother's house when I was five, but when you sang those opening words, it just—" He cut off on a swallow. His grip tightened around her hand.

"I guess that could be right." Cami did some quick math in her head. "Bellini composed it in 1831."

"My grandmother loved that type of music. God, it would fill the house. Especially when she baked her blueberry pies, she'd sing the melodies with my mother. I lived with my grandparents and mother in those early years before, um . . ."

"Before what?" Cami hedged.

Dick hadn't looked at her, hadn't moved an inch except for his hand tightening around hers. He had placed her on his right side, which he often did. He was always so careful to keep her away from his deformed side. Like she was some precious thing who couldn't be trusted near his darker, harsher parts. As if one side was acceptable and one side wasn't. As if she was only good enough to be trusted with the part of him that shone above the surface.

Well, screw that.

When Dick refused to answer her, Cami took his face in her hands and turned his gaze to her. He stood there, his head caged between her fingers and nowhere to look but right at her.

"I see you," she whispered, a slight edge to her tone making the remark harsher than she intended. "The good *and* bad, or however you seem to see yourself. You don't need to protect me, all right? Especially not from you. And if you're not ready to share parts of your past, that's perfectly fine. But I want you to know that you can trust me."

Dick slowly raised his hands and brought them under Cami's forearms to cradle her head and chin in his palms. They just stood there, each holding the other's head, forcing each other to see what they dared not show anyone else. At that moment, Cami was an open book under Dick's inspection. As his eyes roamed over her cheeks, she was aware of every freckle he took in, every insecurity she let show, and in turn, she drank him in as well. His scars were no longer harsh, but comforting. Her thumb smoothed the ridges along his left brow where the scar tissue was most prominent. She picked up on the slight shudder of relief he gave off and relished the barely noticeable way he leaned his head slightly to the left so she could cradle his deformed ear in her palm.

That she was able to calm his storm, soothe his beast, empowered her beyond any stage performance she'd ever given. She never wanted the moment to end.

And then Dick dragged her back to reality.

"In two weeks, I'll be placing one of those rings on your finger," Dick reminded her. "And there won't be a thing standing in your way of singing your heart out and bringing down the house."

Yes, in two weeks, they'd be able to apply for the marriage license and she'd be able to come into her inheritance and pursue her career in earnest. She would soon have everything she needed, everything she'd always wanted.

Then why did her heart feel so hollow inside?

CHAPTER 19

Tension wound itself around Dick's nerves like a boa constrictor. Every part of him felt squeezed, from his knees scraping the theater seat in front of him to his poor balls currently pancaked between his thighs. A man like him wasn't made for a seat this small, that much was clear. But his overall tight fit wasn't the only thing making him itchy.

The last time he came here, Cami's vehicle had been blown sky high and nearly taken them with it. So when Cami had insisted on coming back here for class, over his dead body he would let her go alone.

Though every muscle under his skin was ready to spring, the immediate thought of Cami calmed him back down. Taking a break from scanning the room, he glanced forward. His girl was onstage, score sheet in hand, furiously scribbling some new blocking instructions from the director. He loved watching her work, especially when she wasn't focused on him watching her. As she wrote, her little pencil was nearly eaten up in her hand, she moved it so fast. Her hair hung forward, exposing the capped sleeves of her red peasant's blouse with the tempting tie at the base of her throat. Such a tiny patch of skin to be exposed, so why he couldn't help but focus on it he had no idea.

He shouldn't be staring at her. That wasn't why he was there. A quick shake of his head and he went back to eyeing the surroundings. He couldn't afford to lose focus again. As a reminder of what was at stake, he mentally went through his checklist.

Six exits, two main doors at the back of the orchestra seats, two doors at the back of the balcony seats, and one on each side of the stage. The stage left exit had stairwell access while the stage right exit had dressing room access.

Previous count of total capacity seats: 1,300.

The parking lot immediately outside the theater had been cleared and cordoned off by police, so no unknown vehicles were stationed nearby the building.

All the required parties for today's rehearsal were present and accounted for, except . . .

"Hey there, you were with Cami at the mall the other day, right?"

A tall blond man stood next to Dick in the aisle. His hair was cropped short on the sides but stood tall in the front in a slicked-back quiff. None of the performers were in costume, so Dick didn't know which character this man played, but he recognized him instantly.

"You're Jamie-babe. You were the one with the napkins who rubbed down that soprano wearing the white pants."

A sharp cough escaped the man's throat as he tried to hide a smile behind his fist. His gaze darted around at the people onstage before he returned his attention to Dick. "Yeah, that was, uh, me. I'm James. I play Elvino."

He held out his hand. Dick stared down at the man's open palm. Every other finger had a different chunky silver or tungsten ring resting at its base. Dick didn't know whether he should turn one of the rings like a knob or grab the man's hand and use it to tap out a beat on the back of a theater chair. Not feeling terribly interested in either option, Dick just let the man's hand hang there. Honestly, was he supposed to be impressed with all that hardware? How did he even wipe his ass without getting one of those puppies snagged on the porcelain?

A nervous laugh bubbled up from James as he slowly took his

unshaken hand back. "How about I, uh, just scooch in there next to you?" He nodded toward the vacant seat next to Dick's aisle seat.

Dick turned to his right to look at the empty seat. Yup, there was a seat there. Despite the tight squeeze, Dick kept his knees bumped up against the seat in front of him and just looked back at James. A small talker he was not. Hopefully, this asshole got the hint.

"All right, cool," James said as he hopped over the row in front of Dick and took up the seat in front of him. Once settled, he turned his body sideways and leaned back to address Dick.

Yay.

"So, uh, you're Cami's fiancé?" James asked.

"Yes."

"Wow, a man of few words. Okay, I hear that. It's just a little odd to see you hanging around here all of a sudden, you know? Usually it's just a company-only thing here. Did Cami invite you or something?"

"Yes."

"Huh." James nodded. "Well, Cami's been giving it her all as Amina, eh? I mean, the company's grateful for her to fill in and all. At least until Sandy's recovered and takes it back."

That got Dick's attention. "I was under the impression Sandy's injury prevented her from returning to the role."

"Nah, she'll be back in a week. You'll see. Got the all clear from that nose doc, and a little makeup will cover the bruising. She'll be good as new," James said with a too-enthusiastic nod. "Oh, hey, there's my baby now."

Dick glanced over to the stage right door and saw Sandy trotting out, paper in hand, to speak with the instructor. The smile on the soprano's face was painful to look at, with how it pulled at the corners of her swollen nose. The woman was clearly elated about something. Curiosity tempted Dick to lean forward more, but not out of care for Sandy. No, it was the solemn look on the instructor's face that caught his eye. No smile there, that was for sure. And the way the teacher kept her hands fisted and wrung tight across her midsection was telling.

Mrs. Katro-hoosy didn't share Sandy's joy. What was going on there?

"Good talk, um, sorry, I didn't catch your name," James hemmed.

"That's because I didn't give it to you," Dick said, his eyes never leaving the stage.

"Fucking spazz," James muttered under his breath as he got up and headed toward Sandy. Once he met her onstage, the instructor moved over to speak privately with Cami. They were too far out of range for Dick to pick up on anything, but judging by the ashen tone that crept over Cami's usually vibrant skin, the news wasn't good.

"Attention, everyone. Attention, please," Mrs. Katrukova said, standing in the center of the stage to address the company.

Sandy stood off toward stage right and had the biggest shit-eating grin on her face as she clung to James's arm. Meanwhile, his Cami was on the opposite end of the stage. Immediately, his stomach bottomed out. There she stood, her arms folded across her body in the biggest self-hug her petite frame was capable of. Her bottom lip, usually perfectly pouty and always smiling, hung down in shock. An occasional tremor caused it to shimmy slightly. Her eyes were glued to the floor in front of her.

What had just happened?

Dick shot to his feet, poised to do something. Anything. But what? Was there something he could punch? He was good at punching. Maybe that James guy?

"As you all know, our beloved Sandy had to be removed from the role of Amina due to her injury."

Cami hugged herself tighter at the mention of the accident.

"Stacey was to be our understudy for the role. However, I had just received word this morning that she will be delaying her trip home. She has been enjoying a lovely honeymoon in Europe with her new husband, David, and it is a most well-deserved time for the happy couple. We're so thrilled for them," Mrs. Katrokova added with a single clap of her hands. "Our Stacey has also confided in me her desire to spend this time visiting the European opera houses, rather than returning home to understudy as Amina."

The crease in Cami's eyebrows deepened as she raised her head to face the instructor. The hushed whispers floating across the stage highlighted the collected unease spreading throughout the auditorium.

"This morning, Sandy came to me with a doctor's note regarding her injury. With her permission, I can share that, after this week, she has been given the all clear and can return to her normal performing schedule."

Sandy stepped forward, one hand raised in the air and the other clutched to her chest as if it were already holding a congratulatory bouquet of roses. She was waving.

At people three feet in front of her.

"I'm so glad to be back, everyone," Sandy chirped. "I've missed my beloved Elvino." She cast adoring eyes at that James character.

"Sandy, just one moment, please," Mrs. Katrokova interrupted. "While we're all thrilled that Sandy will be back to full health soon enough, this temporary change in casting has allowed me to analyze some things more intently."

Lemons. That Sandy woman's face soured so fast, Dick would have sworn she'd just choked down a dozen lemons.

"Camilla has been doing a marvelous job filling in as Amina. She has truly stretched her vocal reach as a mezzo, and quite frankly, it has added an element to our production that is not often seen. So, after extensive conversations with our maestro, Mr. Jacobs, we have made the decision to have Camilla continue to perform the role of Amina for the production."

Cami's lips, previously quivering in shock, had expanded into the biggest grin he'd ever seen. Her cheeks must have hurt from how wide and open her smile was. And damn, was he thrilled for her. Happiness was a good look on her. Right then and there, he was determined to keep that streak going. So he clapped. Slow at first, a light pat of his hands coming together. But then he said fuck it and practically pounded his palms in excitement, only stopping to bring two fingers to his lips so he could whistle.

All eyes shifted to him, Cami's included. But he didn't care. No, that wasn't true. He did care. Immensely. Without even realizing it, somehow over the course of his time here, Cami's goals had become his goals. Her hopes had become his hopes. And it went beyond a single achievement. Yes, the money from her inheritance would help both of their situations, but money was money in any time. It brought the power to keep life alive through procuring food, shelter, and more. But it was one note, replaceable and impersonal. Just a needed thing because survival without it was so much harder.

For Cami, though? Money was never about comfort but soaring. Achieving heights one could only dream about. It was an inspiration, a piece of a promise held out to her ensuring she could change her fate. She could come alive, and societal expectations be damned.

Cami was the bravest force of nature he'd ever had the good fortune to lay eyes on. He was totally in awe of her and enamored.

Enamored. In love.

As the words sank in, Cami's bright eyes stayed focused on him amid the theater seats. The smile that had previously lit up the stage softened slowly, but one corner of her mouth still quirked up. As if it would even be possible to seal up the floodgates on her all-consuming joy.

Then she bolted.

Taking a running leap off the stage, she landed in a crouch on the carpet of the theater floor. After a second to regain her equilibrium, she sprang up and ran straight down the aisle toward him. When she closed in, a final jump off the floor had her arms closed tightly around his neck. Her chin rested on his shoulder as she peered out behind him.

With her white cotton sneakers dangling above the floor, Dick wrapped his arms around her slender waist and held her tightly to his body. Her smile, which he couldn't see but definitely felt, was infectious. He couldn't help but grin as he closed his eyes, stepped out into the aisle, and started twirling her around in the small space.

"I'm proud of you, angel," he said lowly in her ear. Her soft curls tickled the left side of his face and neck in the best way, as if she always knew to give that part of him extra love. After a few seconds longer than was probably appropriate, but like he cared, he let her feet skim the ground, giving her the option to stand on her own and separate if she wanted to.

But she didn't.

"I can't believe it." Her words were muffled against his shoulder. "Gosh, I just can't believe it."

"Your mother would have been so stinkin' proud, too, you know," Dick added, recalling the honey blonde specter he saw outside Cami's window that night. He still wasn't sure exactly what he thought he saw or why that memory, of all memories, chose that moment to wriggle its way into his consciousness.

At the mention of her mother, Cami's grip around his neck loosened. The loss stung. He missed the closeness of the connection, her warmth against him. Without issuing the order, his arms made up the difference and tightened around Cami more snuggly. The softness of her body nestled perfectly against his frame. When he held her like this, he was almost tempted to keep her. As if her warm hands had the power to melt the icy shards around his jagged, mangled exterior and smooth them into something worthy. Something worth staying around for.

Something lovable.

By her?

As soon as the thought formed, Cami leaned her head back, her fingers still entwined behind his neck.

The clapping behind them had slowed down. Bodies in the periphery were blurry orbs that dipped low to grab belongings before shuffling off stage and walking down the aisles, passing the two of them to exit.

None of it concerned him. Because Cami was staring straight at him. Her scrutiny was intense, almost too intimate. The theater lights had been brought up and all the seats around them were illuminated. Under the garish lights, around an audience of her peers, he was too open. Too exposed. Would his facial scarring spark curiosity among others? Would he reflect poorly on Cami?

Worried, he dropped his arms from her body. But right as they fell, brushing past her hips on their downfall, Cami stood on her toes and embraced him more tightly. The surprise of her lips crushing against his almost made him fall back against a theater seat. He quickly grabbed her for balance and breathed her in. The warmth, the lightness, the calm, just everything—it all washed over him as their breaths mingled in those slow, burning kisses.

Dick's eyes were still closed when Cami pulled back slightly, just enough for their noses to still touch.

She rested her forehead against his. "Come home with me."

"You got it, angel."

CHAPTER 20

The tires of Mal's truck crunched over the gravel road as Cami rolled the beast to a stop. She normally would park it along the side of the main office building. But tonight, it was too cold to walk the extra hundred feet to the barn. Well, it was too cold and her stomach was doing all sorts of flippity flopping. She was a bundle of nerves . . . and not for the reason she would have thought.

In two weeks, she was going to perform Amina. In front of recruiting managers and talent house acquisition specialists for opera houses all over the world. And as Mrs. Katrukova had pointed out, they'd be coming to see the Rochester production *because* a mezzo sang the lead. Not despite. The notion both thrilled and humbled her.

But that wasn't what made her so nervous.

Cami killed the ignition and just let the keys dangle there for a moment. The cold crept into the cabin quickly, snaking its way through the vents and exhaust systems of the old Chevy. She didn't feel it, though. Inside, she might as well have been the giant red dot on Jupiter for all the fiery storms she had swirling inside her.

When Mrs. K. announced Cami as the lead, the roaring clap that echoed up from the audience seats had caught her by surprise. When her eyes searched out the noise, it had been Dick who was hollering. Dick had been the one smashing his hands together in applause, jumping up and down, and whistling for her. In that moment, he had turned into her number one fan, challenging a stage full of no doubt shocked performers to defy his enthusiasm.

With one announcement, he'd thrown his bet down on her without knowing all the cards and hadn't cared one lick about what others thought. Others who knew more about opera than she did, who were better singers than she was, who were now relying on her performance to launch their own careers. He hadn't cared about any of that. He just cared about her.

She'd had no idea how to process the intensity of it all. Unsure, she'd shut her mind down and given over to her instincts.

And ran to him.

When she flung herself into his arms, dangling like a spider monkey around his neck, the strength leeching off him had been everything she needed. His confidence in her, his awe, his respect. All of it. She'd clung to him and soaked it all in, until it permeated her own thoughts and mindset. And when she pulled her head back to stare up at the man who, with one round of applause, had given her more confidence than years of training? Well . . .

Cami's thought was interrupted when she reached for the keys. Her hand bumped into the back of Dick's hand a second too late. Nabbing the keys, he opened his door but didn't leave yet. When they were tucked in the cab of Mal's truck, they didn't need to pretend to be anyone other than themselves. No cockamamy marriage scheme, no new farmhand from out of town, no underdog leading lady. None of that.

Just two people exploring their own potential for bravery.

Cami reached across the center console and grabbed a fistful of Dick's coat right below the column of his neck. Slowly, she pulled him toward her, mindful of the gear shift, and kissed him. There was no urgency, no frantic jumble of lips and tongues chasing down a fleeting moment. Just a woman kissing a man who lit up her soul in all the ways that mattered.

Dick pulled away and let out a great exhale. Then he cupped the side of Cami's face in his free hand and massaged the apple of her cheek with his thumb.

"I need you to make the first move here, angel," Dick rasped out.

"I thought I already did." A smile teased her lips as she turned toward his hand cupping her and planted it with a light kiss. But he still seemed tense, uncertain. There was a tightness around his eyes. Was it a lack of confidence? Nothing could be further from the truth when it came to Dick. But there was something else. He struggled to hold her gaze for too long. Was he worried about something?

"I'm serious, Cami. I need to know what you're thinking. What's in your head?"

"I'm thinking I want you to come upstairs with me. And stay," she added softly.

"Stay . . . " he hedged.

"Stay with me tonight. And not just to sleep." Her boldness shocked even Cami. A quick gut check came away with no nagging thoughts of uncertainty or impending doom. No doubtful butterflies began swarming in her stomach. Just confidence and contentment, and the desire to go after what she wanted.

And wasn't that just the thing to get Dick's attention front and center? His eyes abruptly sprang up to meet hers.

"You're sure." It wasn't a question.

Progress.

"I'm heading upstairs. When you're ready to join me, lock up the truck," she said before she opened the door and climbed out.

Cami didn't look back. She couldn't. Otherwise, she might lose her nerve.

Singing in front of ten thousand pairs of eyes was as easy as breathing compared to the pep talk she had to give herself as she climbed the stairs to her apartment. Each creak of a floorboard, each groan of the wood was like a kick drum to her senses.

All right, fine. Maybe she was a wee bit nervous.

When she reached the bright red door to her apartment, she remembered that Dick had her keys. Crap. She really didn't want to go back downstairs and embarrass herself by asking for the keys after the "yes-come-sleep-with-me-tonight-and-no-I'm-not-kidding" act she'd laid on good and thick.

A loud thud echoed downstairs.

Part curiosity, part nerves led her to turn around at the top of the steps. Down at the bottom, Dick had his boot on the first stair. Her keys were crushed in his fist. Lightning quick, he scaled the steps two at a time until he was on the landing in front of her door and staring down at her. They stood there like that, understanding swirling around them over what would happen on the other side of her door.

She reached behind her and felt around for the doorknob.

"Wait." Dick grabbed for her hand and covered it over the knob with his own. "If we do this, I need you to do something for me."

"What is it?"

"Call me Richard," Dick said quietly. When Cami didn't respond, he added, "I've been Dick to everyone. But with you, I don't want to be that man. I want to be better with you. Better *for* you. Please."

The desperation in his voice gutted her. She had a million questions about his request. But as the heat from his hand seeped slowly into hers and the small space between them on that landing grew smaller by the second, she didn't care. If it was important to him, it was important to her.

That much she could do.

She nodded her answer as she grabbed the keys from his other hand and turned to unlock the door. After the click, she opened the door and guided him in behind her.

She never let go of his hand.

<hr>

Raw.

Dick was cut open, raw, exposed down to his deepest marrow. As his angel held his hand and led the way into her apartment, he couldn't believe where life had taken him. If she knew the real him, the vile things he'd done over the span of his years, she'd kick him out on his ass and punch him full of holes with the BB gun she kept parked in the barn.

But she didn't, and he was too much of a coward to enlighten her. That was why, for one blessed night, he had asked to be called by his given name. A name that, as a boy, only his grandmother had ever used, and that was only ever spoken in sweet tones and phrases. Dick was associated with all his life's debaucheries, assaults, and failings. Richard was innocent, loved, and treasured.

Dick followed her over to the bed, which was tucked in the corner of her studio apartment. The dip and curve of her waist as she walked highlighted her ample hips, which caused her red peasant's blouse to billow and sway around her. When she reached the bed, the bright red comforter sprawled out on top was a glaring drop zone. Cami walked to its edge and let go of his hand before she turned to face him. She shrugged out of her winter coat and threw it on the floor next to the bed. Boots and socks went next as she toed them off and kicked them over by the coat.

Her hands floated up to the fringes of her forest-green scarf. The deep green brought out the blue of her eyes, almost muting them to a darker, more midnight blue. Like the ocean under the moonlight.

Cami stepped closer to Dick. His lungs tightened up at the proximity. Swiftly, she pulled her green scarf off her neck and wrapped it around his. With her hands on each end, she yanked.

But she didn't have to.

Dick prowled the few inches toward her. The scarf at his neck was a welcome leash to his urges. He wouldn't be rough with her. Absolutely refused to give in to the asshole tendencies other women had sought him out for. And to his greatest surprise, when it came to Cami, none of those urges floated to the surface.

He just wanted her. All of her. He wanted to be the hero she saw him as.

Emboldened, Dick ducked his head, burrowed his fingers through her hair, and captured her lips. Slow, steady strokes explored every corner of Cami's luscious mouth. And to his happiest of revelations, she explored right back. Her hot mouth kissed him with searing nibbles and sweeps. A content groan bubbled up from his chest and escaped between breaths.

Deft fingers tickled up his torso until they reached the rim of the scarf that held him captive against her luscious body. Her hands snaked behind his neck and locked on.

Then he went over.

The two tumbled back on the bed in a cascade of tangled limbs. At some point, he managed to kick his boots off. Firm tugs urgently yanked bulky fabric down his arms. Oh, right. His coat. He was more than happy to take the hint.

Dick sat back on his haunches, shucked off the coat, and tossed the thing to the floor. When his gaze returned to Cami, he was robbed of all sense.

She lay back against her bright red comforter with her mass of dark curls snaking along the pillow. A seductress if he'd ever seen one. Her standard-issue light-blue denim jeans hugged her hips and legs, and while that gave him plenty to appreciate, it was that damn tie at the top of her blouse that held his rapt attention.

That little scrap of string was like the final hundred-yard stretch of No Man's Land. The patch of open fabric that stupid tie held together revealed the slightest shadow and curve of her breasts.

It was like water for his arid throat.

By some stroke of good fortune he was too foolish to figure out, he had been allowed to taste this beautiful angel's sweet mouth. Had held her steady as he stripped away bloody clothes over every curve and mound. And just as the thought crossed his mind, his angel's fingers trailed down his stomach and crossed to her own, where they rose higher and landed on the little string bow at the top of her blouse.

"Richard," she said on a breath. She grabbed one of his hands, took his index finger, and threaded it through the loop.

His cock throbbed against the tight denim he wore. The pain of it was nothing, however, compared to the pain caused by his restraint. If one could die from blue balls, he'd happily succumb if it was what Cami wanted. So, before he pulled on that string, he gave her one final out.

"Last chance, angel," he said through the strain. "There's no going back."

Cami's eyes scanned his face. He knew his expression was tense. Hell, he was practically holding back a tsunami. But when her free hand extended and cupped the left side of his face, all reservations vanished.

"I'm right where I want to be, Richard. You crash-landed into my life and have caused the best kind of disruptions. You made me challenge myself, take risks, live for me and others be damned." She paused briefly while she used her fingertips to rub away the tension at the back of his neck. "I know it's crazy, but I can't imagine anyone else I'd rather be with. I don't know how else to say it. So I'm going to stop talking now and kindly ask that you help me take off my shirt."

Well, shit.

One swift pull and the tie came undone. A canvas of tan skin was spread wide as he loosened the tie completely. His mouth came down a second later. Dick's tongue met the column of her throat as his hands crawled under her shirt. Salty, lush curves greeted his lips. His fingers and palms ran up the sides of her abdomen, raising her blouse in the process. Once her breasts were free and the fabric was bunched under her arms, Cami sat up and threw the garment over her head. Then he grabbed her, brought her chest to his mouth, and suckled at her through her bra. The dark areolas peeked through the white cotton, offering a hint of what he craved.

As he continued to lap at one side, one arm kept her supported while the other fondled and kneaded her free breast. God, they were perfect. Beyond perfect. And the soft moans escaping across her parted lips drove him on. The tension in his cock bordered on distracting, but like hell he'd think of himself before her.

He scooped his fingertips over the rim of the cotton and pulled down, freeing her bound breasts. The sight took his breath away. But more than anything, he loved chasing the noises she made. Every slight squeeze or gentle scrape of his teeth had Cami making the most delectable little mewls. The ups and downs of her breaths, the rise of her moans, was the most perfect melody he'd ever heard.

"Richard, I want you," Cami panted lightly.

Still lost in the nectar of her body, he hadn't even registered the slight tickles of her fingers trailing up his chest to remove his shirt. When the fabric was free of his head, he looked down to see Cami leaning back, supported on her arms, completely nude from the waist up. The mischievous twinkle in her eyes was all the encouragement he needed.

And then he was on his back.

"Whoa! Angel, what are you doing?"

"Something I should have done a long time ago," she said as she wriggled out of her jeans and, oh, God, yup, her underwear, too.

The time for slow had clearly passed as Cami's hands went to Dick's belt. He helped her make quick work of his bottoms. Then their hands were on each other again. Mouths, tongues, and fingernails scraped along torsos. It was all a frenzy of lust, emotion, and desperation.

"Cami. God, Cami, I need to be in you," Dick said between breaths. His mouth devoured her breasts as they danced in front of him, her lithe body straddling his. A hand, incredibly firm for its size, gripped his cock and began to pump.

"Oh, fuck." Dick's head dropped back on the pillow. Through slitted eyes, he saw Cami take his cock in her two slender hands. The motion was too much, though. He couldn't last.

And then the tight warmth around his cock, coupled with Cami's moans, had his eyes shooting open completely.

Cami was on top of him, miraculously taking all of him into her delicious body. She was stunning, a goddess of sensuality, confidence, and every other fantastic specimen on earth his pea-sized brain was too drained to come up with in that moment. As her hips slid forward and backward, her breasts swayed with the motion. Her hands, which had previously driven him wild when they were all over him, were snaked through her thick hair. He brought his hands to her waist, if for no other reason to feel a closer connection to her. Though he didn't think that was possible.

He was in heaven. There was no other way to describe it. And when she increased her momentum, urging her hips faster and higher, he completely shattered. His release shot out of him with no warning. The crest had risen so fast, he nearly lifted Cami off the bed entirely. And while he came in hot spurts that felt like nonstop streams, Cami arched her back and squeezed him unimaginably tighter.

They stayed like that, both of them tense and sweaty as they rode out their passion. Dick soon melted into the bed, but not before his angel collapsed on top of him. A sheen of sweat coated her olive skin, adding to her already celestial glow. Their chests rose and fell in sync.

Cami's delicate cheek lay plastered against Dick's chest, and he took the opportunity to wrap her tightly in both arms.

"Just so you know, there is no way I'm letting you go, angel. I can't pretend with you anymore. When we sign those marriage papers in two weeks, I'm not going anywhere after that."

His heart soared when he felt the edges of her lips curl up into that smile he loved.

"Sounds good to me."

CHAPTER 21

Sharp neighing pierced through her mind's fuzzy morning fog. Bright light shone into Cami's apartment and spotlighted the top half of her bed in a whole lot of rise and shine. A quick peek through squinted eyes revealed she had neglected to shut the blinds before she went to bed.

Crap! The horses! She never did her night checks last night.

But wait . . . her alarm hadn't gone off.

The black radio alarm clock on the stacked milk crates serving as her nightstand revealed it was six fifteen in the morning. Her alarm should have gone off at six.

The enveloping warmth at her back and the soft puffs of breath along her neck brought her back to the present.

Saturday. It was Saturday morning, which meant she hadn't had to do night checks last night. Part of her barter arrangement with Mal was that Cami would get Friday and Saturday nights off.

She was blissfully allowed to stay right where she was, and stay she did. Though the laser-focused sunbeam blasting her in the face wouldn't do.

Before she turned over so her back could shield out the sun, a snug, warm arm was locked firmly against her belly. The undersides of her breasts brushed softly against the tickly arm hairs.

Dick— Richard still lay snuggled against her, with soft snores fluttering out on each breath. The memories of their time together flooded back. Cami peeked over the edge of the bed, and yup, piles of clothes strewn about confirmed it for her. She and Richard had slept together. The slight soreness between her legs attested to the fact, but she couldn't recall a time when, despite the slight discomfort, she had ever enjoyed herself so much or been so happy.

Perhaps the leading lady mindset had needled itself into her own psyche because, in the bright early morning sunlight, Cami couldn't hide from anything. Last night, she'd taken charge in a manner that was completely foreign to her, but it'd felt so natural with Richard. When she was around him, she could be the uninhibited woman who had no problems going after what she needed.

And she had needed him, in more than just the physical ways. He had offered commitment. Real, honest-to-God *commitment*. Did she want that, though? With Richard? Well, heck, they were already getting married on paper, weren't they? Plus, aside from her mother and Mal, no one had ever gone to bat for her the way he had. He was her hero in all the ways that mattered, and though the man could be infuriating at times, she was often at her happiest with him around.

"I can hear your wheels turning there, angel," Richard said in his gravelly morning voice.

Cami smiled widely as she turned in his arm, grateful for an excuse to trade in her sight of the glaring sun for a view of Richard.

It was always chillier in the maintenance barn, but one of the benefits of having a second-floor apartment was taking advantage of the rising heat. Richard lay on his side with the covers pooled around his waist. The V-shaped shallow groove along his abdominal muscles dipped down beneath the covers underneath his arm, but the expanse of his hulking chest cradled Cami in a protective cocoon.

She could wake up like this every morning and have absolutely zero complaints.

"I was just thinking about last night." Cami freed a hand to feel the slight blond stubble forming around his square jaw. Her slight tickles made him twitch a bit.

"Mmm. Any part in particular?" he asked as he squeezed her

tighter. The hardness of his arousal could easily be felt through the many layers of blankets.

"All the parts, actually," she said, looking down at his bunched-up chest. Her darn fingers had somehow found their way there and were tracing lines around his pecs. Seriously, did all parts of her body have minds of their own now?

"Do you need to take that pill thing again today?"

Curiosity at his strange statement had her puzzling at his words until the pieces clicked into place. Sometimes, it was so easy to forget that he wasn't from this time. "Oh, yes. I usually take it at breakfast time. No worries there."

"That is certainly an invention of modern medicine I have no trouble getting behind. How does it work, exactly?"

"Uh . . . " Cami had briefly mentioned she was taking a birth control pill. He, of course, had no clue what she was talking about, but she hadn't been about to break down the nitty-gritty of pharmaceutical advancement when her lady parts were screaming to get their biological mating dance on. "It's a bit early in the morning for that conversation. But maybe once I've had breakfast, I can tackle it," she said with a small laugh. "Are you all right with eggs and toast? It's probably all I have right now. Saturday is my grocery shopping day."

"I'll get there, but first, I want to make sure there's no confusion about last night."

"Confusion?"

"About what I said, about us. I meant it, angel." He snaked a finger around a tuft of her hair. "A lot of strange shit has landed my way over the last few weeks, but I can't imagine moving forward and slogging through any of what's ahead without you. You're it for me."

She stared at him a moment longer and took in his solemn expression. He was serious. Actually serious. For him to bring it up in a morning-after haze meant it must have been real. All of it. He wasn't kidding about what he said after they first had sex.

"I have questions." Her directness surprised even Cami. But if she was going to continue down this road, emotions would not win the day. She needed facts, details. She needed to know all the rules of engagement.

"Hit me." He nodded sternly. The sun's rays had begun to creep slowly up the bed and were just about to crest over Richard's shoulder. They would soon illuminate his face. The imagery of a police commissioner questioning a perpetrator under a bright spotlight blossomed in Cami's mind. There was one thing she had wondered about.

"Your name, you said Dick was associated with vile things you'd done. What did you do?"

The slight bob of his Adam's apple caught her eye before his gaze fell to her hand still toying with the lines on his chest. She really did know so little about him.

His solid hand grabbed hers and held it close against his chest. His other arm, still stretching across the dip in her waist, pulled her toward him more tightly. The hard knob of his chin rested just over her shoulder as he hugged her close and faced the window.

It wasn't lost on her how he chose not to make eye contact.

"I love you."

"Wait, what?" Cami tried to push away and look at him.

"No, stay still, Cami. I need to say what I need to say. And if, when I'm finished, you never want to see me again, I'll get gone real quick. But I'm done with the secrets, and I need you to know. I don't have any more room in my life for regret, especially if I'm making room to put you in it. So please, will you stay silent and listen to what I have to say? Just for a moment?"

The dip in his voice was ominous and had replaced all the butterfly flutters in her stomach with sinking dread.

"You're scaring me here."

"Shhh, nothing to be scared of." He stroked her back in long, soothing motions. "I swear on my life, I will never ever give you a reason to fear me. I'd sooner slice off my own arm than cause you any pain or worry."

Again, all the warning bells and triggers she was so used to relying on were staying quiet. She wasn't truly afraid, at least not for herself. But from her position against his chest, she could easily pick out his increasing heartbeat against her ear. *He* was scared, and that thought made her hair stand on end.

"All right, I'll listen," she said, but not before she placed a soft kiss against his chest. She had no idea what he needed to tell her, but she would support him. He had done no less for her.

Cami's head moved along with Richard's chest as he inhaled greatly. Her hair fluttered under his breath as it left him.

"Before I came here, in my own time, I was not exactly well-loved. No, that's not true. Certain people loved me, but only for what I could do for them. When I was five years old, my mother left me in the care of my father. She had gotten pregnant quite young, and when my father refused to marry her, that made life quite difficult for her. But when I turned five, she dropped me off at his door, announcing she had an opportunity for a proper marriage to a man who would take care of her. Unburden her of the charity from my grandparents and the dependency of a young son. So, for the years until I reached adulthood, I lived under his house. I'll spare you the details, but suffice it to say he was not as caring or loving as what you've told me of your mother."

Cami's own heart rate climbed with Richard's as he continued the story.

"I was the root cause of everything wrong in my father's life. I was an added expense, something that had to be fed and clothed with money that he would have far preferred to go toward whiskey and cards. My presence turned into the reason for his misfortune. And he took it out on me. Most times with the belt across my back, sometimes by not feeding me. After a while, when I began to grow and was just on the cusp of adolescence, I realized others saw me that way as well, as a hulking menace, and it was beneficial. I made friends, though I would use that term loosely, in seedy circles. Learned how to cheat at cards, pickpocket money, and lie through my teeth.

"I hated it so much." Richard's words came out choked. "But when I reached manhood, the persona I had crafted for myself became lucrative and enabled me to leave my father's home. I had money, though none of my own. I had all the cigarettes, whiskey, and women a young man could want. Once I grew out of my lanky boy years, I had sprouted quite big, you know? Well, my size brought more . . . attention. Men would pick fights with me, and one or two punches later, they'd be ass-down in an alley while I'd be going through their pockets, richer for their misfortune at having picked the wrong man to mess with."

The coppery taste of blood invaded Cami's mouth. She had bitten through her tongue without realizing it to keep from crying. She swallowed it away as Richard went on.

"Women followed," he said with a sniff. "God, Cami, did I have women. Most of them got off on my size. Bedding a brute for a night of thrills while their husbands were off tending to their own mistresses was a popular attraction, apparently. The money was good, and I hadn't thought much of it in those years. But there were times —" He broke off as he gripped her harder. His fingernails dug into the skin of her back. "There were times when I couldn't look myself in the eye for what I had done."

Richard was crying now, his voice a mess of quivering consonants and vowels. His hot tears fell down Cami's back in searing streaks. She struggled to hear him, to make sense of his words.

"There were times when . . . Fuck!" he shouted. "I've hurt women, Cami! Those who asked for it as some sort of sick thrill. I allowed it . . . and I'm so goddamn sorry for all of it!"

Cami lay there, naked, vulnerable, and clutched to that man's chest as he revealed the ugliness of his past.

"It all came to a head when I tried to kill a man in my old Army regiment. The man I thought was responsible for my scarred face and hearing loss. But he wasn't. It had been a misunderstanding, and I was too enraged to listen. I almost died in that fight with him. Hell, I was sure as the day was long that I wasn't surviving the fall in his well after he tossed me into it. But at the last second, when I finally made my peace, I didn't hit the water. No, instead I woke up and landed here."

The tension in his arms lessened as he slowly released Cami to look at her, but he still kept her close. His eyes were red and bloodshot. An unshed tear hung precariously from the tip of his nose before it dropped onto the sheets between them.

"You are my second chance when everything that makes sense to me says I don't deserve one. But I'm here, with you, and I'm so fucking grateful for whatever force allowed that to happen."

Richard rose off the pillow and sat back on his heels in front of Cami. He let the covers fall and never took his eyes from hers. Even though he was completely naked, he made no move to cover up. Instead, he just took her hands and leaned down to rest his forehead on top of them.

"That's all I've got now. As I said, I'll spare you the brutal details because no good would ever come from hearing those stories, but now you know me. I've got no more secrets. And that man who I was, who did those disgusting things, you need to know he died in that well."

Cami looked down at Richard's sandy blond head as he slowly raised it. "I'm a new man. I just want to do right by you, and I will follow you to the ends of this earth if you'll still have me. But I don't expect anything from you now or ever. I love you, angel. And all I ask in return is for you to keep on singing."

A loud banging at Cami's downstairs door stole her attention away from the man before her. "Cami? You up there?"

"Shoot, it's Mal. Why the heck is she up now?" Cami scrambled out of bed and reached for her clothes on the floor. "Coming!"

"Mr. Donnelly just called!" Mal hollered. "He's on his way to talk to you. Said it was urgent, or otherwise he wouldn't be here so early on a Saturday. He should be here in about thirty minutes."

"All right!"

"Oh, and bring Dick with you," Mal added. "He asked for the both of you."

Coffee. She was going to need a boatload of coffee.

CHAPTER 22

Mr. Donnelly sat on the couch with his stack of papers sprawled out on the glass coffee table centered between them all. "I'm sorry, but end of day Tuesday is the absolute latest I can extend our arrangement. Beyond that, I'll need to close the application for your inheritance fulfillment."

"What? Why? You said we had another two weeks to provide you with the marriage license application!" Cami couldn't get the questions out fast enough. Dumbfounded, she crossed her arms and gaped at Richard, who stood next to her, leaning against the small desk that occupied the office's seating area. Mal hung back and copped a squat at the bottom of the steps. No, she wasn't particularly part and parcel to the details of the conversation, but Cami knew full well that anyone who bothered Mal off-hours with business that didn't immediately concern her quickly found out that it did.

"Miss Foster, I told you from the beginning that the possibility for this to pass through without a legal marriage application was tenuous at best." Mr. Donnelly held his hands wide in a placating motion. His stupid glasses slid farther down his stupid nose, and Cami wanted to rip them off and punch him in his stupid face.

"What happened?" Richard stood next to Cami. His arms were

crossed over his chest, and the scowl on his face was sour enough to spoil milk.

Mr. Donnelly removed his glasses and placed them on the coffee table before pinching the bridge of his nose. "My colleague who works for the county clerk's office was not able to offer the leeway I had hoped, despite my best efforts at persuasion. It would seem that the small favors I had done for him professionally over the years were not enough to convince him to look the other way on certain items pertaining to your inheritance bequest."

The wood desk behind her groaned as Richard leaned back against it.

"Tits on a toothpick," Mal muttered. All eyes in the room flew to her. "What? Oh, don't look at me like I'm not supposed to know about your little plan." Mal waved a finger between them. "Ain't nothing in this world Cami doesn't share with me, and what she doesn't share, the rest of the town does. So you best be gettin' back to figuring out your next steps instead of focusing on me and how I know what I know."

"Mr. Donnelly, we need more time. In two weeks, I have my first performance as the leading heroine in *La Sonnambula* at the conservatory, and it'll be in front of a dozen or so talent scouts for opera companies around the world. I just need to hang on until then. If I land a spot in a company, I need my inheritance to fund the training necessary to keep me there. There's no telling how prominent a role would be offered to me in the future if I get placed. I will still need the funds to keep my training competitive if I find myself stuck in the ensemble again. Please, is there anything we can do?" Cami didn't like how desperate she sounded, but they hadn't yet come up with a plan to get Richard a social security number for the marriage application.

"Like I said," Mr. Donnelly reminded them as he pushed his papers back into his briefcase and clicked the locks on the side panel of his briefcase in place, "you have until the end of day on Tuesday. My contact at the clerk's office will be returning from vacation on Wednesday. The office is managing on temporary help for the first two days of the workweek, and I am confident I will be able to get the appropriate signatures from someone less familiar with the process. But that's all I can offer."

Cami let out a dejected sigh and thanked the attorney before he left the room.

Once the three of them were alone, Mal spoke freely. As if she needed a reason to do so. "You two want to tell me the full story here? Cami, I know you were going to get hitched so you could claim what your mama left you. I don't like it, but hey, you're a grown woman who can make grown choices. And grown mistakes, I'll add, but that's none of my business."

Cami raised an eyebrow at the jab.

"Why can't you two apply for the marriage license right now? What's stopping you?"

Cami and Richard stood next to each other. Neither of them said a word, and she very much felt like they had been caught looking at a dirty magazine together and had been sent to the principal's office to wait for their parents.

How would they explain Richard's time traveling to Mal? It certainly wasn't Cami's place to reveal that secret, regardless of how close she was to the woman. And especially not after Richard had just laid himself bare to her. Gosh, she still hadn't had a moment to process all he'd told her.

Cami walked over to the coffee pot in the corner, put a coffee filter in, and began scooping out the grounds. There was too much being thrown at her this morning, and she was way too undercaffeinated to handle it.

"I need some documents for the application, but I no longer have the originals. It's taking some time for the copies to be made," Richard said. Amazing how he didn't flinch at Mal's question, and he delivered his response without an ounce of hesitation.

Had he lied to *her* at all, and she just hadn't been able to see it?

"What's the holdup?" Mal asked.

"Delay's on my end, in my home city."

"You said you were from Baltimore, right, Dick?"

"Yes, ma'am. There was a fire at the clerk's office in the district I was from. I'm waiting to get word on what notarized documents survived the fire. I'm hoping my birth certificate made the cut."

"If proof of identity's the issue, why not just use your social security card? A passport, driver's license? Any of those should do the trick," Mal said as she rose off the stairs. The disbelief in Mal's voice rang loud and clear.

"I've never had the good fortune to travel overseas, Mal. And I'm sure you can appreciate the mutual benefits that come with paying your ranch hands in cash. I've noticed you do that for several of us, and I'm grateful for it. And my license to operate any mode of transportation extends to horses only, I'm afraid."

Cami nearly poured her cream all over the counter. She hadn't yet turned around to look at them, but she knew a face-off when she heard one. If Mal had a tail, she'd be slapping that thing against the banister in warning. Cami took two coffees and turned, hoping to give them out as peace offerings.

She was not prepared for what Mal said next.

"Oh, I've been meaning to tell you two. I spoke to Gerry last night. Tami and their baby girl are all doing fine, so mama and baby will be staying in Florida another week or so. But Gerry's coming back to work at the end of next week."

The floor fell out from under Cami. She looked at Richard, but if he felt anything about it, he didn't show it. Just the same old scowl he had on earlier, though his arms seemed to be clenched across his chest more tightly than before.

Mal walked over to Cami and took one of the coffees in her hand. "Looks like after next week, we won't be so short-staffed on the ranch anymore, Dick." Mal never made eye contact as she brought the mug to her lips to blow at the steam. "You've been a huge help around here, but when Gerry comes back, I won't be needing you to stay on."

Cami's chin hit the floor a second before the porcelain mug she was holding.

160

Camilla's burly lunk stormed out of the office building and trotted down the field to where the stables were. From the distance, he hardly looked so hulking or intimidating. No, he looked like just another ranch hand who was all muscle and no mettle. Though this one was far uglier than the other meatheads he'd come across in his day.

The man lowered the binoculars from his eyes and leaned his head back against the headrest in his truck parked along the county road next to the ranch. He watched as the ranch hand brought the horses out of the stable. He took turns unbridling each one before he released them into the fenced-in pasture. Then he took out a pitchfork and began relocating some hay or straw or some other yellow grass thing the man couldn't be concerned with.

No, what he was most interested in was how to ensure that brute wouldn't get in his way again. As if right on cue, the lovely Camilla walked down the front steps of the office building the ranch hand had just left. She huddled down in her coat as she walked briskly toward the maintenance barn next to the stable. The two exchanged a glance before she went inside.

The man still couldn't figure out how the ranch hand had saved Camilla from the car bomb. He had taken great pains to make sure she was otherwise engaged so he could plant it in her car. Yes, he'd admit the design was rudimentary; nothing more than a collection of simple propane tanks, gasoline cans, and consumer-grade fireworks. But they were effective. Or would have been if that meathead hadn't nabbed Camilla out of the way before it detonated.

He never thought it would be this difficult to sideline the poor little orphaned opera singer. She'd started out as a nuisance and had quickly turned into a legitimate obstacle. He had come too far to be left behind at the eleventh hour.

After another thirty minutes, the man noticed that Camilla had not yet left the maintenance barn. Interesting. The ranch hand was still outside, so what was keeping her so long in a maintenance barn? Surely, the ranch hand could go in and get whatever he'd need from there.

Movement upstairs caught his eye. Grabbing the binoculars, he peered up at the large bay window. In front of it, Camilla stood looking down at the pasture. She had changed clothes, and her hair was wet. Did Camilla have lodgings in the top of the maintenance barn?

He dropped his binoculars and picked up the papers sprawled out on his passenger seat. Thumbing through, he located the one depicting the original elevation drawings of the horse breeding farm from fifty years ago. He scanned his finger along the page until he found the maintenance barn in front of him.

But the drawing in his hand only listed one floor.

He looked down at the papers on the seat again and, peeking underneath, noticed another set of elevation drawings of the property he hadn't seen before. These were newer, only from five years ago, and contained two drawings: one for the first floor and one for the second floor/attic space. The man held up the second drawing and examined the different room configurations. It was a large open space, but it had a door to a stairwell and a closed-off bathroom.

Camilla must live there.

And judging by the fact that the building had originally been erected in 1938, he suspected the main supports weren't what they used to be. A new plan began to form in his mind, yet as he watched the ranch hand tidy up his piles and hang his tools up, he realized the need for contingencies. Since the car explosion, that ranch hand had been stuck to Camilla's side like a bad case of herpes. He'd made it nearly impossible to get her alone.

But perhaps that was the problem. He was still thinking in terms of going after the intended target when, in actuality, there may be an opportunity to kill two birds with one stone.

The man placed his papers and binoculars on the seat next to him and turned on his truck. As he pulled out onto the main thoroughfare, heading toward Rochester proper, he made a mental note of the exit for the nearest home supply store.

CHAPTER 23

The white oval bar of soap in Dick's hands slowly sullied in color as he handed it back and forth over the sink. The gentle lather bubbled up over his knuckles and wicked away the black and brown grime of his day job. A quick rinse under the faucet and his hands came away clean. Well, mostly clean. There was still the crud under his fingernails that he hadn't managed to wash away. No matter how much he lathered, rinsed, and repeated, the stains were still there. Short of scraping them off with a blade, he didn't know if they'd ever wash away fully. Visions of his tarnished adolescence floated to the surface and mixed with the swirl of the murky water.

Baltimore, Maryland - 1903

The sting of the belt across his bare bottom caused his teeth to clamp down on his tongue. He stood with his arms outstretched toward the wall, his back toward his father. A warm, coppery wetness pooled at the base of his mouth when the next blow came. Thankfully, this would be the last. While his father never failed to highlight his many shortcomings, Dick did know how to count to three. The lashes never went higher than that. Probably because his father lost interest in his own game.

Dick was only thirteen, yet he decided at that moment it would be his final whipping from his father. He was still a boy in many ways, but he was also on the cusp of his adolescence. He didn't know why that thought mattered to him, but he held on to it like a lifeline.

Already, he was getting bigger. His ankles had begun showing beneath the hem of his trousers, not that his father would care enough to provide new ones. The arms of his linen shirts, once baggy and lifeless, had begun to fit more snugly around his budding biceps. His voice, as well, had begun to change. And he needed the change, needed the hope that came with it.

The muscles in his arms relaxed from their bunched state as he heard the jangle of the belt buckle fall back into place at his father's gig line. The hot breath Dick had been holding ghosted through his teeth as his trembling hands fell down at his hips. He slowly raised his trousers up over his raw skin, the fastening at the waist more cumbersome to secure due to the adren-aline surge.

"Don't think I won't know if you dip into my whiskey again, boy," his father said, stomping toward the door that led out of their second-floor apartment.

The shock of the slam behind him traveled up Dick's spine, a billiard ball of tension finding home in the pocket at the base of his skull. It had been one swig, one slight sip that tempted his interest in rebellion. Oh, he knew he'd get hell for it. But should he even care anymore? A few more years and he could be out, a man grown . . . at least in the ways that mattered to him.

Dick clenched his fists at his side as the wall in front of him cushioned his forehead. He hadn't moved from his standing position yet. At one point, before that day, he had wondered if he would ever be able to move on from his circumstances. Rise above his raising, and all that. Yesterday, he would have said no. Today, however, he felt hope. Hope that there was more on the horizon for him than being the son of an abusive father and a mother who'd abandoned him.

But he would keep that kernel close to his chest. Until then, he would be content to play the part expected of him.

On newly steady legs, Dick walked over to his father's whiskey stash above the stove. His iron fist clenched around the neck of the bottle. The smooth rim of the glass caressed his lips before the liquid burned down his prepubescent throat. The harsh bite of the alcohol slowed his swallow, but it wasn't too bad. He was getting better at taking the burn, as well as other things his father would disapprove of. With practice, he would learn to stand on his own. By knowing his place within people's expectations, he could move through the channels he needed to before, God willing, he came out whole on the other side.

A horse neighing outside grabbed his attention. He glanced quickly at the front window of the bunkhouse before grabbing a towel to dry his hands. Cami was probably out doing her night checks. She always liked to let the horses out in the paddock for some final fresh air before tucking them in for the night. The idea was absurd. Hell, they were horses, not pets. They didn't need a lap and a warm blanket to curl onto each night. But apparently, Cami felt differently. It was just another glimpse of her warm heart and highlighted how his heart, in contrast, was as warm as a frozen cow patty on a steel shovel.

Hands dry, he walked over to the front window and peered out to the field in front of the barn. He rested his forearm high against the windowpane and just watched as the horses moseyed about. Come to think of it, a nighttime walk didn't look like that bad an activity. Maybe Cami was onto something. The movement looked soothing and would go a long way in helping him dig out of this hole.

He had been avoiding Cami since Mal gave him his marching orders yesterday morning. Next Friday night, he was getting the old heave-ho. But worse than that, he had absolutely no clue how to climb the veritable mountain of shit that had been stacked in front of him. Dick's chest tightened every time he recalled the pain in Cami's eyes when she realized time had run out on their marriage game. He wouldn't be able to give her what she had been relying on, and it gutted him that he had put that anguish on her face.

Hell, maybe it was better that his time on the ranch had an expiration date. Because even if he could miraculously figure out how to procure a social security number in two days, what good would it do if he didn't have a place to live? For as much as he had come to enjoy Mal, it was crystal clear the woman's trust toward him had waned once some of the cracks in their facade started showing.

Then there was the whole bare-his-soul-to-the-woman-of-his-dreams bit that was also left unaddressed. Well, he could remove that burden from her shoulders at least. He could walk away from her, right? If he needed to, he could just leave . . .

"No!" A loud snap rang out through the bunkhouse as Dick slammed the toe of his boot into the baseboard of the wall. His forehead dropped onto the windowpane. Great breaths left him in hurried succession. The wood by his foot had splintered slightly but not so badly that he'd have to immediately answer for it.

A slight shadow moved across his periphery. When he raised his head, he noticed the horses were gone, presumably all penned for the night. But the shadow trotted toward the bunkhouse. Instantly, he recognized Cami's shape, even through the bulk of her winter coat. As she trudged up the three porch steps to his door, stomping out the muck from her boots, he exhaled and ran over to grip the doorknob. Before she could knock, he opened the door.

Cami stood before him, flushed from the cold and breaths puffing out of her chest. Her delicate fist was held in front of her, poised to knock but never given the chance. The temperature was freezing, as evidenced by the frozen horse shit littered around the pasture. But the starkest evidence was right in front of him: rose-kissed cheeks and misty, round eyes were nestled inside the fuzzy hood of Cami's egregiously loud purple winter coat. The thing wasn't even fastened all the way. No wonder she was shivering.

But she wouldn't come in. They just stood there, unspoken words swirling in the frigid air between them. He didn't want to do this, whatever *this* would turn out to be. Dick had done enough ripping the bandage off. The sight of his angel, though, standing before him with half-frozen tears threatening to fall, shredded his insides. Before he could usher her in, she piped up.

"I haven't seen you," Cami said hoarsely, her hand still raised and very much on the too-damn-cold side of the door.

"Inside," Dick said with a head shake, stepping wide for her to enter. When she hesitated, he looked back at her, dropped his head with a sigh, and shuffled toward her across the threshold.

He really did hate the cold. "I'll listen to whatever you need to say, but I've got one condition."

"You've got a condition now?" Cami snorted. "And what would that be?"

"That you rip into me on the *other* side of the frozen tundra. My sensitive skin can't handle those kinds of elements," he deadpanned with his hands on her shoulders. "Though I'm not complaining about these sweatpants you talked me into getting. A bit tight in the ankles, but they keep the twig and berries from getting frostbite."

Unamused, Cami shrugged off his hands and stormed past him. Dick smiled to himself as he closed the door. He would never tire of getting under her skin.

"Why do you have to be so infuriating sometimes?" Cami threw her coat on the coatrack and kicked off her boots by the door.

"All part of the charm, angel."

"Yeah, well, bottle that lightning back up for a second, will ya?"

"You got it." Dick leaned his shoulder against the bunk bed support beam and crossed his ankles. As he stood there, he watched Cami pace across the room. Dick wasn't entirely sure her cotton socks wouldn't catch fire due to her friction and speed. That is, *before* she managed to wear a hole through the room's woven rug. Rarely had he seen her so stuck for words, and surprisingly, it was an uncomfortable sight. Her front teeth nibbled the tips of her usually dainty fingernails while her free hand crushed and tugged at the hem of her tunic-length sweater. None of this painted the picture of the confident woman he knew. He wretched at the thought of him robbing her of that.

"Cami, it's fine if—"

"I'll take it."

When they both fell silent to let the other talk, Dick took his opening. "I'm sorry, what? Take what?"

"You," Cami said, her eyes square on him as her front teeth bit her bottom lip. "All of you. As you are."

Yeah, he was going to have to check his hearing again. Because it sounded like . . .

"The things you told me, they're unbelievable." Cami resumed her pacing.

"Look, I know I've done terrible things," Dick hedged, rubbing the back of his neck.

"No, let me finish." She threw out her hand toward him. "They're unbelievable because I haven't seen a single indication that you could possibly be the horrible man you think you are."

"It's not my desire to force my past on you, but I can't hide from the things—"

"Arrogant, yes. Bossy, yes. Uncouth, oh, *God*, yes." She began to tick off her fingers.

"Well, I wouldn't say—"

"And you don't smile ever, unless you're doing that smart-ass smirk thing. You don't engage in conversation, every mare on the ranch has a sixth sense when it comes to squishing your balls into bits—"

"All right, I get it."

"You use your size to intimidate, you eat your hot dogs wrong, and sometimes you don't shower as often as you should."

"Enough, lady! I get it!" Dick clenched his lips together as he stared down at the grains in the wood floor, half wondering whether his castrated balls had rolled under the bottom bunk.

"But I'll keep you anyway."

Yup, his balls were still there. And so was his head because the damn thing volleyed back up to face Cami in double time.

"Wha . . . What?"

Cami shuffled across the floor, her black socks rasping slightly against the wood grain, and stopped mere inches in front of him. The corners of her eyes quivered with the threat of tears.

"Since my mother died, I've been on my own. Sure, I've got Mal, but she's more like a crazy protective aunt who only doles out wisdom if you catch her between biker runs and vet visits. She helps when she can, but she's not my mom. She can't tell me why it feels so wrong for me to rely on others and accept their help . . . or why it feels so right when you offer it to me."

Dick's tongue felt so swollen, he struggled to draw in a breath. Or maybe it was the increased heart rate pounding through his chest cavity that hindered the whole in and out thing. A panic attack, maybe? Because he couldn't tear his gaze away from her if she was a fireball threatening to sear his eyelids off.

Cami took a step closer and grabbed his hands, which were hanging limply at his sides. Would she comment on how cold his fingers had turned?

"You saved my life, Richard. And yes, you physically got me away from that exploding car. But more than that, I think you saved me from the life I was going to have, the one I was hell-bent on chasing after. And maybe . . . you showed me something better instead," she said with a slight shoulder raise.

Her purple tunic was hanging loosely off her right shoulder, and a flash of a bright pink strap caught his eye briefly. But his attention immediately shifted back to hers when she squeezed his cold hands, massaging away the chills with the pads of her fingers.

"You're helping me realize I don't need the money to live my dream. I think I just need the trust and confidence you have in me, someone to look at me like you do, and it took me some time to sort that out. I think I finally understand why my mother made the decisions she did with my inheritance. All this is to say, Richard, I like you just fine. And I'm going to keep you."

Warmth slowly crept into his fingers, enough that he felt confident he could grab his gorgeous woman's face in his hands and not frighten her away with the chill. With palms spread wide on either side of her face, he bent down and met her warm lips with his own. In his hands —hands he had previously used to fight, cheat, beat, steal, and worse —he held his most precious angel. He was beyond grateful, and not a little bit shocked, she hadn't turned tail in the opposite direction. But as her arms snaked around his waist to hold him closer to her, he was done asking the whys.

"I'm still marrying you," Dick said when their mouths finally parted. "Nothing's changed for me."

"But I told you I don't need the money anymore."

"Don't . . . care . . ." Dick said through intermittent kisses. "I'm here in this time for a reason, and I'll find a way."

Cami leaned back a bit, examining his declaration with a stern inspection of her own. "How?" she said with a head shake and an all-too-brilliant smile just for him.

"I am a very determined man. One who is highly motivated."

"Oh, is that so?"

"Absolutely. I've heard amazing things about wedding nights." He wagged his eyebrows.

A mild slap tickled his stomach as the back of her hand brushed across his black T-shirt. There was no malice in it, but he couldn't ignore the thrill of the sting. Yet, when the playfulness halted abruptly, Dick glanced down to see Cami eyeing the floor, her brows deeply furrowed.

"What is it?"

"There's something else." Still no eye contact.

"Hey." He used his thumb and index finger on her chin to gently raise her eyes to his. "It's about Gerry coming back, isn't it?"

Her eyebrows arched into a sad V as she gave a slight nod. "I went to Mal, tried to talk her into keeping you on. I got her to admit that her emotions unjustly played a part in her decision, but regardless, she just doesn't have the horses to breed right now to justify keeping on another ranch hand. And Gerry's been with her for years." She shrugged her shoulder slightly. "What will we do?"

We. She said we. Not just what will he do, but what will *we* do.

Finally, he'd found someone to walk beside him, and he didn't have a clue how to blow through this obstacle tearing them apart.

But he would find a way. And like hell he'd have her worry over it.

"When you're performing your opera, do you focus on the finale during the whole performance?"

"No, I take it one scene at a time, one aria at a time." A smile crept across her face as she caught on to where he was going.

"Sounds like a heck of a plan, angel."

They were both taking a leap of faith in trusting the unknown. But since faith had landed him in his siren's arms, the idea wasn't as uncomfortable as it used to be.

"There's someplace I want to take you," Cami said.

"Anywhere." Dick wrapped his arms tighter around her waist.

"There's an outdoor market in the city that's open year-round. One of the vendors there makes the best Amish friendship bread. My mother and I always used to go and treat ourselves once a month, but I'd love to take you."

"Sounds like a date, doll. I can't wait to see it."

Her beaming smile was almost as bright as the outside light on the bunkhouse porch. As Dick cradled Cami to his chest, outside the front window, he could have sworn he saw a flash of red hair illuminated in the porch light.

CHAPTER 24

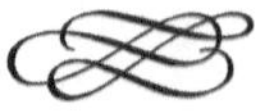

Mouthwatering aromas wafted up from each booth as Cami and Richard strode down an aisle at the Rochester Homestead Market. The market grounds were immense and just as Cami remembered from when she would come with her mother on Sundays.

Cami leaned into Richard's side, and his firm arm snaked around her waist as they walked past the city's local homestead bounty. One vendor had a cast-iron kettle over a small portable burner and was doling out piping hot cups of homemade apple cider to passersby. Another booth had cheeses all lined up, with many cut into small sample pieces and pierced with toothpicks. They were all made with sheep, goat, and cow milk from the seller's family farm. To go with the cheeses, little butter crackers were spread out on saucers, with tiny jars of homemade jam—complete with tiny plastic spoons—adorning the rim of the plate.

As the crowd grew thicker up ahead, Richard's warm hand tightened around her hip. It was a comforting gesture she allowed herself to lean into wholeheartedly, whereas, previously, she would have shied away from the dependence.

Man, did everything feel right. She hadn't realized it until this weekend, but the weight of it all had been immense. The pressure of added vocal training, while much needed, had been a tipping point. Between getting into the conservatory for lessons by seventy thirty a.m., training on her own until rehearsals started at noon, tutoring Mrs. K.'s son as part of a barter arrangement for lessons, and then her nightly ranch duties as part of, yup, another barter for living arrangements, she was exhausted.

But as Amina, all of that didn't matter. As Amina in front of talent acquisition specialists from opera companies all over the world, it didn't matter. And as Amina, pouring her heart out into her performance with Richard's penetrating gaze empowering her from the audience? Well, she couldn't keep her feet on the ground if she wanted to. Because when he pushed her and pumped his strength and encouragement into her heart each day, he made sure there was no room left for self-doubt or worry. His love was so immense, and she finally learned to embrace it . . . and love him back.

"I meant what I said, you know," Cami said as they walked past a vendor selling satchels and coin purses made from dyed wool fibers courtesy of their sheep farm. "If this performance goes well next Saturday night, I won't need the money for private vocal training. If I get picked up by an opera company . . . God, can you imagine?" Her voice squeaked higher as her hands squeezed more tightly around his rock-hard bicep.

"Someone's excited." Richard chuckled as he steered them around a group of kids running down the aisle with bags of kettle corn in their hands. A tall, thin gentleman who Cami guessed was somewhere in his midforties called out after them as another group of kids trailed behind him. Cami remembered the field trips the local schools would take here on Monday mornings. She grinned at the memory of the sugar high from the kettle corn before being corralled under the 4-H tents around the corner to observe how dairy farms operated.

"Well, I can't help it. I never thought I'd make it here. I only ever thought I had one way out. And don't get me wrong, I was willing to work my eager little tail off to get there, but thanks to you," she said with a nudge, "I can see another way."

"First of all, if you keep talking about your eager little tail, a man's bound to get all sorts of ideas. Now, I'm happy to oblige, but you promised me Amish friendship bread. I won't have you thinking I've got a one-track mind when, in reality, my mind has two tracks firmly laid: sex and food. And lest you think my mental infrastructure is a one-horse landscape, let me assure you that those two roads definitely intersect." He smirked. "And secondly, no one's happier for you than I am about your role. You'll knock 'em dead, doll. But I don't want you to put all your eggs in one basket. A good soldier keeps their skills sharp and their knives sharper. And there's no better use of your inheritance than honing your craft. Keep at it with the lessons."

The bite to the air around her felt a little harsher, like how a bee sting felt on bare skin instead of through layers of bulky clothes. Her steps slowed a tad while the people around her seemed to speed up. When Richard noticed she had ground to a halt, he looked back at her.

"I thought you believed in me, that I could pull it off," she said so quietly he had to tilt his head down to hear her.

"Oh, angel." He cupped the sides of her neck. "There's nothing I believe in more strongly. But I also believe in trusting your gut. If your gut told you all these years that private tutoring will take you to where you want to be, I wouldn't throw all that hard work away on a whim. Weren't *you* the one to tell me about your worries of getting cast in an ensemble role for a company, despite your debut being a lead role?"

The weight of her words being thrown back in her face hurt. Suddenly, the lure of the sweet cinnamon bread was losing its appeal.

The jerk was right.

"Hey, look at me," Richard said, extending his thumbs so her chin was urged northward. "You've got the makings of greatness. You'll get there, and I can't fucking wait to cheer you on every step of the way. And that money your mother left you? It's only going to take you higher. I promise, we'll get there."

The frigid morning air snaked through Cami's nostrils, glided down the back of her throat, and seeped into her bones. He was right, darnit. And as she looked up at Richard, she allowed herself to acknowledge the changes in her life. Wisps of his sandy blond hair peeked out beneath his navy-blue wool knit cap. The collar of his tan leather winter coat, part of his ranch attire, was popped up around his neck. He was so hunkered down in his coat, his scars were hardly noticeable. But they were there, and much to his unspoken credit, he never made excuses for them. Never leaned on his handicap instead of his strengths.

Yes, Cami was poor. Yes, she didn't have the wealth of operatic training her peers did. Yes, she had landed her big break. But did all those yeses negate the need for hard work?

As she stared into the eyes of the man who had helped her make sense of it all, yes, she realized she still needed money. And didn't that just take the wind out of her sails and leave her stranded in a dingy with one oar?

Determined not to let the thought ruin their morning before she had to head back to rehearsal, she switched gears. "The Amish baker's booth is at the end of this row. You hang tight here a minute, and I'll be right back."

Richard curled his lips in and gave a quick shake of his head. "All okay, angel?"

"Yeah, I'm okay. Just want to take a minute to clear my head before I introduce you to my favorite winter breakfast treat." Cami backed out of his arms and let them drop to his sides. The scowl on Richard's face hid nothing. "I'll be right back, I promise. I just need a moment."

He remained silent but just gave her a single nod as a sign of acquiescence.

Cami turned, threw her hands in the pockets of her coat, and crunched down the gravel aisle of the market.

If only cinnamon sugar could solve all her problems.

Dick squinted as the last of Cami's purple winter coat was swallowed up by the crowd. Was he foolish to let her go on her own? The market was bustling with an eager midmorning crowd, despite the cold. Plenty of onlookers and dark corners for people to hide in, if they needed to. What if someone recognized Mal's truck? Cami had been driving it for two weeks. It would be easy to find her.

As his wheels continued to spin, he had to take a deep calming breath to tamp down the anxiety. She would be fine. Of course she would be. A walk of a hundred feet down a public market aisle in broad daylight wouldn't kill her. No one knew they were here. There was safety in numbers.

Dick crossed over to a silver pole supporting a nearby booth's canopy and leaned back. He banged his head in time with the hammer of his nervous heart, shut his eyes, and repeated his mantra. She would be fine . . . She would be fine . . .

He still didn't like it, though. None of it. When she'd stepped out of his arms and walked away from him, he could see clear as day how her self-doubt had slipped in between the mental cracks. It was apparent in the three little worry wrinkles that formed between her brows, and the way her top teeth nibbled her lower lip. All small tells that he had learned over the last few weeks.

She was nervous, and he still had no solutions to offer.

"Interested in anything to read, sir?"

A singsong voice behind him broke through his moment of mental character bashing. Dick stepped away from the support pole and turned around. An older woman stood under the booth's canopy and was surrounded on all sides by six-foot-long tables laden with books. She wore a knit cap on her head with a fuchsia pom-pom bouncing from its center. Her long silver hair cascaded down her shoulders and almost reached her elbows. A white puffy vest fitted over a long-sleeve emerald sweater. Beyond that, the rest of her was blocked by stacks and stacks of books. Her expression was expectant, and Dick realized she had addressed her question to him.

"Uh, no thanks. I'm not much of a reader."

"Oh, nonsense." She waved her hand in front of her face. "I find that people who say they don't read really mean they just haven't found their favorite type of book yet. What are you interested in? You look like you know a thing or two about the outdoors. Perhaps a book on hiking or camping?"

Dick peered down the aisle to see if Cami's purple coat was on its way back. Nope. No such luck.

"I'm really not interested," he said, though his boots slowly carried him closer to the tables. The din of the crowd behind him was loud, and he didn't want this woman straining to hear his refusal.

"Do you work on a farm?" she asked, rummaging through her stacks, no longer meeting his gaze.

"Yeah, I do, but . . . "

"I've got *just* the book, then! Now, where did I put that thing . . . ?"

The woman gave him her back as she sorted through the tomes behind her. The sign on the table read "Billoughy's Booksellers: Proprietors of Regional, Trade, and Historical Volumes."

Yeesh, just the name was heavy enough to be buried under.

He could have walked away, left the woman to her bound stacks of paper, but something next to the sign caught his eye. A navy-blue hardcover book, protected by a thin plastic film, stared back at him with the title *Accidental Marriage: A Guide to Common Laws in the Commonwealth*. Intrigued, he picked up the book, which seemed heavy for its size, and opened the front cover.

As his eyes skimmed over the inside cover's book description, his heart rate began to climb until it nearly busted his eardrum. His thick fingers thumbed through the worn pages to the first chapter. The cold air slammed against his teeth as his lips stretched into a great smile.

"There, I've got it! *Farming and Agriculture in the Colonies* seems right up your alley." The woman held the newfound book high in triumph.

"How much for this one?" he asked, still not looking at her.

"Price should be on the back, I believe."

Dick flipped it over, and sure enough, a fluorescent sticker stood out with "$11" scribbled on it in pen.

"I'll take it." He rummaged through his pockets for the wad of cash he had on him. He uncurled the bills and threw them down just as the smell of warm cinnamon wafted his way.

"Have I got a treat for you, mister," Cami said with a smile. "And it's still warm. Come, I saw an empty bench at the end of the next aisle."

Dick tucked the book inside his jacket and zipped things up nice and tight before following Cami. The grin he kept to himself, though, because if what he'd read was true, he may have just found a solution to their problem. But of course, one door didn't open without a window slamming down firmly, and usually on his fingers. He needed help, and with his limited resources, there was only one person he could turn to.

He just hoped Mal wouldn't go for his nuts the way Rosetta had.

CHAPTER 25

"C'mon back . . . C'mon back . . . Oh, let's go already! You've got plenty more space to back those tires up. No need to worry you'll crush my dainty toes or some nonsense. I want these damn rail boards installed some time *before* my fat ass is pushing up daisies. Don't be afraid of hittin' the gas, buddy!" Mal's deep voice broke through the sudden grind of a truck's engine ramping up.

As Dick rounded the corner of the stallion pen that was buried at the back of the property, he was having second thoughts. Of course, Mal would be in a pissy mood. Why would things be easy for him? Hell, she reminded him of one of his colonels back at Camp Meade in Baltimore. The bastard ran four a.m. perimeter drills in the summer because the only thing that put a smile on his face was working up a sweat harder than any heat the sun could bear down later in the day.

As his boots trudged along in the muddy tire tracks, he thought back to his own time. All those lowlifes, drunks, and nightwalkers he'd mingled with would be long gone now. He'd never see them again. The notion was oddly uplifting, though, like a lanced-off wart on a major appendage. Nah, he wouldn't miss them. Those days were far behind him. Literally.

Yet, as the weight of time's passage began to settle on his shoulders, other pangs flared up. He'd never see Helen again. His half-sister, who was really his only family, had been the primary source of comfort through his adult years. Yes, he had mended things with his mother, which was how he got to meet Helen and his other half-siblings, but there was always tension below the surface with her. He wasn't a puppy who, after a few short weeks of rearing, could be cast aside to a new owner. But he had never confessed that to his mother for fear of losing what he had. So he took what he got, and the few family relationships he cherished had served him well.

Strange how he thought of his time before Cami in the definitive past tense, whereas only a few short weeks ago he was still solidly in the 1919 frame of mind, with 1988 being a million years in the future. His steps faltered as the realization of his circumstances slammed into him with full force.

His home was here. Not in 1919, in seedy bars with fixed card games. Not with a sweet-on-the-surface mother and a drunk father whose whereabouts he couldn't recall. But here, with Cami. The world he occupied today was right and natural for him. The vehicles were thrilling. The labor was tough but honest. He was right where he needed to be.

"Mal! Hey, Mal!" His shouts barely registered over the growling engine as he trotted toward the truck laden with wood planks.

Mal's head jerked to the side when she registered her name being called. "All right, that's far enough. You can kill the engine and start unloading these puppies. Over there is fine."

She gestured with her finger before turning her attention to Dick. "Hiya. Been meanin' to come find you. The boards finally arrived for the stallion pen. Price of lumber nearly knocked me over, but what can I do? The five-foot posts are to spec, and no way do I want to be installing rails in pasture that's more frozen solid than Frosty's snowballs, but I don't have a choice. The fences need to be repaired now. No owner's going to trust me to breed their stud if I've got holes in my—"

"I'm in love, Mal. And you need to know that."

Crashing planks of wood sliding out of the truck's tailgate filled the deafening silence. The man unloading the wood stood in the bed of the truck with his hands empty and his mouth hanging open like a fish. Mal's expression wasn't that far off either.

"Man, you're asking for a life sentence with that one," the worker mumbled with a nod toward Mal before picking up the planks.

"What? No, not Mal! Cami! I'm in love with Cami. Oh, for Christ's sake," Dick muttered. "Mal, I need a minute with you. Please."

"Just, uh, keep unloading those boards," Mal said to no one in particular and followed Dick to a nearby oak tree. The bark had clearly been leached out of her bite.

Dick meandered over to the tree and leaned against its trunk, bracing himself with the sole of his boot. Despite his mental rehearsals and bravado, when he was face to face with Mal knowing what he was about to ask, he had never been so tempted to turn tail in his life.

"Look, I didn't mean to blurt it out like that, but the truth is . . . yeah." He cupped the back of his neck, still unable to look her in the eye. God, the woman was five feet, if that, and he couldn't even face her.

Because he knew she was right not to trust him.

"People love all kinds of things, Dick, and for a variety of reasons. They love a pair of jeans that hug 'em just right. They love a puppy for licking their face and keeping their feet warm. They even love vehicles for loyalty and dependability. It's a throwaway word most of the time," she said with her arms crossed. "Which makes me wonder what your reason is for using it."

Dick gripped the ends of his hair and pulsed his fist before letting go. How to proceed? What could he reveal? Then it dawned on him. Why couldn't he just tell the truth? His truths.

"When I first stumbled onto your ranch, I was in bad shape. I had done things I wasn't . . . proud of," he hedged. "I had a criminal life, where the only outs offered to me were prison or the Army. I took the Army and had half my face blown off as part of the privilege." He peeked up in her direction as Mal slowly lowered her arms. Her gaze landed on the left side of his face. But instead of shying away from the scrutiny, he purposely held her attention.

"Cami found me, and then Rosetta nearly castrated me until Cami reeled her in. She took me to the barn, patched me up, and even put a call into you on my behalf. But the kindness didn't stop there, even though it was infinitely more than I deserved. Seeing her day in and day out, working with her, hearing how far she'll go to sing on stage—well, somewhere along the way, her dream became my dream. And to my great surprise, she kept throwing her kindness my way. So much so that I couldn't help but believe it, believe in her, and see myself as she saw me."

"And how does she see you?"

"As a man." He shrugged. "A man who's made mistakes but was given the trust of an angel not to fuck up again and ruin this second chance at redemption. Not as a monster or as the seemingly never-ending list of terrible things I've done."

Dick was grateful for the cold as the biting wind quickly dried up the glassiness in his eyes.

"I'm going to marry Cami," he said, his chin up and his hands clenched at his sides. "Yes, it may have started as an arrangement, but that's all over for me now. I'm in this for the long haul, and nothing would make me happier than to live out my days losing my voice each week as I cheer her on from the back row. And I will make it so she never has to worry about money again. She's mine to protect and provide for in all ways, even when her smart mouth tells me otherwise."

Mal stood there and said nothing. Her scrutiny was debilitating. But he just stayed stock still and accepted it. He needed her to examine every wrinkle in his pants, every calloused fingertip, every strong muscle, and every gnarled scar.

"Go ahead and measure my worth with what you see. Just know I'm hers completely."

Her silence was maddening, and Dick had to curl his fingernails into his palm just to keep from punching the tree in frustration.

"You're wrong." Mal shook her head.

His stomach hit the floor. *What? No.*

"Let me just—"

"There's no way on God's green earth you'll be able to afford even a nosebleed seat at one of the concert halls that girl's destined to perform at." She smirked as she walked closer to him. "But if you're lucky, she'll keep you around anyway."

A sharp laugh burst out of him.

"You think I don't see the writing on the wall with you two? How happy she's been since you came around? But screw the happiness. The motivation, the intent, the drive. She's pushed herself harder these last few weeks than I'd ever seen her. Her star is just gearing up to explode. It's only a matter of time before she shoots across the sky. *Oomph!*"

"Thank you so much," Dick said through his bear hug around the little spitfire. After he let some of her circulation come back, he played his ace. "There's one thing I need your help with."

"Don't ask me to say no to Gerry. I wasn't lying when I said he'd be coming back, you know. But I like you, Dick, despite my better judgment, I guess. If you and Cami can make it work, you can stay at the bunkhouse until you find lodgings. I can't pay you, though. Money's tight, and Gerry's been my man for years."

"No need to pay me." He reached into his coat pocket and pulled out the blue book from the market. "Because I think I found a way for Cami to collect on her inheritance without jeopardizing Donnelly's reputation or connections. But I need your help talking things through with him."

He gripped her hand and cupped it around the book's spine. The curious expression on her face, followed by the raised eyebrows and lit-up eyes as she read the inside cover, gave him hope he hadn't felt in a lifetime.

"Hey, buddy!" Mal hollered over her shoulder at the worker still unloading the rail boards. "Drop 'em and scram. I've got an errand to run while I can still feel my lead foot, and I don't have time to be babysitting the delivery."

"Whatever, lady," he muttered as he jumped out of the truck's bed and ambled over to the driver's-side door.

"C'mon. Donnelly's firm closes in another hour."

Dick tried not to allow himself to gorge too thoroughly on the hope and excitement coursing through him. But that didn't last.

For once in his life, he would grab happiness by the reins and ride her until they both collapsed.

184

CHAPTER 26

"Ouch!"

A drop of blood welled up on Cami's fingertip. She quickly put the pad of her finger in her mouth and used her tongue to soothe the pinprick.

Her hands hadn't stopped shaking since she arrived at rehearsals late that morning. With one week to go until opening night, the disasters in her court kept piling up. Her nightgown costume, for the third time this week, had inexplicably wound up with tears.

The first time, she'd asked Mrs. Katrukova if she knew anything about it. When the woman had no clue and clearly no patience for it either, Cami had just used her portable sewing kit she kept in her purse to repair the fabric. The tear was minor and only involved reattaching a small portion of the collar.

The second time, the bodice had been ripped down the front slightly, which wouldn't have been noticeable to the audience, but it put Cami's chest on display more than was appropriate for the role. She couldn't understand how it'd happened but chalked it up to a careless custodian who may have snagged the garment on a vacuum handle by accident when it was hanging on the back of the door.

That morning, however, was different. When Cami came into her dressing room, the costume had been torn halfway down the back of the garment. No amount of coincidence could have explained that.

And the occurrences kept piling up.

The day before, after she finished up performing Act I in full dress rehearsal, she came back to her room and couldn't tear the wig off her head fast enough. She had quickly grated her short fingernails over her itchy scalp. The relief was instant but fleeting. When she peered down at the wig's inside netting, there were patches of sweat that appeared tan in color. A swipe of her finger came away with a beige residue, which promptly began to burn and irritate her skin. Again, Mrs. Katrukova hadn't seemed concerned and directed Cami to the costume department for a new wig.

The final blow came when, ten minutes before she was called on stage, her staging notes, which she *always* kept in the flap of her olive-green canvas bag, had gone missing.

Cami pulled the white thread taut, knotted it, and bit off the excess with her teeth. It was a miracle she hadn't bitten off her finger as well, she was shaking so badly. With her mending finished, her mind drifted from the deliberate sabotaging acts to what she had tried so hard to forget.

The explosion.

For a week and a half, she had put the incident out of her mind. Had basked in the intoxicating—and sometimes frustrating—glow that was being in close proximity to Richard Stevens. She had never met a more infuriating man . . . and couldn't imagine anyone else holding her hand while she stared down the barren runway from which she'd launch her career.

Cami exhaled a nervous breath as her eyes drifted closed.

The smell of gunpowder, which Richard had recognized.

The sharp hit to her gut as he hoisted her over his shoulder and fireman carried her away from her car.

The crushing weight of his solid body and the tiny tremors that shook it as he shielded her from the falling, scorching debris.

Exhausted, she caught her head in her hands. Her mother hadn't raised an idiot. And that was the problem. Because on the one hand, Cami knew she was being targeted somehow. But on the other hand, her mother's written words finally burst through Cami's armadillo armor and hit home.

Find your gem.

A deep sob burst free, and stupid cowardly tears began falling, dampening her denim-clad thighs. She had found her gem. Richard's love and support raised her higher than any pep talk she could have given herself. Funny how, when she finally learned she didn't need her inheritance money to achieve her dreams, she'd fallen for a man she wanted to marry anyway.

"Oh, Mom. I wish you were here right now. Because I think I love that silly brute." The words were choppy and garbled. She hadn't spoken out loud to her mother in ages, but fear and uncertainty always made you want your mother, didn't they?

She could do this. She had earned the part of Amina, darnit. Had lived, breathed, and eaten Bellini's words since she was barely tall enough to look over the back of a theater seat. She would not be bullied, nor would she force Richard to risk his life again when he had gone through so much trauma already.

Decision made, she zipped up her bag and planned to call Detective Peters at the Rochester PD as soon as she and Richard drove back to the ranch. If they thought there was nothing to be concerned about, then at least she had the confidence backing of law enforcement to tamp down her paranoia.

Leaving the dressing room (after she triple-checked the new location of her stage notes), she hoisted her bag high on her shoulder and walked out the stage door to the parking lot. Richard always waited for her around the front, having preferred to keep an eye on the truck. Once she rounded the corner and saw his sandy blond hair, she picked up her pace.

"Boo!" She jumped onto his back and flung her arms around his neck. The forced cheer she emitted immediately overtook the dread that had been dogging her down moments ago. His warm hands covered hers as she pulled herself up a tad higher and gave a peck on his cheek. It had become their routine. "Did I scare you?"

"The only thing that scares me is the thought of you *not* hanging on my neck and kissing me every day." He reached around behind him and managed to wrap his arm around her waist. A sharp tug had her turned around in his arms, with her body front and center against his. "That and how low you let your fuel level get in Mal's truck. The poor vehicle's practically licking the spare drops of gasoline out of the tank just to chug our asses here. Would it be so terrible to treat the lady with some respect? At least buy her a drink, angel." Richard's light-hearted scolding cracked when Cami landed another kiss on his mouth.

"You know," Richard hedged as he squeezed her closer to him, "Mal's been letting me drive the ranch trucks around the property. I've got the hang of it, and I think it's high time I test out my skills on the open road." He wagged his eyebrows. "Want me to drive us home?"

"Uh-uh, mister. No license, no driving on public roads. Yet another detail we'll have to figure out, but we've got plenty of time for that." She grinned playfully. A dull thwack on her tush had her jerking in Richard's grasp. "Ow!"

"Slave driver. Now, c'mon." He settled her feet on the ground. "Let's head back. Mal and I have a quick errand to run in town."

"Oh, yeah?" Cami opened the driver's-side door and climbed in. "What's the errand?"

"It's a surprise."

At the mention of a surprise, Cami let the truck keys dangle in the ignition and turned to him. "What's the surprise?"

"Well, if I told you, it wouldn't be a surprise, would it?"

If she could roll her eyes any harder, she would have. But her curiosity was piqued, so she'd oblige. Throwing the truck into reverse, she backed out of her parking space and exited the conservatory's campus.

Thirty minutes later, she pulled the truck home into the gravel driveway and hopped out.

"Oh, there you are. Great timing," Mal called from the main office's doorway as she locked it behind her. She stuffed the key in her pocket as she hobbled down the short steps and over to the truck.

"Where are you guys heading to?"

"Town," Mal returned as she climbed into the seat Cami vacated.

"Well, yes, I figured. But where exactly?"

"Downtown." Mal was fidgeting with the seat, making Cami's preferred tiny legroom even tinier for herself.

"Nice. Real mature. Well," Cami said with a wave, "have fun, you two."

The truck U-turned around her and headed out onto the main highway. Excited at the prospect of being alone on the ranch for a few hours—in other words, not worrying about bothering anyone with her rehearsal singing—she jogged the hundred feet over and back around to the maintenance barn.

As she neared the front door of the building, a familiar scent emanating from the stables next door tickled her nostrils. The acrid smell made her cough. Her eyes burned and began to tear slightly. When she looked up, a thin, barely visible plume of dark gray smoke floated out the back of the building. Her mouth went dry as she dropped her bag to the ground.

She whipped her head back around at the road. Damn. The truck was long gone on its way to town. Right on cue, neighs and whinnies began to echo out of the stables.

A fire had broken out at the barn, and she was all alone at the ranch.

CHAPTER 27

The frozen barn door creaked its resistance as Cami threw her weight into heaving it open. A loud clang resounded when the thing finally slid home. Panting heavily and squinting at the stable space she knew better than anyone, she balked. Things didn't make sense, and too many questions flooded her mind.

A hazy mist quickly began to thicken. The smoke was rising, though she didn't see or feel any heat yet. Where was the fire coming from? In their spooked states, the horses were kicking up storms in their pens. Bits of straw floated in the air from the bucking and slamming of hooves. If she didn't get the horses free soon, they'd hurt themselves. Likely break their ankles at the very least. The worst-case scenario was something she didn't want to contemplate just yet. And thankfully, they only had six horses penned in these stables tonight.

Cami opened the barn doors wide and ran to the first stall, slipping on the straw as she came to a stop. Her fingers shook as she tried to work the latch. "Easy, girl. Easy. You'll be out in a sec."

Ginger, the chestnut mare, whinnied and kicked at the stall door. Cami threw the door wide and patted Ginger on the rump. "There, go. Go!"

The mare ran out of the barn, not needing to be told twice. When Cami moved two stalls down to the next horse, an orange hue rose up in her periphery. There, in the back of the barn, around where they kept the extra bales of hay and other feed, she saw the first licks of flames.

Crap.

She turned back to the stall, unlatched the door, and sent the horse running after Ginger. The sight of the flames sent her into a panic. Should she finish getting the horses out and then call the fire department? Or run to the small office at the front of the barn first and make the call?

Beads of sweat began to form along her neck and trickle down her chest. Her mind had already become frazzled from the adrenaline and heat. Why was she struggling with this? She was *alone*. She needed to call for help immediately, without hesitation. But it wouldn't take long to get the horses out. Once they were free, she would do what she could to protect the building until fire officials showed up.

Crap! What should I do?

She glanced back toward the fire, and her breath hitched. The flames, which had only been chest high a moment ago, had leaped to two more hay bales. Tendrils of fire snaked in all directions. As Cami looked around in fear, her pulse hammering loudly in her ears, she was hit with the obvious: the whole place was one giant tinderbox.

With Plan A quickly abandoned, she worked down the line of stalls to get the horses free. The final stall was closest to the flames. Cami's fingers shook as she fought with the rusted metal on the gate's latch. The fire's heat bore down on her neck. The mare frantically kicked and neighed while turning in circles. The gate's metal was warm to the touch and proved harder to maneuver than the others.

"I'm trying, girl. Hang on. Just . . . hang . . . *on!*" A deep grunt tore through Cami as the rust on the latch finally broke away and the metal slid home. As soon as she cracked the gate, the horse bolted out of the barn, knocking the gate—and Cami—to the side.

Caught off balance, Cami fell to the ground. Her hips crunched against the floor first. The rest of her body bounced hard. The slam of her shoulder against the ground sent a shooting pain all the way to her teeth.

Get up, dammit! Get up!

Once she got her feet under her, she rose slowly. Her legs had never stopped shaking. Determined, she screamed through the pain. All her remaining strength was shunted into her quivering thighs as she prepared to run to the office to call for help. Her canvas sneakers took two steps before the creaking of splitting wood reached her ears. When she looked up, the support beam directly overhead snapped. Cami threw everything she had into halting her steps. When the beam came down, it crashed into the stall she had just wrenched open.

Hot air filled her lungs as she stared down at the beam in front of her. Flames quickly engulfed the wood, like vultures to a fresh kill. She covered her forearm over her mouth and turned in a circle, hoping for a clear exit. Panic and oxygen warred for space in her brain.

She was well and truly trapped.

"I still can't believe Donnelly's on board." Dick shook his head back and forth before resting his elbow against the truck's armrest and gazing out the window. "This is going to work. I can feel it. I know she said she put the inheritance from her mind, and believe me, no one's happier than I am to see that girl realize her full potential, but this will help her so much."

Dick couldn't remember the last time his cheeks had hurt so much from all the smiling. Hell, maybe he could get a job as one of those creepy clowns at the Ringling Brothers Circus, if it was still around. Lord knew he wouldn't even need the red face paint he was smiling so much.

"I have to admit, you definitely surprised me." Mal gestured toward the windshield as if she were speaking to the glass instead of Dick. "And the fact that Donnelly thinks he can pull it off is amazing. You know," she said, peering at him, "that was some ace-in-the-hole maneuver if I've ever seen one. You thought this whole thing up from that book you showed me?"

"I'm not due that much credit. I never knew of the concept of common-law marriages before I saw that book. But from what

Donnelly said, he knew of a few places that still honored those arrangements. Washington, D.C., was one he mentioned."

The car grew silent as he mulled things over. Would Cami be happy if they moved to Washington? Would *he* be happy moving to Washington? That would be so close to his former home. Would it bother him? Sadden him? What would it stir up? As the thoughts piled up, a quick shake of his head scattered them to the wind.

Nah, he'd be just fine wherever he landed as long as Cami was happy. That affirmation made a soothing warmth settle within his chest.

He'd definitely be fine.

His mind turned to the next phase of his plan. Now that he knew *where* and *how* he and Cami could make their marriage work, he needed to research opera companies in the area. Surely, if the number of talent scouts invited to the conservatory's production was any indication, the medium was more widely popular and available to the people in this time. There had to be a company of some sort based in the nation's capital. If he could just find out the name of the scout in attendance at the show, he could talk Cami up to them, plant a bug in their ear. He could—

"You ever going to tell me why you won't marry Cami good and honest?"

Dick's tongue caught in his throat at Mal's comment. Her directness hit him like a ton of bricks. He admired the quality when other people were on the receiving end of it, sure, but now, that truck's cabin just got a hundred times smaller.

Shit.

"Of course I'm honest with her."

"That's cute. Not what I said at all, though. Let's try that again. Why do you need to run off to D.C. to get hitched under some law that doesn't actually require it to be spelled out in writing?"

His jaw ticked under the accusation. How much could he reveal? And why the hell were these seat belts so damn constricting? He couldn't imagine why vehicle manufacturers would want their passengers tied down to the seats. He wasn't a teetering trunk that could bounce out on the slightest bump lest it was strapped down. The truck had handles he could simply grab onto, after all.

But the lying had become exhausting, and it wasn't something he wanted to keep up in his marvelous second chance at life. He was just soul-weary. So he said what he could to satisfy Mal and prayed to God it would be enough.

"I can't provide all the information asked for on the marriage application," he said softly into his window, his breath fogging over the pane.

"What are you missing exactly? You've got a name, don't you?"

Here goes nothing.

"I don't have a social security number." The weight of the words sat on his chest when they left him. His index finger erased the fog on the window to fill the quiet.

Please end it there, Mal. Please.

"You know," Mal said as she fiddled with the heater's nobs, "I've had plenty of people come through my ranch over the years who, for one reason or another, weren't cozy with Uncle Sam. But they kept their head down, were honest in their work, and always took care of their loved ones regardless. So know this, Dick, it makes no difference to me what your circumstances are as long you take care of Cami. Now, she ain't my daughter, but she definitely gets her stubbornness from me. Can't look out for her own well-being either if it slapped her in the face and spit on her shoes."

"Huh?"

"No matter," Mal dismissed. "Just know that her mother died tragically when Cami was eighteen, and that girl's been coasting along just as tragically ever since. I've seen how you've knocked the rust off her caged-in self-confidence. If you can keep her happy, that's all that matters in my book. And hey, feel free to invite me to the honeymoon if you go to the great state of Hawaii. A mai tai on a beach doesn't sound half bad."

Shocked, Dick whipped his head around to face Mal. "Hawaii's a state?"

He quickly scanned what he knew of US geography from his time. Yup. He still came away with forty-eight states. So, Hawaii was no longer a sovereign territory. Interesting. A slight shudder rippled through his stomach at what other important facts he didn't know.

"Boy, what kind of schooling—"

"Mal, the barn!"

Dick's and Mal's eyes went wide at the same time once the truck cleared the tree line next to the highway. As the ranch came into view, tendrils of black smoke wafted up to the sky right above the main barn on the property. The barn that housed the stables where the horses currently onsite for breeding were kept.

The barn that was right next to where the woman he loved lived.

Mal's foot hit the gas. The truck lurched forward and careened down the gravel road toward the ranch. Dick leaped out of his door before the truck came to a full stop.

"I'll call the fire department. Go get Cami and the horses!" Mal yelled. She slammed the door and ran toward the main office.

Dick's heart squeezed tight in his chest as his feet ate up the grass under him. When he rounded the corner toward the barn, the sight of the horses out in the pasture put him slightly at ease. But only slightly.

As he pointed at each one, satisfaction settled in him a bit. All were accounted for. But he'd trade in a thousand dead horses if it meant saving Cami's life.

When he got to the barn, the main doors were thrown wide open. No flames were visible from the front, so he ran into the barn through the doors. Once inside, the heat instantly assaulted him. His lungs tensed and burned at the foul onslaught of smoke, like he was sucking on an exhaust pipe. Billowing black funnels of smoke poured up toward the ceiling from the back of the barn. While still potent at the front, the worst of the smoke definitely hadn't reached him yet.

Squinting through the haze, Dick could see the burning flames at the back. The stables, which he confirmed were all empty, had their gates flung wide. Beyond that, he couldn't see much.

Then a faint sound of grunting broke through the din. He turned his head to the left so his right ear could hear better.

"Cami!" he yelled in between coughs. He heard her, he was sure of it, but he couldn't see her, dammit. He ran forward with his head down and his arm covering his nose and mouth.

"Richard!"

His name in her raspy voice guided his direction. Behind the stalls, a ceiling support beam had snapped free and fallen. The wood was completely consumed in flames and blocked his way forward.

Directly behind that beam was Cami, holding her sweater's collar over her nose and mouth. Fire at her back threatened to consume everything. Piled hay bales at the rear of the building were its closest fuel source. Soot caked her face and clothes. Parts of her hair looked singed and shortened. Wide, panicked eyes stared back at him through the conflagration.

"Hang on! I'll get you out. Just stay low and I'll come to you!"

He whipped his jacket off and held it over his head. The beam had fallen diagonally, leaving a larger gap on the left side. Fire still swirled around it, but he didn't have a choice. He could crawl under if he was fast and stayed low. The smoke made seeing harder, but he'd get to her even if it meant burning off the other half of his face.

He scrambled toward the beam and got down on his belly. Elbows under him, he prepared to army crawl under the flames. His jacket rested on top of his head and back. He hoped like hell it would offer some protection.

As fast as he dared, he inched forward on his stomach. His lungs were beyond grateful for the clearer air closer to the ground. Oppressive heat pressed down on his back. Even through the layers of winter clothes, his skin began to tighten. Finally, after what felt like an eternity, his feet cleared the underside of the beam. He allowed himself a moment to exhale before he rose to his knees.

Gloved hands latched tightly around his ankles. Confused, Dick tried to look behind him but was blocked by his jacket overhead. Before he could remove it, his legs were jerked back. He fell forward, his chin hit the floor, and he was dragged backward under the flaming beam.

"No! Richard!" Cami's screams registered as he threw the jacket from his back.

Just as he became free of the fabric, a hard slender object struck him in the back of the head. His teeth clamped down on his tongue.

Pain and dizziness overwhelmed him. His head *thunked* to the floor right before his eyes slammed shut.

Straw scraped against his cheek as he was pulled backward out of the barn. Between the dizziness and lack of oxygen, his muscles didn't have the strength to listen to his brain's commands.

Cami was still trapped in there.

Cold grass cushioned his skin as he was dragged over the field outside of the barn. Frustrated, he managed to crack his eyelids slightly. The bright light of the outdoors sent a stabbing pain to his head. And his body was still being pulled. The motion added to his dizziness. Nausea threatened to join the party.

But the one thing he could make out through his hazy vision was Mal. As he was dragged past the main office building, Mal's unconscious body lay sprawled at the base of the steps leading up to the office. From the looks of her position on the ground, he didn't think she'd even made it inside to call for help.

"All right, sir. In you go." A loud grunt preceded a man's hands wrapping around his torso. Another set of hands grabbed his legs. Tears leaked out the corners of his eyes as he dry-heaved. Everything in his vision was black, but Dick didn't know if that was from the smoke, what the men wore, or his mind closing the curtain on him.

His back smacked against hard cold metal. Footsteps landed next to his good ear and walked around his head. The loud slam of a tailgate resounded around him, but all his senses had become severely muted.

"Nighty night, buddy."

The blunt jab of a fist struck him in his cheekbone. Dick's head jerked to the side. His poor neck was ill-equipped to hold its ground. Hot, flaring pain bloomed up in his cheek before muted edges of darkness began to descend on his consciousness.

The last image in his mind before he succumbed to the pitch-black abyss was of Cami, alone, screaming his name as she was lost to an inferno.

CHAPTER 28

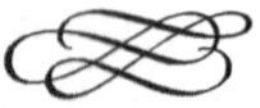

Her daughter was burning. Amid the crackling wood and roaring blazes, Leanne's precious only child was trapped in a fire of Leanne's own making.

Because this was all her fault.

The white vapor of Leanne's aura mingled with the orange-and-gold flames as she watched on, powerless to stop the elemental onslaught. Feverish screams erupted from her throat as she hollered Cami's name, but her daughter never heard. Her ethereal fingers gripped the emblazoned wood beam blocking Cami in. Leanne heaved against the wood and braced her heels against a nearby crate.

Nothing.

"Cami!" she cried as she slumped to the floor before floating over to her daughter.

Cami could neither see nor hear her. Leanne was too frazzled to concentrate hard enough to make her body appear corporeal. And even if she could, it wouldn't do any good. Spirits could only show their presence to mortals for a brief second before their auras dispersed. For the first time in her spirit afterlife, she cursed her lack of existence.

Leanne was helpless as she looked on in horror. Cami had removed her coat and was waving it around at the flames in a futile attempt to keep them at bay. Sweat and grime coated her skin as she ducked low every few moments for a fresh breath of hardly clearer air.

The images in front of Leanne blurred as tears overtook her vision. Her spirit trembled as helplessness overtook her.

She should have never meddled with time. If she had left well enough alone, Cami would have never met Dick. Her daughter wouldn't have been alone on the farm and wouldn't have been a target for some deranged lunatic with a pyrotechnics obsession.

Despite her short mortal life, Leanne had learned that grief was immortal.

"Leanne! Oh, no . . . Cami!" Roberta formed at Leanne's side in a hasty shimmer. "What happened? Where is Mal?"

"Knocked out in front of the office," Leanne sobbed. "She'll be fine. She's breathing. But Cami—" Her breath hitched.

"Is she alone? Someone must be nearby. C'mon, Leanne, *think!*"

"No, Mal's still out cold, and Dick was taken."

"Where's Gerry?"

The ranch hand's name broke through the fog in her brain. *Gerry. Of course!*

"Roberta, yes, Gerry!" Leanne cried. "He's been away, but I think I know where to find him."

"Is he nearby?" The worry and uncertainty flashed in Roberta's icy-blue eyes, a sharp contrast to the blaze around them.

"I don't know. Wait . . . the airport! I remember overhearing Mal talk about Gerry coming back tomorrow from Florida. I don't know if she meant he was landing tomorrow or coming back to work tomorrow. But I have to try and find him."

"Go! Quickly!"

Leanne's spirit vanished out of sight before she caught Roberta's last word. She had to find Gerry.

She just had to.

***

"C'mon . . . C'mon. Where are you?"

Leanne hovered anxiously over the two-lane county highway exit sign. This exit was the only one for miles on this stretch between the airport and downtown Rochester. If she had any chance of getting to Gerry, this was the best spot to do it. The sign was lit up sufficiently, more so than the standard streetlights dotting the highway. She'd need that light to make her plan work.

Up ahead, a beige Toyota Celica meandered down the highway, barely hitting the speed limit. It was long past rush hour, so the traffic was mild and what few cars passed weren't racing down the strip anyway. Leanne recognized Gerry's car from her time watching over Cami on the ranch. She hoped like hell he was tired, banking on the fact that he'd be tempted to pull over for some coffee and food before heading home.

The car's headlights flashed across the exit sign but just enough to illuminate its offerings. She needed him closer. Just a little closer. Leanne's spirit form floated above the ground, mostly tucked behind the sign. She needed him to see her at just the right moment.

Hold on, Cami. Mama's sending help.

A gulp caught in Leanne's throat as she held back a swallow. The Celica's tires drifted slightly to the right, then snapped back forward. Leanne recognized the motion of a driver fighting sleep. Good. She could use his disorientation to her advantage. He just needed to get a little closer.

Finally, beams of muted yellow flashed head-on at the exit sign as the car began to turn off the highway. Leanne's spirit form moved faster than mortal eyes could track, positioning herself next to the sign's support pole. The beams of light shimmered where they hit the metal, like heat radiating off scorching pavement.

And then they landed on her. While she would never possess a solid body again, she hoped the vision of an ethereal, floating woman would jar the exhausted man enough to skip his coffee run and head straight to the ranch.

Especially when that vision appeared directly in front of his car.

Like clockwork, Gerry yanked on the steering wheel and swerved back onto the highway. Relieved, Leanne hovered her transparent form over to the road and watched as the car changed course, heading in the direction of Mal's ranch.

***

Cami's throat was so dry and irritated, she hardly had it in her to inhale anymore. The wool sweater she held over her mouth helped but barely. Her lips were cracked like mosaic glass, and her skin had sweated out every spare ounce of liquid in her body. Breathing had become the hardest thing to do. Harder than standing, blinking, or crying. But she had to keep breathing. Had to keep fighting.

Because her last memory on this planet would *not* be someone taking Richard away from her.

She lay low on her belly, her sweatered hands covering her mouth, and scanned her surroundings for a tool, anything to get herself out of there. As she rested her chin on the scratchy wood floor, staying low as possible, a cool breeze tickled the left side of her cheek. Not a breeze, exactly, but a subtle change in air temperature.

Air that was definitely a million times cooler than the hell she was in.

She whipped her head around to the left and briefly dropped her sweater below her nose to help scent out the sensation. A foot away from her was a thin crack in the wall. Not a crack, but the bottom gap of the door for the overstock storage closet.

Of course!

The stable had a two-way storage closet used for overstock items and small-engine appliances. One side of the closet had a door that led into the stable, and the other side had a door that opened to the outside. Gerry had the outside door installed a few years back so he could easily get out the Weedwacker and small mower without having to bother the horses. She'd forgotten all about it because they hardly used it in the wintertime.

Cami threw every ounce of remaining strength into lifting her arm up to reach the door handle. Every muscle in her body was heavy and exhausted beyond movement, but her survival instincts told her body to shut the heck up. Hesitantly at first, she tapped the black iron handle. Thankfully, it was cool to the touch. That meant the fire hadn't spread to the closet. Yet.

With a renewed sense of determination, she gripped the handle, depressed the black iron latch with her thumb, and pulled. A slight crack was all she could manage from her position on the floor. The wooden door was too heavy, or maybe it was her depleted muscles that weren't up for the job her body needed them to do. Slowly, she rose, ignoring the pain in her lungs. Instead, she let the sweater fall from her nose and mouth and, with two hands, gripped that handle with all she had.

She yanked. The wood groaned and moved slightly, but not enough to clear the door jamb. Heat made things expand, she recalled, so the bloated door was more tightly sealed against the doorframe. As she adjusted her grip on the handle, thoughts of Richard assaulted her, reminding her what awaited on the other side.

Tug.

Richard holding her hand at the public market.

Tug.

Richard feeding her a bite of Amish friendship bread.

Tug.

Richard saying he loved her.

That last memory flew from her mind as the door yanked open and she plopped back on her butt. Cool, stale air quickly mingled with the stagnant heat of the barn. Elated, she scrambled on her hands and knees through the door. Bits of dried leaves and loose pellets of horse feed supplements crunched and poked her knees as she crawled through. Once her feet cleared the doorway, she turned around, grabbed the handle, and slammed the door behind her. It wasn't a tight fit by any means, but it kept the smoke out. At least for the moment.

Cami sat there, plunged in the darkness with the handle of some pointy lawn tool jabbing her in the leg, and just breathed. She sucked in great gulps of air so fast, she didn't know if her dizziness was still from the smoke or her rapid breathing. She hardly cared because the more she breathed, the more her senses sharpened and her heart rate slowed. But she was far from safe. Cami couldn't recall exactly what

Gerry kept in the storage closet, but she would bet there were all sorts of highly flammable fuels stacked around.

With her hands held out before her, she palmed her way a few feet through the darkness until she reached the outer wall. She sighed when her fingertips came away cool as she gripped the other door handle. She summoned another surge of strength and pushed. This time, the door flew open with ease. Cami tumbled out, tripping over the lip of the door jamb, and fell onto the dirt path between the stable and the maintenance barn.

Cool air, fresh and clear, cascaded over her. She was free. She did it. A pride she didn't think she was capable of welled up inside her. Her eyes stung and prickled as would-have-been tears threatened to form. Her body was so logy she hardly thought she could stand. But if she knew anything, it was that she had been a master of underestimating herself.

Richard had taught her that.

Slowly, she rose to her feet and then put one shaky foot in front of the other. Her surroundings were blurry, and she definitely had to stop to close her eyes and stand still a few times, but eventually, she closed in on the main office building. Even though her apartment was closer, stairs were not something she was willing to contend with. Baby steps in a straight line while fighting back a pounding headache? That, she could do.

When she rounded the curve in the path, her already laden stomach sank even further. Mal's motionless body lay at the base of the office front steps.

"Mal," Cami croaked. "No!"

Shuffling as quickly as she could, Cami closed the distance between them. When she reached Mal, Cami all but collapsed on top of her. That was surely her last time being upright. Exhaustion weighed her down as her clumsy fingers searched Mal's throat for a pulse. A gentle thrum patted against Cami's forefingers as she pressed them to the column of Mal's neck. Relief caused her to bite down on her bottom lip, nearly splitting it.

"C'mon. Wake up. Goddammit, wake up! You're too stubborn to go out like this." Mal was facedown on the ground, with her head facing to the side. Cami didn't have the strength to move her, but she certainly had the strength to administer not-so-gentle pats across the woman's pale cheek.

Mal's short eyelashes fluttered at the assault.

"That's it. C'mon." A few more pats, gentler this time, and Mal's eyelids slowly opened like lazy drapes not eager to let in the sunlight. When those glassy orbs landed on Cami, they lingered until Mal's mouth finally caught up with what she was seeing.

"Cami? What the . . . Christ, my head is pounding." Mal squinted her eyes shut again as she curled her legs into her.

"I know." Cami shifted so the woman's head was in her lap. "The barn, it's all gone. I don't know how."

She glanced back in the direction of the barn. Giant black funnels of smoke rose up from the building, thicker than she remembered from moments ago.

Gone. It was all gone, or it would be in a few more minutes. And if she didn't get up and call the fire department, that fire could spread to her apartment. She inhaled a great breath as she tried to reposition Mal's head so she could get her legs out from under her to stand.

Her muscles collapsed under her faster than a crumbling Jenga tower. And Mal wasn't in much better shape.

"Cami? Mal? Holy hell! What's going on? Are you guys all right?"

Cami turned her head toward the voice she recognized. A man in a puffy light-brown leather coat, worn blue jeans, and work boots trotted over to them. The streetlight on the gravel driveway illuminated the beige Toyota Celica.

"Gerry! Call the fire department!"

The man stalled in his tracks before he even reached them. With a nod, he ran past and took the three front steps to the office in one giant leap before heading inside. A moment later, Gerry's heavy footfalls stomped down the steps and skidded to a halt at her side.

"They're on their way," he said as he crouched down, his eyes swinging back and forth between her and Mal. "I just landed at the airport a short while ago. I was going to stop for a coffee and groceries first, but decided to come to the ranch instead. And it's a damn good thing I did. I pulled up and saw this huge fire from the road!"

"The horses," Cami rasped out, suddenly remembering them. Her eyes flew to meet his. "I got them out, but they're probably running spooked in the paddock. Mal's probably got a concussion, but she's awake."

"I'm on it. Stay here."

Gerry's worn hands gripped her shoulders and drew her into the most comforting hug before he got up and ran to get the horses. Maybe it was a form of trauma, or maybe it was a by-product of staring death in the face and winning. But as she sat there, with her lungs and throat beginning to calm down, one thought raced through her mind.

Richard had been taken. And she would bring him back.

Because she'd gotten a good look at the bastard's face who grabbed him.

A short time later, the fire department and ambulances arrived on scene. Their hoses were quickly connected to the ranch hydrants, and the first flames began to sizzle when the water made contact.

But that did nothing to quell the flames of revenge raging inside of her.

"These are some pretty fancy digs." A low voice resonated through Dick's addled mind. The voice was deep, gruff, and not one he recognized. But the cold metal against his cheek and the throbbing ache in his head made it hard to concentrate. He couldn't recall his own last name if he wanted to.

"It's my family's estate. What can I say? Old money likes to spread out and make itself known."

That voice he knew. It was higher and had a pitch to it, one he had come to recognize at Cami's rehearsals.

Dick cracked his eyes open. The steel frame in front of him, coupled with the cold metal against his front, added up to a ride in the bed of a pickup truck similar to what he had begun to drive at the ranch. As his senses slowly came to, he tried to move his hands and sit up. Sharp needles prickled at his wrists. The burning bite of rope rasping across his skin slowed his movements.

Bound. His wrists were tied behind his back, which didn't surprise him. What did surprise him, though, was James, the tenor from Cami's production, sitting down by Dick's head, with one lanky leg bent at the knee and the other outstretched. He was clad in all black, with a hood pulled over his head. Tufts of blond hair peeked out from underneath.

Dick groaned. "Hiya, Jamie-babe."

No use in playing dead. Besides, he wasn't the run-and-hide type. His face full of scars from his run-in with German machine gun shells kind of made that point.

A deep chuckle came from down by Dick's feet, followed by the voice of another man. "Jamie-babe? That's a new one."

Ah, so James had help. Figured.

"My fiancé's pet name for me. I hate it, but I love her money, so . . . " he said with a shrug. "Now, let's get him out of the truck, Matty."

"Whatever you say, Jamie-babe."

"If you want to get paid, you'll let that die right there," James warned.

The man's smile flattened out as he jumped from the truck. For the second time in as many hours, a firm grip clenched around Dick's ankles. A strong, jerky yank backward and Dick was out of the truck. He anticipated the maneuver, thankfully. A last-minute twist allowed him to land on his shoulder, rather than the faceplant he would have otherwise been destined for. A cloud of dust puffed up around Dick's head, which wasn't helping his irritated throat.

"Now, Mr.— What did you say your last name was again?" James asked as he jumped down from the truck.

"Stevens," Dick coughed out. "And I didn't."

"Right. Mr. Stevens. We've got a problem, I'd say. Well, actually, you're the one with the problem."

Dick shook his head out and managed to get his feet under him. Once he was upright, he took in his surroundings. The sun had already set, but there was plenty of outside lighting around the perimeter to get a feel for the landscape. Off in the distance, a large building sprawled out across an expansive property. Not far from the main house, for he didn't know what else to call it, were landscaped rolling hills with sandbanks and steep bunkers. Though he hadn't seen many, he knew what a golf course looked like . . . and that was it.

What he wasn't prepared for was the gated-off area he stood in. A wrought-iron fence lined several hundred feet around them. But the grass he stood on was shorn and maintained. Were they in a meadow of some kind? Why gate it off, though? Behind him and to his right, a large mound of dirt had been piled up, but he didn't see where it had come from. And then he saw them.

Headstones. He was standing in a cemetery.

Thoughts of morbidity immediately brought his mind back to Cami. *Shit! She's still trapped in the fire!*

Turning, Dick leaped for the driver's seat of the truck before he remembered his wrists were still bound.

"Oh, please, don't even bother. There's no use in trying to save her. We're forty minutes away and well-hidden on my family's property. Cami's long dead by now. But please don't worry. You won't be far behind, I promise."

Forty minutes. He had been out for forty minutes? Dick mentally assessed the best possible survival odds for Cami. None of them gave her forty minutes to live. With the blaze as high as it had been, with the barn's structure failing, and the oxygen getting eaten up, she had five minutes at most. *Maybe* ten if she stayed low, covered her mouth, and slowed her breathing.

But no one else knew she was there except him. Dick dropped to his knees. His body, for all he had put it through, completely gave out.

Cami was dead. His angel . . . dead.

Tears, warm and foreign, tickled the slopes of his cheeks and landed in the dirt before him. He inhaled great rasping breaths as his world, his second chance at life, crumbled on top of him. As the torrents of grief kept pelting him, he was aware of his captors looking on.

He'd kill them. James and the hired thug. He'd kill them both, bound hands or no. For his angel, he'd blot out the sun and lay waste to everything else. He just needed to know one thing.

"Why," Dick growled as he stared daggers at James. It wasn't a question, but a statement of fact, and Dick dared him to say otherwise.

"Because it should have been *me* who soared!" James whirled on Dick. "*Me* who commanded that stage! *Me* who the director fawned over! But did they? No."

He turned his back to Dick. "Cami and I had a lot in common, you know. Despite my talents as a tenor, they were never quite enough to lift my career as high as I needed. This estate," he said with a sweep of his arms, "the money that built it is nearly as old as our great country. The Lowell family, my family, made its immense fortune selling gunpowder during the Civil War. By World War I, we produced virtually all of the gunpowder in America."

A memory poked through the recesses of Dick's mind. Stacks of wooden barrels on the ammunition carriers bound for France. Rows and rows of gunpowder barrels stamped with the same white letters: *Army Cannon Powder - Lowell Manufacturing, Ltd.*

"Needless to say, my family knows a thing or two about blowing things up."

The jab made Dick see red. Rage blinded his vision. He nearly got to his feet, ready to charge into James, when the man continued speaking.

"But as the third son in line for the family fortune, and add to that the fact that said son had no interest in gunpowder, ammunition, or weaponry, and, well, you can imagine the disappointment." James turned back to face Dick. The other man was over by the truck, leaning against the tailgate and cleaning out the grime under his nails with his utility knife.

"I wanted to sing. From the moment I heard Luciano Pavarotti take down the house singing nine high Cs in *La Fille du Régiment*, I knew that was for me. The highs and lows, the emotion, the adoration from a grand stage. I could drink it up and never have my thirst quenched. But my error, however, was in thinking my parents would support a career pursuit other than what supported them all these years. I quickly learned what it was like to go my own way without their support, financial or otherwise. So I struggled, floundered, trained on my own, but could never reach the heights I needed to . . . until I met Sandy."

Dick slowed his breathing and allowed the rush of oxygen to help his brain strategize. Apparently, Jamie-babe thought it was story time, which was fine by Dick. He needed the time to think.

"Sandy was your typical opera diva: phenomenal voice, holier-than-thou attitude, access to the best vocal coaches and trainers, and a strong love of pretty boy tenors with eager cocks. It didn't matter that

I would soon be broke. It didn't matter that I would rather dress in festooned costumes and pour my emotions into song than dig out the gunmetal grease from under my fingernails." James peered at the man by the truck in disgust. "I wasn't good enough to excel on my own, not at the level needed to keep me in the comforts I was used to. But Sandy was. I kept her fucked and flourishing, and in exchange, she recommended me as part of her doubleheader. The tenor to her soprano. And it was working . . . until little Miss Impoverished gave Sandy a busted nose and cracked teeth."

"The explosion, the fire, Cami . . . this was all some revenge scheme because you suck at singing and Cami didn't?" Dick backed up slowly, giving himself space to process, space to panic and explode. "You killed my *wife!*" The roar that erupted from within surprised even him.

"Wife, eh? I wasn't aware you two made it official. But at any rate, it's time to move on. "Oh," James said with a raised finger as he walked closer to Dick. "I probably should just clarify a point. You know, I never meant to hurt Cami. Oh, no, not at all. I would have been more than happy to just take her out of contention with an accidentally sprained ankle or mild carbon monoxide poisoning."

"Fight me, you fucker!" Dick drew himself up into James's face. He was done talking. Done listening to hows and whys as the asshole ran his mouth. Chest heaving, heart pounding, Dick all but ignited on the spot.

"And *that's* why I had to go the more drastic route. You're too much of a guard dog. Always lapping at her heels, sniffing around for out-of-the-ordinary scents. It was too risky to get close to her. So I had to go in a different direction. Regrettable, perhaps, but necessary." James turned around to address his thug. "Matty."

The man by the truck looked up at James but didn't say anything.

"Payment's in the duffel bag under the driver's seat in the cab. Once we're finished here, load his body into that hole, cover it up, and the bag is yours."

Dick leered at Matty as the man gave a quick nod and stepped away from the truck, closer to Dick. A flash of light danced in Dick's periphery. Straight ahead, James gripped a gun. The weapon's body glowed with occasional glints from the moonlight. The pistol was aimed directly at Dick's head.

"Nah, man. A job like this, I take payment upfront." Matty walked over in front of Dick toward the driver's seat. As soon as their paths crossed, Dick attacked.

He rushed at Matty, jamming his shoulder directly into the man's throat. The sharp gasp and wheeze had Matty falling backward. Dick slammed down on him, crushing Matty's torso and preventing him from moving. The compression of the man's bones under him, the futile strain of his muscles, was satisfying. In the assault, Matty's utility knife slipped free.

Dick turned onto his back and tried to grab the knife with his bound hands. Cold metal kissed his palm as his fingers gripped the hilt. He turned onto his right side for a better angle, then flipped the blade quickly. Matty lay beside him, still gasping. The sharp edge of the blade slid under the rope's fibers.

But because his good ear was facing the ground, Dick wasn't able to hear the two gunshots fire.

CHAPTER 30

Cami lay huddled up under a blanket on a stretcher in the back of the ambulance, gripping the oxygen mask to her mouth like the literal lifeline it was. The rig was parked on the gravel driveway, and its back doors were wide open. Her view of the action caught in the ambulance's floodlights was gut wrenching.

The fire department had yet to contain the fire, but it was much improved. The only saving grace in the whole thing was that they'd managed to contain it to the barn alone.

Some great consolation that was.

Crackling and hissing drew Cami's attention as another ladder was raised over the back of the barn. A firefighter was up in the bucket, dousing the remaining flames.

"We're taking your friend over to the hospital now." An emergency medical technician appeared around the back door of the ambulance, leaning his elbow against the edge of the vehicle.

"Good. Tell Mal I'll come visit her first thing in the morning. I want her to rest and get whatever care she needs tonight." Cami said the words, but her mind was elsewhere.

"Are you sure I can't convince you to go with her?" The EMT stared at her, his eyebrow raised with that it's-your-life-not-mine look that highlighted Cami's stubbornness and, yeah, maybe a touch of stupidity.

But she had passed their cognitive test, and legally, she was in her right to refuse medical attention.

Do you know what your name is?

Cami Foster.

Do you know where you are?

Hell.

Do you know who the president of the United States is?

Reagan.

Despite the grumbles of disapproval from the EMTs and Gerry, she'd never lost consciousness, so she was still allowed to sign off on her release. Even if everyone around her thought she was an idiot for doing so.

"All right, then. Just be sure to call your doctor in the morning so they can check up on anything we can't detect in the field." As in, *we respect your right to be an idiot, but your doctor ought to know, too.*

"Thanks. I appreciate all the help, but I think I'm good for now. The oxygen helped immensely." Cami unwrapped the blanket from around her shoulders and swung her legs over the side of the stretcher.

The EMT extended his hand and she took it, slowly stepping down. "Call us if you need anything."

"Will do."

With Mal safely taken care of, Cami walked over to the main office.

She was a woman on a mission.

Once she was alone in the room, urgency hurried her movements. Cami walked over to Mal's desk and began searching.

"It's got to be here somewhere." Cami's brittle fingernails did their best to leaf through the stacks of papers and catalogs Mal left buried in her desk. When her hand skimmed across a thick periodical she hoped was what she was looking for, she yanked it out of the drawer.

"What are you doing? And why the hell are you not going to the hospital with Mal?" Gerry stood at the office door, his arms crossed over his chest, with a boatload of disapproval in his eyes as he glared daggers at her.

"I'm fine. And I promise I'll get checked out tomorrow. I just need to find an address right now. Please help me? I think I know who caused the fire."

That was all it took for Gerry to get with the picture and start digging through the office. They had been at it a good ten minutes with no sign of progress.

"Why the heck would Mal keep every Ames department store catalog for the last year in her desk?" Cami sighed in frustration before tossing it to the ground.

"Beats me, especially since I've never once seen Mal within a hundred feet of that place." Gerry was over at the bookshelf along the wall, sifting through piles of papers as well. When the next stack he moved revealed a three-inch-thick bound directory with a glossy yellow cover, he smiled. "Found it!"

Cami whipped around, scrambled to her feet, and grabbed the phone directory out of Gerry's hands. She brought it over to the coffee table and laid it open. Her index finger scanned gray newsprint pages for the Ls.

"Are you sure it was him?"

Cami's pulse pounded in her ears as she flipped through the pages, swiping past the advertisements and commercial listings until she got to the back where the residential phone numbers and addresses were.

James Lowell, the tenor she had been rehearsing across from for the better part of two weeks, had been in the barn as it burned around them. She was sure of it. When Richard's hulking body squeezed under that beam, a dark shadow had risen up behind him. Cami hadn't gotten a sense of what she was seeing at the time. But as Richard attempted to rise to his knees, two long arms clad in black had reached out and grabbed his ankles. Then his body was pulled back under the beam.

Away from her.

The blaze around her made it hard to see. The oranges and yellows of the fire mingled with the thick, black smoke to scramble her senses and choke her throat. But when the man who grabbed Richard rose to his full height before he turned, the profile was unmistakable. The recognition was a gut punch that almost made her vomit. A long, patrician nose stood out starkly against the fiery background. Awareness of the slicked-back quiff that was James's signature hairstyle, short on the sides and longer down the middle, settled over her. She hadn't seen him long, only a moment, but every cut and curve of that face was as familiar as the halls of the conservatory. Heck, she had even kissed that pale cheek as his enamored fiancé, Amina!

"London . . . Loppetti . . . ah, Lowell! Gerry, grab me a pen from the desk."

Cami uncapped the pen with her teeth and jotted down James's family's address on the back of her hand. The cold ballpoint pricked and tingled against her tight, irritated skin, but she didn't care. All the burning, dryness, and shortness of breath in the world wouldn't keep her from getting to Richard. And she had a pretty darn good idea of where James had taken him.

"You're sure he's there? This Richard guy?"

"Definitely." Cami hadn't yet filled Gerry in on who Richard was, but one of the wonderful qualities about Gerry was that he never pried. And it was that lack of nosiness that always made her feel comfortable sharing with him. "Everyone at the company knows about James's family's estate. It's all he ever talked about when Sandy let him get a word in. From what he described, the place is huge. And he's well connected."

"Cami, we should tell the police. They can look for him, go after this James person. You were just in a fire, for Christ's sake!"

"No! There's no time. Every off-duty copy and volunteer firefighter this side of the Genesee River is out there trying to contain that fire. I need to find him now. Before something happens to him. God, Gerry, if something did, I'd never forgive myself." Cami looked up at Gerry. Her body couldn't produce any more tears if it wanted to, but that didn't stop her anguish from rising to the surface.

"I love him," she said, sniffling. "I need him, and leaving him behind is just not an option." She nodded her chin in defiance, though she knew he wouldn't fight her further.

"All right." He sighed. "We'll go. Let me grab some waters from the fridge. You need to start chug-a-lugging. Wait for me in my car. I'll be right there. Maps are in the glove compartment. You're navigating."

Every step was excruciating, but Cami bit her lip and kept moving forward. She would get through this because the only way she'd be able to heal fully was when Richard's strong heartbeat was against her ear and he was wrapped safely in her arms.

<hr>

Pain, bright and blazing, flared near his left shoulder. Sulfur and carbon permeated the air. He was in a position he'd been in before in the forests of France, when a German shell blew up too close to his head. This time, however, the trauma and memories didn't haunt him. Other images seeped into the forefront of his mind.

Images of a beauty with curly hair mesmerizing him on stage with her song.

The way her skin pebbled as he lightly skimmed his fingers over the curve of her naked hip.

The cute wrinkle that formed between her eyebrows when he needled her delicate sensitivities.

The sound of his birth name falling from her lips.

One by one, his memories of Cami assaulted him. They slammed into his consciousness with vigor and purpose. But instead of dragging him down into darkness, twisting each positive experience into angst and a bottomless depression, his mind calmed. Each thought he conjured lifted his heart. With each breath he willed himself to take, each flutter of his eyelids he forced his eyes to make, the darkness stayed at bay.

"Cami," he rasped out, staring up at the sky full of stars. Was she up there? Twinkling in front of him, sending down her love and encouragement? His angel . . .

"Matty, get up, dammit!" A panicked, shrill voice broke Dick from his daze.

He registered the hard lump next to him very quickly. After all, he knew a dead body when he saw one. Matty's right arm and leg were sprawled across Dick's body. Heavy, lifeless limbs weighed Dick down. Not the embrace he'd prefer, given the circumstances, but at least it was one less person he'd have to kill tonight. Which reminded him.

James.

Boots crunched down at Dick's feet as James came closer, no doubt to inspect his handiwork. From the quiver in the man's voice, Dick got the impression Jamie-boy hadn't intended to shoot his hired help. Well, Dick would make sure to keep the bad day train moving for him.

Dick slipped his eyes closed as James drew closer. A sharp kick to his calf sent a painful jolt to his body, but he kept stock still during James's little proof-of-life test. He needed him to come closer. Dick accelerated the play dead routine and took a deep, though discreet, breath in through his nose and held it. Chest rise was not his friend, and he'd keep it to a minimum.

The weight of Matty's limbs was dragged off Dick, and he was thankful for the increase in blood flow.

"What a fucking waste. Well, at least the hole's already dug. No reason I can't kick in two bodies."

Warm wetness pooled at the back of Dick's neck. A dryness invaded his throat, and his lips began to feel tense and parched. He ticked his jaw and fought through the weakness that permeated his limbs. A quick flex of his left arm told him it was usable but barely.

Hang on just a little longer. C'mon, you asshole. Get in close. Nice and close.

Grunts and pants, greatly muffled by his hearing loss, barely registered, but not the complete loss of weight and warmth on his left side. James must have moved Matty. Subtle vibrations through the ground alerted Dick to James's position. On his left side. Shit. His reflexes on his right side were stronger. But like hell he'd give up this opportunity.

Light puffs of air tickled Dick's nose. James was above him, close enough for Dick to feel his breath.

It was go time.

Dick's eyes shot open and locked in on James next to him. He reached up with his left arm and grabbed James by the throat. As he squeezed, blood poured out of Dick's open wound. Before James could react, Dick swung his right arm around toward the tenor.

The flat of the blade in his hand glinted in the moonlight.

In a quick slash, Matty's utility knife scraped across James's jugular. Dick leaned in hard and sliced deep. Blood sprayed out and painted Dick's face. He released James. Bright red crimson flowed between the man's fingers as they helplessly clutched his throat. James fell to the ground with a thud. Gurgles and gasps wheezed through his mouth as the life drained out of him.

Dick had no interest in the writhing going on down by his feet. And he certainly had no interest in touching the gun that was on the ground by his knees. Back in his time, police detectives fingerprinted weapons and crime scenes. It was all the rage in criminal investigations. He had to hope modern police still used the same metrics, if not something better. Still, no way he was touching that gun. There was, however, another weapon he needed to take care of.

A few feet away from him, on his right, lay Matty's body. Dick was thankful he didn't have to stand up just yet. He was content to stay on his knees for as long as possible, so he crawled toward Matty. Dick fumbled around at the lackey's belt and let out a sigh of relief when he found the knife sheath. After a bit of nimble finger work by pulling his jacket sleeves down—again, trying to minimize his presence on the dead man's body—he managed to open the sheath, wipe down the knife handle, and slide the blade home, but made sure to leave it open and sloppy. Satisfied, he had no choice but to finally get his legs under him and try to stand.

Slowly, his gait shaky and his breathing heavy, he walked toward James's stilled body. After he fumbled around in the man's pockets, hard metal and rough edges caught against his fingertips.

Car keys.

The means to an exit in hand, he hobbled over to James's truck and climbed in. A quick check under the seat confirmed James's duffel bag delivery, but Dick wanted no part of it. With his hands still covered with his sleeves, he heaved the thing out the window in the direction of James's body.

Coherent thoughts were leaving him. Blurriness crept in at the edges of his vision. He needed to make it back to the farm. Worry and sadness tightened around his heart.

She was gone.

But he would get back to her regardless. If only to say goodbye.

Dick threw the keys in the ignition and fired up the truck. It was a much newer vehicle than the ones he'd practiced on at the ranch, but he'd figure it out. He had to. One problem, though, was he had no idea how they got here, or where the property was in relation to what he knew. A quick glance down at the driver's door revealed wads of folded paper sticking out of the rigid pocket. Curious, he grabbed one stack of paper and smiled when the words "Rochester Street Map - Easy to Read!" stared back at him.

He unfolded the map and scanned for landmarks and streets he knew. Thankfully, map reading hadn't changed much since his time. He had never been more grateful for the easily transferable skill. Once he got his bearings, he tossed the paper to the side, not caring a whit about folding it back up.

Dizziness and sleep threatened to pull him under as he backed out of the cemetery area and turned around to exit the property the way they came in.

He just needed to get to the ranch. But the drowsiness was becoming harder to fight. As he turned out onto the highway, his left foot slipped off the clutch when he tried to shift the truck into fourth gear. Sensation in his left leg was fleeting, yet he tried again. He managed to successfully depress the pedal, but when his right foot stepped back on the accelerator, Dick's eyes dropped closed.

The vibrations jarred him awake.

But not before the truck careened into a giant oak tree.

CHAPTER 31

Cold water slid down the back of Cami's throat as rows of trees sped by her. Her lips were still cracked, and she had difficulty getting a good seal around the rim. Dribbles leaked out of the corner of her lips. She blotted them with her coat sleeve.

"Easy, girl. Slow, tiny sips at first. Your body needs to work itself back up to speed." Gerry sat behind the wheel of his Celica as they ate up the exits on the highway heading east. The estate should have been coming up soon. From the maps, the thing looked massive. Acres upon acres of privately owned estate had filled out the property lines. The size of it had her worried. Slight pricks shot up through her cheeks as she bit down on her lip a bit too hard.

How would she ever find him? And what if she was wrong?

Dread and worry returned with a vengeance. But she tamped them down, picked her head up, and kept her eyes on the road. The solid yellow lines on the side of the road flashed quickly in her periphery and provided a comforting reminder of the speed Gerry was driving. She needed fast.

"It should be up here somewhere, I think." Cami peered out the window, looking for a break in the tree line.

"Looks like we're not the only ones having a bad night."

Gerry's comment drew Cami's gaze over to his side of the road up ahead, where a large black pickup truck had crashed into a tree. Smoke rose up out of the smashed-in hood, which had narrowly missed a head-on impact. The front passenger's compartment had taken the brunt of the damage, with its windshield, front fender, and entire cabin crunched in.

Cami squinted at the truck as they approached. Her eyes widened when recollection dawned on her. "Gerry, stop! That's James's truck! Stop the car!"

"How do you know that?"

"Because I've seen it parked at the conservatory tons of times before. That's his truck!"

Gerry slammed on the brakes and pulled off to the side of the road. But before Cami could undo her seat belt, he grabbed her hands. "If that's his truck, why the hell are you running toward it? He tried to kill you! Set the barn on fire and kidnapped a man. And you want to go in there guns blazing?"

"Look at that truck. You think anyone survived that? A dead man isn't a threat to me. But if he *is* in there, and he *is* still kicking, I want to know what he did with Richard. So, are you coming or not?" She scowled at him before she undid her seat belt and leaped out of the car.

Cami was done playing games.

She ran across the road, grateful for the lack of traffic at that time of the night. She had no weapons on her, but once she got a better look at the truck, she was pretty sure she wouldn't need them anyway. As she crept around to the driver's side of the car, the body of a man lay slumped over the steering wheel. His head was facing the passenger's seat, so she couldn't get a good look at him.

"Here," Gerry said, handing her a flashlight.

She spun the beam around to the driver's-side door. The light settled on a mass of sandy blond hair that was half matted with blood. The coat, stained with rust-colored splotches and fresh crimson streaks, was the same beige leather coat she'd grown used to for the last few weeks.

"No . . . Richard!"

Cami lunged forward and wrenched the door open. Blood caked

the back of his head and trailed down his entire left side. Despite the noise she made and the occasional road noise behind her, Richard didn't move. Her trembling hands gripped his shoulders and neck as she carefully laid him back against the headrest. His eyes were closed, and his lips were slightly parted. Shallow breaths flowed in and out of his lungs, but she could clearly see he wasn't getting enough chest expansion. She fumbled around his coat collar, and her hands came away coated in red.

"Oh, God. Gerry, he's been shot! He's breathing but barely. We need to get him to the hospital." Cami couldn't breathe, couldn't think straight. "Oh, please, Richard. Hang on. I'm here. Just hang on a bit longer. I love you, and I'm not going anywhere."

"Put pressure on the wound while I bring the car around."

Cami nodded as she shrugged out of her jacket and pushed it against Richard's shoulder. She was doubtful it would do anything, but she had to hope. She just got him back and like hell she'd throw in the towel now.

While she waited for Gerry to return, she looked Richard over. Dull bruises had begun to form under his eyes, and black soot marred his features. Blood trickled out of his nose and dripped off his upper lip. Her heart squeezed in agony at the sight, both for what he had endured and what may yet come to be. Again, she shook the thought away.

She leaned forward into the car, as close to his right ear as she could get. Her thighs strained to support her in the awkward position. The tips of his blond hair tickled her cheek as she got closer.

"I'm here, Richard. Stay with me a bit longer. I love you." She let the words seep into the cabin of the truck and hoped he heard them.

A car engine revved behind her. Gerry pulled up and jogged over. "He really shouldn't be moved, but there's nothing to help it. We need to get him breathing again. Any potential cervical spine concerns would have to be back-burnered."

Cami nodded for lack of anything better to say. She was fresh out of words.

Once they both heaved Richard out of the truck, they managed to carry him over to Gerry's car.

"Hop in the back and he'll sit next to me. Just hold him upright from behind while I drive."

Cami flipped the back of the passenger seat forward and slid in behind it. She grabbed the seat back and yanked it toward her, repositioning it for Richard. After a moment of a few tricky maneuvers, Gerry got Richard in and belted. Cami's hands were immediately around Richard's neck as she kneeled on her seat. There wasn't a seat belt in the world stronger than the grip she had around him.

As Gerry floored the Celica and scooted out onto the highway, Cami positioned her head on Dick's right shoulder. His chest rose and fell shallowly, but every other inhale he took seemed a bit fuller than the one before it. Was he improving? Should they stay and try to do CPR? Indecision had caused her to remain trapped in the burning barn, instead of calling for help.

No. Richard needed help. She wouldn't make the same mistake again. God, she hoped like hell she was right this time. Instead of dwelling on it, she hugged him as tight as she dared and kept her lips close to his right ear.

In the absence of any medical training, and with an abundance of stress and panic, she offered the only thing she could.

She sang.

The fog was endless. When Dick tried to focus and get his bearings, the oppressive mist stretched in all directions. Bits of numbness had started to fade and made way for all sorts of bite-down-on-a-stick-so-you-don't-eat-your-tongue kind of pain. As he mentally assessed his injuries, a faint humming sounded off to the right. Not a humming so much, but a melody.

Dick turned his head and subconsciously sought out the song. He'd heard it before, though he didn't know the words. Memories were teased to the forefront as the song went on. It comforted him, calmed the flare-ups, and gave his wandering mind direction amid the endless fog.

The voice, the words. Soft Italian libretto sung in gentle feminine tones. Well, shit. When did he get all fancy with words? The events of the last twenty-four hours flooded back to his consciousness. Cami trapped in the burning barn. James tearing Dick away from Cami. The knife wound. The truck crash.

A great inhale rushed into his lungs, and he moaned on the exhale. Damn, that fucking hurt.

The voice stopped. "Richard?"

Of all the sounds he'd thought he'd never hear again, Cami's voice was at the top of the list. But, no. She was dead. Died in the fire. She had to be.

Right?

Hesitant yet oddly hopeful, Dick strained to open his eyes. A harsh, overhead light threatened to clam them right back up. He blinked uncontrollably.

"Oh my gosh! Richard! Shoot, the lights. Hold on."

That was Cami's voice. But how? Was she alive?

The room's lighting dimmed, and his eyelid fluttering stopped. One or two more solid blinks and he was able to keep his eyes open fully.

And, boy, was he glad he could.

Above him was a giant mass of dark brown curls hanging down, threatening to tickle his chest. The beautiful face at the center was the most radiant thing he'd ever seen. His angel leaned over him with the brightest blue tear-rimmed eyes. Her smile reached from ear to ear. Delicate teardrops slid down her cheeks and crash-landed onto his heart.

All questions flew out the window as he reached for her face, hoping she was real. Soft, smooth skin met his hands as he sat up to hold her, kiss her. His body, however, protested. Sharp pains from all sides caused him to groan into her mouth when he desperately wanted to be doing other things to it. A soft chuckle escaped her lips.

"Easy," she said as she settled him back down onto the hospital bed. "You've got a lot of healing to do."

"How?" he asked, nearly breathless. "Cami, how are you alive?" The words came out on a wince, and he wondered if he should take that as a sign not to look a gift horse in the mouth.

"Shh. We can recap my near-death experience once we've gotten over yours. You almost died, too, you know." She nearly choked on the words. "I came after you, figured out where James may have taken you. But before I got there, I found you on the side of the highway in James's pickup truck. You lost a battle with a tree, and you were in bad shape."

A sob forced its way through her steely demeanor. "Richard, you were shot. In your shoulder. The surgeons operated on you for over two hours. The bullet hit your collarbone, and chips of bone were driven into your tissue and around your shoulder. They removed what fragments they could, but your collarbone will have to heal on its own. And you punctured your lung, but thankfully, it was a small pneumothorax. They took out your chest tube not too long ago once your lung started to inflate fully on its own."

Dick sat there for a moment and absorbed her words. He had no idea what a pneumothorax or a chest tube was, but he sure as shit knew about bullets and bones. The throbbing pain that stretched out across the expanse of his left shoulder and chest gave credence to her story. He had no idea what the healing time frame was for those injuries, though. When he got himself blown up overseas at the end of the war, he had been out of commission for months. He'd needed to relearn so many things. Walking, hearing, seeing. How long did he need to be holed up in recovery again? If so, he'd be useless to her. Utterly useless.

"Ah, Mr. Stevens. You're awake! How are you feeling? Your wife was confident you'd be waking soon." A blonde woman came into the room wearing a baggy light-blue uniform. Her hair was tied back, and she had a stethoscope draped around her neck. She was smiley and chipper as ever, as if Dick was holding a bucket full of ice cream and was about to serve up a sundae bar.

"Who are you?" Apparently, his manners had died along with the demolished truck.

"Apologies. I'm Kathy. I'll be your nurse until seven p.m., and then Johnny starts his shift in this wing."

Dick's head throbbed, partially from the pain and partially from stimulation overload. This woman, in the men's pajamas, was a nurse? And who the fuck was Johnny?

Then something she said finally registered. *Your wife was confident you'd be waking soon.*

Wife.

Confused, he turned to Cami. A smile tugged at her lips as she kindly asked the nurse to give them a minute.

When they were alone again, Dick addressed the elephant in the room. "You told her you're my wife?"

"Absolutely. When we brought you in here, you had no wallet, no money. No identification of any kind. The easiest thing to do was to say you were my husband. Are you angry?"

"Angry? How could I be angry? Angel, I'm the happiest man alive! I'm only slightly annoyed that you beat me to it. I had plans, you see."

Cami came over and sat on the edge of the bed. Dick wrapped his arms around her waist. It hurt like hell, but damn if he'd let her know it. He was right where he needed to be and didn't plan on moving an inch.

"Oh, plans?"

"Oh, yes," he said, hugging her small frame to his body and planting a kiss on her sternum. "They involve going to bed with you each night and waking up next to you each morning. There's stuff that happens in between, of course, but I'm still working on the details."

"I bet you are." She chuckled, then kissed his forehead.

"One thing's for certain, though."

"What's that?"

"Don't ever stop singing."

A radiant smile spread across Cami's face. "I love you, Richard."

And just like that, Dick was gone for good.

CHAPTER 32

The hard mattress underneath Cami did little to help her lack of sleep. Sure, she had slept on worse, but she sure as heck had slept on better, too. When she first moved into her apartment above the maintenance barn, she'd made do with a futon for the first six months until she could scrounge up enough for a real bed. That futon was killer. Talk about your lumps and bumps.

But she certainly wouldn't complain about her lack of sleep this morning. Soft snores rumbled against her ear. A warm, strong arm was wrapped around her waist, securing her tightly to the firm body at her back.

A week ago, Richard had been discharged from the hospital, with specific instructions for his recovery. His confusion at the news had baffled Cami, until she realized that Richard probably didn't know how much modern medical advances improved surgical recovery times. And she'd also be lying if she said she didn't enjoy playing nursemaid a bit. But now that he was in his second week of recovery, he had improved greatly. He no longer needed her help when getting into the shower, and more often than not, he preferred to join her in the kitchenette when she prepared their meals. His stamina had progressed, as well, and he was able to stand for longer periods of time without getting winded. He had even ridden a horse again for the first time two days ago.

Mal had become the mother hen Cami never thought the woman was capable of. Every other day, she dropped off bags of food and clothes at the bunkhouse, where she and Richard were staying since there had been some minor damage to the maintenance barn from the fire. Thankfully, the fire department deemed the building habitable, but she still preferred to stay with Richard in the bunkhouse for the time being.

But man, Cami had never worn so much borrowed flannel and eaten so many veggie burgers in her life. Since James had attacked Mal, the woman had developed a new lease on life, apparently. She convinced herself that her being out of shape (her words, not Cami's) was why James got the jump on her. Ever since then, she'd switched to a vegetarian diet and started running (well, speed walking) laps around the ranch at random hours of the day. The poor horses never knew when to expect her and got spooked more often than not when she'd round the corner out of nowhere while they were out in the pasture.

"I hear you thinking, angel." Richard's gravelly voice always sounded that way first thing in the morning. And, boy, did she love that she knew that.

"How can you hear someone thinking?"

"I can't. I can only hear *you* thinking."

"And how is that different?"

"Easy. When you think out loud, your breathing changes. And you always free one hand so you can make small gestures with your fingers." His body tensed up behind her as he stretched his limbs out.

"I do not." But then she looked down and noticed how one hand was still tucked under the covers, but the other was free and tapping against the mattress.

Know-it-all.

Cami turned in his arms and nestled her hands against his warm chest. Her fingers drew small circles through the light hairs as he held her closer. "I was just thinking about James."

"I told you. Don't waste your energy on worm food. I've got you, and he's not coming back."

"I know. I just can't believe it all. And I'd be lying if I said I don't have anxiety about what happens next. How can I possibly start over at the conservatory after what James did?" She searched his eyes for an answer to the question that had been knocking around her head for the past two weeks.

"First of all, you're not starting over." His arms returned to rest around her. "And take that from someone who traveled through time with nothing except the mud on his boots. Second, think of it as more of a rebirth. A do-over. Except, this time around, you've got something you didn't have before."

"What's that? A sexy man in my borrowed bed?"

"True." He pointed his finger at her. "But also, this."

Richard rolled over and reached so far under the bed, Cami was sure he'd fall off. His mild grunts and groans made her worry he might aggravate his injuries again. Just before she was about to pull him back, he rolled back up to her.

A manila envelope was clasped in his hand, with the address of Mr. Donnelly's estate firm in the top left-hand corner. In the middle was her name. No address.

"Go on, open it."

Cami sat up in the bed and unbent the fastening on the envelope flap. "What is this?" As she pulled out a stack of papers, her eyes skimmed over the top of the first page.

"This is what you've wanted. What I promised you."

Cami's eyes flew across the page as she read the words she never thought she'd see. Emotion swelled in her throat, but she swallowed it back down.

"Enclosed within are the official behest documents outlining the formal distribution of properties and/or monetary assets to Miss Camilla Foster, daughter and sole heir of the deceased Mrs. Leanne Foster . . ."

The words beyond the first paragraph turned into a blurry mess. Tears dotted the bottom of the page, narrowly missing the attorney's official signature. Richard took the papers from her hands and handed her a tissue, lest she turn everything into a splatter of illegible scribbles.

"How? I don't . . . " She shook her head.

"Before the fire, do you remember how Mal and I were running into town for something?"

Cami's throat tightened up as emotions threatened to shut down her vocal cord superhighway. She couldn't risk speaking, so she nodded furiously.

"I had an idea about how we could make our marriage work and get you the inheritance that's due to you. But I needed Mal's help navigating things." He shrugged his shoulder and glanced down.

"What did you do?"

Richard took a deep breath and brought his head up. His eyes darted around the wall a bit before settling on her face. Were those . . . ? Was he . . . *nervous?*

"I'm not from this time, Cami. I don't have access to the required documents needed for a modern-day marriage license. For all intents and purposes, I'm a figment of history with no proof I exist. For the longest time, I couldn't figure out how to marry you legally. But when we were at the public market, I came across a book on common-law marriage. With Mal's help, I dug a little deeper into the subject. It would seem that, in certain parts of the country, common-law marriage is recognized as legally binding."

Cami leaned her head to the side and squinted a bit. "I've never heard of it."

"Me neither. But basically, in parts of the country where it's honored, all the couple has to do is state their intent to be married by . . . what were the words?" He cocked his head to the side briefly. "Ah, 'mutual and express agreement,' I believe was the expression." Whatever nerves were there before vanished in a flash when that smug expression appeared. "There's no formal marriage license needed. No risk of denial because I don't have a social security number. None of that. So, I floated the idea to Donnelly, with Mal's help. He didn't see a reason why that wouldn't fulfill your mother's terms of inheritance. Once he was satisfied, he drafted the release documents."

Richard's words finally sank in. Like a freaking sponge.

"You should get the bank draft within thirty days. But there's—"

Cami flew the covers wide and crashed into Richard. Her arms clamped around his neck as her mouth found his. A carousel of overwhelming emotions whirled through her mind. Tears filled her eyes as she kissed the one man who had single-handedly given her the world. Warm, comforting fingers traced up the nape of her neck as she memorized every delicious curve and angle of her new husband's mouth.

Because that's what he was. Her husband. In all the ways that mattered. And he had found a way to give her that, despite his tattered past, murky present, and unknown future.

Richard managed to tear his mouth free. "Wait, angel. There's one more thing you need to know."

She tried chasing his mouth, but he pulled away. She sat back with a frustrated pout. "What?"

"As much as I'd love to nibble that delicious bottom lip of yours, I need to tell you one more thing."

"What more could you possibly have to tell me?" She wanted to jump her husband, dammit. No more talking!

"New York doesn't recognize common-law marriages."

Her face fell as the other shoe dropped. Not just dropped, sank like an iron anchor through rotten floorboards.

"But . . . Washington, D.C. does."

Huh?

"What are you saying? That we have to move to D.C.?"

"There are other states that honor common-law marriages: Alabama, Colorado, Iowa, to name a few. But none that have top-notch opera companies like D.C." He handed her back the manila envelope and nodded at her to look inside again.

Cami pinched the bottom edge of the envelope and held it upside down. She shook the papers out and a glossy, red-and-black trifold brochure landed in her lap. When she turned it over, *The Washington Opera* stared back at her in prominent gold letters.

Before she could even open it, Richard elaborated. "They just took on a new general director a few years back. Apparently, his aim has been to lure young artists and cultivate their talent. There are a bunch of names in there of who they've brought into the company in recent years. They don't mean anything to me, but I'm hoping they mean something to you."

Cami skimmed the opera company's overview, passed over the maestro's bio, and gazed at the industry talent who had been acquired in the last few years. *Gian Carlo Menotti, director of* La Boheme. *Daniel Barenboim, conductor of* Così Fan Tutte. *Plácido Domingo, debut tenor in* Goya.

Plácido-freaking-Domingo!

She could hardly keep the drool contained. These were names she knew but would never dream of working with. They were all rising stars in the opera world. Highly coveted names and reputations. To even say her name in the same breath as theirs was an honor.

Holy freaking cannoli!

"I had no idea." She slapped her palm across her forehead. "I . . . I don't know what to say." She looked up at him, shaking her head in disbelief.

"A Washington talent scout from the company will also be at your performance. I called and made an inquiry," he said, rubbing the back of his neck. "Regardless of what you decide, you'll blow them away." His grin gave away his own excitement at what he'd managed to pull off.

"Richard, this is too much." But she couldn't keep from smiling.

"Nah, it's nothing you don't deserve." He took the brochure from her hand and placed the papers on the floor. Her neck lolled against his hands as they bracketed her face. "You gave me back my life, in more ways than a simple guy like me can say." His Adam's apple bobbed on a nervous swallow. "What do you say, angel? Will you be my wife?"

As he waited for her response, an uncertain, nervous look took residence on his face. He looked like a puppy who was promised a treat but wasn't sure if there was one left in the bag for him.

She was more than happy to put him out of his misery.

"Nothing would make me happier than marrying you."

His face finally relaxed, and the breath she hadn't realized he was holding rushed out of him.

"But I have a condition."

"Oh? And what's that?" He cocked his eyebrow.

She leaned forward and peppered soft kisses against the side of his neck. His left side. "Stay in bed with me until lunchtime," she whispered.

A low growl bubbled up from Richard's chest. He quickly grabbed her wrists and laid her down on the bed. As he rose over her, he nibbled and licked his way from her mouth to the column of her neck, only halting when he hit the roadblock of her T-shirt.

"You drive a hard bargain." He moved both of her wrists into his left hand.

A thrill shot through her when his fingers climbed their way up under the hem of her shirt. The backs of his knuckles lightly caressed the underside of her breast, taunting and teasing with each contact.

"What can I say? I appreciate the art of the deal." Her words came out almost breathless as her eyes fluttered closed. When his hands left her body, she opened her eyes in confusion.

Richard was still over her, his arms braced on either side of her body. The widest smile graced his face as he looked down at her. "Marrying you was the best damn deal I ever made."

The remainder of their clothes was tossed to the floor as they kicked off the blanket from the tiny bunkhouse bed. Her mouth never left his, as if she feared separation of any kind would magically shatter the love she was drowning in.

Closer. She needed him closer.

"Now," she said against his mouth. "I need you now, Richard."

"Yes, ma'am."

Cami drew her hands down Richard's rock-hard torso, relishing every nook and cranny of abdominal muscle her fingers encountered along the way. She would never tire of his granite physique, or how adorably ticklish he could be when she found the right spots.

She loved learning all his right spots.

Smooth skin bumped the back of her hand. The head of his shaft greeted her, almost weeping in anticipation as it stood at attention. Obligingly, she gripped it and simultaneously gave it a slight squeeze while wiping her thumb over the tip.

"Oh, sweetheart. I'm not going to last long if you keep that up," he groaned, his eyes closed.

She eagerly guided his cock to her opening. A quick slide of the tip up and down was all it took to get him wet and ready. And that was good because she was beyond primed. A tight ball of tension was building in her core. Her tummy flutters had quickly turned into roiling anticipation. Eager as ever, she notched him at her entrance while his hands splayed out on her hips. The tips of his fingers pressed into her skin, and the slight roughness of the contact excited her. He flashed her a wicked grin, and she had never been so happy for him to take it from there.

Without warning, he jerked his hips forward, embedding himself to the hilt. Cami gasped at the welcome intrusion. They stayed like that for a moment. The fullness was immense, both physically and emotionally. As Richard slowly slid out, the loss was acute. A slow, languid stroke back in had her whimpering. She couldn't anticipate his torturous methods, and the unexpected combinations drove her wild. When he shifted, she'd slow down, only for him to speed up and grind at an unrelenting pace. Her body was overloaded, and her lack of knowing what came next only heightened her build up.

Her hips jerked against his and, finally, met him at the same pace. Together, they hurried their movements. Each snap and rise took Cami higher until every sensation exploded from within. She arched up from the bed as Richard whipped his hips against her in a frenzy. A deep groan erupted out of him as he fell on top of her. He roared against the crook of her shoulder as his hips jerked with a few final thrusts. Heavy, hot breaths rushed out of them both.

Once her heart rate began to settle, he slipped free of her and reached for the blanket from the floor. With one hand, he tossed it over Cami's naked body just as she registered the chilly winter air in the bunkhouse.

He always knew her needs better than she did.

And she knew he always would.

The magnitude of love she had for this man couldn't possibly be described by a single moment, conversation, or day. It was everything. *He* was everything. And she couldn't imagine seeing another sunrise without him by her side.

CHAPTER 33

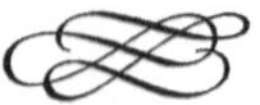

One Month Later

Dick's back was ramrod straight against the theater chair. And despite his bulky size, he managed to keep his knees bent at a ninety-degree angle so as not to disturb the guests next to him. The white bow tie cinched around his neck, an accessory to the tuxedo Mal had helped him pick out, did wonders for keeping his chin parallel to the floor as well. He didn't even mind the tightness in his shoulders and arms from the trim fit of the suit coat.

Oh, hell. Who was he kidding? He could have chewing gum stuck to his sole and bug bites on his butt and he'd still be glued to the vision on stage. After weeks of delays due to James's criminal investigations, the conservatory's production of *La Sonnambula* was finally premiering.

His Cami, the conservatory's first mezzo-soprano singing a lead soprano role in an operatic production, stood in the foreground of the stage. A giant spotlight illuminated her movements as she danced around. Amina's happiness was evident in Cami's radiant smile and soulful vocal expression. She was singing her final aria, *Ah! Non giunge*, where Amina had just been roused from her sleepwalking after Elvino placed a ring on her finger.

Dick had asked Cami about that part of the opera before, how challenging it must be for her to sing of doom and gloom one minute, then turn around and leap joyfully about the stage in glee the next. It gave him whiplash just thinking about it.

"That's part of the fun," she had told him. "When Amina sings, '*Ah! Non giunge uman pensiero / al contento ond'io son piena,*' she's literally saying, 'Human thought cannot conceive of the happiness that fills me.' It's easy to get swept up in the emotion because it's so unbelievable. That's why it's my favorite opera. Because despite everything, love wins the day. And there's absolutely no way to explain it further. It just is."

A smile slowly stretched across Dick's face as her words drifted through his mind. A silent chuckle broke free when he realized his own journey was not too dissimilar from Amina's. It had been some time since he mulled over the events that had led him here. There was a point where the questions of his time travel plagued him. The green dust on his pants in the well, stumbling through time, the image of what he swore was Cami's mother out by the oak tree.

After a time, trying to come up with the hows and whys of it all had become too exhausting. Maybe it was never meant to be explained. Maybe—and this was a *monumental* maybe with a side of no-way served over you've-got-to-be-shitting-me—he was just meant to finally be happy.

No questions or explanations necessary.

The thought was both sobering and freeing.

"I can't imagine how these women doll themselves up like this on a regular basis. I've got so many sequins up my ass, I'm liable to poop out a rainbow."

Dick let out a roar of laughter before he quickly clamped a hand over his mouth. The people next to him, thankfully, were polite enough not to shush him. Though based on the thinned lips of the old patron sitting next to him, the man heard every word and was probably desperate not to blurt out laughing himself and embarrass the missus.

Like Dick had just done.

"Mal, for what it's worth," he whispered, "I think you look stunning." He leaned over toward Mal, readjusted the teal shawl draped over her shoulders, and patted her back. "It's almost over, if it helps matters. Besides, Cami hasn't seen the finished product yet. You wouldn't want to rob her of her only opportunity to see you glammed up."

"That girl is lucky I love her so damn much." Mal grunted as she kicked off her heels and rounded her shoulders back as if she were gearing up for the last leg of a race.

"You and me both."

Roars and cheers erupted in his right ear as the audience around him rose to their feet. Dick jumped up and immediately drew his fingers to his mouth. The shrill whistle he blew out penetrated the clapping, but just barely. As Cami stood on stage, her hands clasped with her costars, her eyes scanned the crowd. He knew she couldn't see him, but that didn't stop him from jumping like a fool and cheering for her as if she were a winning prizefighter. He may not know much about opera, but Dick sure knew how to cheer on a sure thing.

And he was never surer of anything in his life.

As he pumped his fist in the air and the crowd noise around him continued its standing ovation, Dick was struck with how different their circumstances were from a month and a half ago.

The curtain finally closed as the house lights were brought up. Audience members slowly began to collect their things and shuffle out of the aisles.

Dick reached down to his feet and grabbed the bouquet of flowers he had been hiding. "Want to come with me to congratulate our leading lady?"

"You go on. I've only got enough concentration left in me to get myself safely to the truck in these heels without falling on my ass. Give her a kiss for me, and I'll be waiting for you two in the truck."

"Don't ever change, Mal," Dick called behind him as he jogged down the center aisle, ducking and shimmying in between the oncoming pedestrian traffic. When he arrived outside her dressing room door a few minutes later, he lightly rapped his knuckles against the wood. It took all his strength not to bang the door down and sweep his girl up in his arms. He was so damn proud of her.

"Come in."

Dick turned the knob and let himself in. Cami sat in front of her vanity mirror. The lights around its edge cast her in the most ethereal glow. Her dark curly hair had been freed from its wig and even the soft strands seemed lighter and more exuberant.

Just like his angel.

Cami turned around in her chair. She had already changed into her regular clothes, but her stage makeup remained. Not that Dick didn't appreciate the fluttery eyelashes and lipstick, but she could have been wearing war paint and she'd still be a knockout.

"Should I be feeling envious of all the other bouquets in this room?" He tilted his head toward the vanity, on which sat two flower arrangements, and another rested on the dresser behind him next to the door.

"Of course not." She walked over to him and took the flowers he offered. Her arms circled around his neck as she stood on tiptoes, rubbing her nose against his. "Yours is the biggest anyway." She teased his mouth lightly with brushes of her lips.

"Size *does* matter, right?"

"Whatever you say, love." Cami peppered his mouth with soft kisses.

"Seriously, angel." He drew back and cupped her face. "You blew them all away tonight. I couldn't be prouder of you. Sky's the limit, babe."

Cami's radiant smile melted him. Softened all his hard edges into jelly. He was utter goo in her arms. It was the best feeling in the world.

"I couldn't have done it without you." A light knock at the door interrupted the moment. "Come in," Cami said.

"I'm sorry to intrude, Miss Foster." A short, balding, mustachioed man in the standard black penguin suit shuffled into Cami's dressing room. He held out his hand to her in introduction. "My name is Vincent D'Angelo, and I'm the artistic director at The Washington Opera." Dick took a step back, more than happy to let this man shake

Cami's hand. "I very much enjoyed your performance this evening," Mr. D'Angelo said as he clapped his hands together. "I was quite enamored of your take on Amina. Truly breathtaking, my dear. The accomplishments you brought to the role as a mezzo were outstanding. You should be very proud of yourself."

"Thank you, Mr. D'Angelo. That means a great deal." The blush on Cami's cheeks made Dick smile.

"Well, I should get right to it, then." The man reached into his back pocket and presented Cami with a business card. She took the card and briefly stared at it before returning her nervous attention to her visitor.

"My opera company is undergoing a bit of a renaissance, if you can imagine such a thing in the opera world." He chuckled. "Since I took on the position two years ago, I have been fostering collaborations with outstanding artists and emerging talent. It has become somewhat of a hallmark of our productions, as it were. My interest has always been in new theater works and innovative productions. And what I saw tonight, Miss Foster, was certainly innovative and a breath of fresh air, if I may."

"Thank you. I . . . um, I'm so glad you enjoyed the performance." Her chin still struggled to stay off the floor. Damn, did she look cute when she was flustered.

"Miss Foster, I'd like to invite you to Washington to interview and audition for a role in our company. I'd certainly love to hear more of your singing, and I have some ideas for other expanded roles for mezzos that I hope may interest you."

"Oh, my . . . um." Cami looked down at the card in her hand, then looked back up at Mr. D'Angelo.

"No need to answer now. My contact information is all there on the card. When you have some time, please don't hesitate to connect with me. I'd love to chat further."

"Yes, yes! Absolutely, Mr. D'Angelo. Of course!" Cami furiously shook the director's hand before she put the brakes on the enthusiasm. When the door closed softly behind him, Cami jumped into Dick's arms and squealed into his ear.

His right ear.

Dick's laughter joined the noise as he spun her around. "I guess that answers the question of what you should do with the inheritance payment Donnelly gave you last week." He slowed his spinning but never took his arms off her.

"What's that?"

"Looks like we'll have to start looking for places to live in D.C."

"Oh my goodness, Richard!" She placed her hand over her forehead. "Are we really doing this?"

"Believe it, angel."

As Dick wrapped Cami up in another strong hug, he bent his head down into the crook of her neck and inhaled. He was home. In the arms of the woman he loved and who loved him back. He never wanted to be without this feeling again.

Peace was a glorious thing.

EPILOGUE

Three Months Later

" S unglasses. Where the heck did I put my sunglasses?"

Richard leaned back against the kitchen counter, his arms crossed over his chest, smiling in amusement. Cami had just started her third lap around their living room, opening the same end table drawer she'd searched through twice before looking for her sunglasses. Every time she bent over to scramble through the same drawer of card decks and butterscotch candies, he'd get a prime view of her generous backside.

He bit back another groan as the contours of her tight denim skirt highlighted her hips when she closed the drawer and scooted across the room again. It was a sight he'd never tire of. Good thing, too, since this time tomorrow, Cami would be his wife. Legally married by D.C.'s standards. And that was more than good enough for him.

"On top of your head, angel."

Cami halted midstep. Her hand flew to her head, and sure enough, her fingers crashed into the thick black glasses, smudging the lenses in the process. "I swear I'm losing my mind. I just keep feeling like I'm forgetting something. Oh, makeup! And . . . shoot. Did I pack my hairspray?"

Cami ran into the bathroom. Knocks and slams rang through their apartment as Richard left her to pack up what he assumed was the remainder of their small bathroom. A deep chuckle rumbled through his chest as he glanced around the space they now called home.

True to his word—and research—common-law marriage was well and truly alive in the District of Columbia. Richard learned that the notion had actually been oddly freeing for Cami. It had taken a huge weight off Cami's shoulders, eliminating the hassle of red tape while still giving her everything she could have wanted in a new marriage. At the very least, it paved the way for an easy apartment rental, that was for sure. When Cami had begun inquiring about available units for rent, the mention of her and her fiancé as tenants got her much further than when she'd called as a single person, before mentioning Richard.

Likewise, Cami's time at the new opera company had been a dream come true. Mr. D'Angelo's creative approach to casting and direction was truly innovative. For the first time, she told him how she had a renewed excitement for some of the classic pieces she'd previously thought of as status quo. Mr. D'Angelo was playful, experimental, and always asked for input from the performers. Cami had been beyond grateful for the transparency. She even went so far as to recommend that a trumped-up baritone try crossing over and singing some lead tenor arias. Those workshops had been her absolute favorite, and Richard got a thrill out of seeing her come home so happy each night. The comfort and ease with which she went to work every day was a breath of fresh air for him to witness as well. She fell into her new routine flawlessly.

Richard's adjustment, however, had been more gradual. Since there weren't any active productions open yet for casting, as they were still in the early developmental stages, he couldn't exactly sit in on rehearsals as he'd done before. With Cami working during the day, he took some time to wander and explore their new city as it was now. It wasn't that the changes bothered him. They didn't, not so much anymore. What unhinged him at times had been the lack of purpose he struggled with. Feeling untethered had been unsettling, and a part of him worried such a void might make room for old haunts to find him.

One day, however, that all changed. He still recalled the curious expression on Cami's face when she came home to the apartment to find him kicking off his muddy boots and wriggling out of his dusty blue jeans. He never came home looking so dirty. And the little crinkled V between her brows at the sight of him had never looked so cute.

"So, I may have gotten a job today." He shrugged, as if jobs were handed out to everyone like lollipops at a bank, and walked his boots over to their backdoor balcony before smacking them together to get the mud off.

Every morning, he and Cami would ride the Metro together to drop her off at the opera house. But during the day, he would walk the streets of the city, slowly exploring. A few blocks away from the performance center, he'd discovered Oak Knoll Cemetery. It was small and quiet, and benches lined the sidewalk outside the cemetery's wrought-iron fence. He sat on those benches often, looking in at a cemetery that, more than likely, should have included him.

Each day, he would notice an elderly groundskeeper moving through the property. The man would weed and mow and perform general landscaping maintenance on the graves and surrounding areas. For lack of anything better to do, Richard would sit and observe. It became his form of recreation and grounding. And comfort. Dirt he knew, weeds he knew, even the back-breaking shoveling enticed his lazy muscles. Since moving to the city, he'd missed the exertion and exercise of daily physical labor.

A few weeks later, the old man's knees had buckled underneath him while Richard had been watching. On instinct, Richard hopped the fence and aided the man as best he could. But when it became apparent the work was too much for the elderly man, Richard stepped in.

And he did that for weeks. Every day, he'd say goodbye to Cami and then show up to help the old man, who Richard learned was named Jack McCafferty and, as he suspected, was the primary groundskeeper for the cemetery. Richard would trim back the ivy for him, uproot the invasive vines, and remove the dying flowers left behind by loved ones. His unofficial help quickly turned into more expected assistance. Jack offered to pay him, always trying to slip folded bills into Richard's back pocket. And he would always refuse. Eventually, Jack had begun walking Richard through laying out the plots for burial and the steps for digging them out and filling them in. The tasks were hard but rewarding and deeply fulfilling. And not something he wanted to see Jack injure himself again trying to take on.

"I spoke to Jack today," Richard said as he walked back in from the balcony. "He wants me to take over. Officially. He and his wife want to retire and settle down in Tennessee somewhere. Besides, he said the work had become too much for him for a while. So, he offered me his position . . . as head groundskeeper."

The day he'd shared that news with Cami had been the day he officially learned to let go of his past.

A number of the graves in the cemetery were for World War I veterans. For each of those graves, he took meticulous care of the aesthetics, ensuring every footstone and headstone of a fallen soldier had the ivy and grass trimmed back and was swept free of debris. Even if a family only paid for seasonal care on a grave, instead of perennial care, Richard maintained the graves anyway. The sense of comfort it brought him was immense. These small acts were his way of offering solace to future generations of loved ones. To highlight a soldier's worth, even in death, with those small dignities.

One such act still weighed heavy on his mind and his heart.

He had been working in the cemetery as usual, clearing a particularly persistent patch of ivy off a few headstones, when a prickle at the back of his neck caused him to look behind him. In the far west corner of the cemetery, not too far from where Richard was kneeling, a patch of graves stood out in stark relief to the ones around them.

That area was one he rarely ventured over to, as they mostly housed those who'd died prior to the Revolutionary War. Rows of uneven rusty brick stone, worn smooth with age, made up the small landscape. Except one of the headstones, the very far plot all the way in the corner by the fence, could hardly be seen.

Curious, Richard grabbed his tools and walked over to the grave. The sight kicked his heart. Thick, green moss coated the base of the headstone while weeds and grass at least a foot high obscured any visibility of the names buried below. The stone itself was so sunken in, it barely registered a foot and a half above the ground at all. The engraved words, what ones he could make out, were hardly legible. But four words he could make out, and they nearly toppled him over in the grass.

Wife and son of . . .

The next twenty minutes were spent meticulously clearing the overgrowth from the headstone. Some of the ivy branches had been so thick, his garden shears struggled to break through. But eventually, he rocked back on his heels, dragged his gloved hand across his sweat-slicked brow, and exhaled.

Here lies Emily Brannigan and Elliot Brannigan, beloved wife and son of Thomas Brannigan.

A great sadness rose up in him at the realization of a mother and her infant son being buried in the same grave. He squinted at the grave's markings again but was unable to make out the dates. All he could tell for sure was that they'd lived and died in the 1700s.

At least they could rest in peace.

As Richard rose from his kneeling position, a blurry ripple of light off to his right caught his eye. When he glanced over, a faint image of a woman holding an infant danced across his vision. Her dark brown gown covered her legs completely, and a laced-up bodice lay over a long-sleeve white shirt. Her long auburn hair was tied back in a plait, and in her arms was a tawny blanket wrapped around a sleeping baby.

Richard quickly glanced at the sky to determine what hour of the day it was. The high glare beating down on him confirmed the peak of the afternoon. The heat was getting to him, clearly. He had worked straight through the day without a break to eat or drink, and his care-lessness was catching up with him. When he glanced back down where the woman had been, a faint wisp of her figure still remained. Richard squinted at the vision and let out a brief gasp when the woman gave him an appreciative nod and smile before vanishing before his eyes.

He quickly shook his head and threw his tools in his bag before calling it quits for the afternoon. Though, for some reason, he was more than content to bask in the newfound satisfaction that lingered with him throughout the day.

"All right, I think I'm good to go." Cami sauntered up to Richard's side and snaked her arm around his bicep.

He gave her a brief flex just to see those delicious lips curl up into the smile he knew he'd get. She loved hanging onto his arm, and he loved anything that would keep her smiling at him that way.

Forever.

"C'mon. Let's go get married."

***

Cami sat on a folding chair conspicuously placed around the corner from the gazebo where her hulking, handsome, soon-to-be husband stood. Every now and then, she'd risk a peek at their makeshift altar.

As if peeking every ten seconds would somehow convince the butterflies in her stomach to take a hike.

She spun her head around again, placed her hands against her stomach, and exhaled. The delicate lace was soft on her skin, and when the nerves kicked into high gear, she'd calm herself down by tracing each intricate swirl with her fingertips. It was oddly soothing.

"All right, my dear. Let's go put the poor boy out of his misery and get you two hitched." Mal stood near Cami with her hand outstretched.

"We're really doing this, huh, Mal?" Cami stood and rested her sweaty palm in the crook of Mal's elbow as the woman led her around the corner.

"I don't know what you're talking about. You two were as good as sealed months ago. Nothing's going to feel different tomorrow, except for maybe a slight hangover from the party and a little extra soreness down under."

"Mal, come *on!* It's my wedding day! Do you have to bring that up?" Cami rolled her eyes as they walked closer to the aisle.

"My dear, if I don't bring it up, who the hell will?" The smirk that pulled at the corner of Mal's lips took all the fight out of Cami.

Well, that and the breathtaking sight of Richard in full tuxedo regalia right in front of her.

The cut of his suit was sharp and clean. Each crease was firmly starched and pressed into submission. The buttons on his waistcoat narrowed his hips even more and highlighted the immense breadth of his chest. He clasped his hands behind his back as she and Mal slowly walked toward him. His lips were closed, but even from a distance, she could see his nostrils flare slightly as if he fought to hold back his emotions.

She had never been more grateful for her veil. The privilege of seeing his love for her reflected back so keenly, while her expression was shielded from view, well, it was her final moment as Cami Foster, and a bit hard to reconcile. That woman, with all her doubt and lack of self-worth, would be left on the lawn she'd just tread across.

As her white kitten heels climbed up the small gazebo steps to her new husband, she was Camilla Foster-Stevens. Confident, motivated, and completely humbled by abundant love. (And with a new kick-ass stage name to boot.)

As Cami passed her bouquet off to Mal, she quickly scanned the guests standing on the lawn. In total, there were fifteen people. Small, intimate, and absolutely perfect. Her guest list was pretty much Mal, Gerry, and an assortment of Mal's biker buddies, with a few of Cami's newfound opera friends sprinkled in. She was acutely aware that Richard wouldn't have anyone from his family here, so she wanted to keep it small.

The officiant asked the guests to take their seats. Cami looked up at Richard as he slowly lifted her veil. Words flowed from the officiant, and at some point, she recalled saying, "I do," but her attention had been wholly consumed by the gorgeous pillar of strength she had the good fortune to clasp hands with and love unconditionally.

"I now pronounce you husband and wife."

Cami didn't even have a chance to wipe her tears away before Richard's warm lips were pressed against hers. The cheers and whistles from the peanut gallery made her laugh, and she unintentionally broke the kiss.

"Fine, break it off if you want, angel, but as soon as I get you back home, you'll have to tie me to the bed to keep my mouth off you," he whispered so only Cami could hear. "I've waited too long for you to come along into my life and I'll be damned if I let you go."

"Can't we just enjoy the moment without bringing up the idea of tying someone to a bed? We *just* got married, after all." She laughed as he swung her up into his arms.

"I know. That's the point." He winked.

As he carried Cami in his arms down the lawn to the town car, she couldn't help but smile.

The first act of her very own opera was just beginning. And she was determined to give it a happy ending.

For the second time in recent memory, Leanne was frustrated she couldn't feel her tears as they streaked down her face. Sure, her fingers wiped them away out of habit, but there was no satisfaction in the maneuver. The only way she registered them at all was because of her blurry vision.

But she'd happily cry all the dry tears in the world if it meant she could witness her daughter's wedding day, even as a spirit.

"I've got to give it to you, Lee. Your plan worked." Roberta stood next to Leanne on the sidewalk lining the park where Cami and Dick said their vows. Close enough to witness the ceremony but far enough away to avoid temptation for Leanne. She wasn't alive anymore, and standing next to her daughter would only pour salt on an old wound. It wouldn't sting so bad as it had when it was fresh, but the reminders of the trauma didn't benefit anyone either.

"I regret nothing." Leanne blurted out the words through tight lips. Every stupid word in that will, every agonizing rejection her daughter experienced by virtue of her poverty, cut deep. But she firmly believed in Cami and desperately needed her daughter to learn the lessons Leanne had run out of time to teach.

"C'mon." Leanne draped her arm around Roberta's shoulder. White wisps floated off her skin and enveloped her sister in sisterly affection. "I'm in the mood to ride this lover's high. Want to see the original *La Sonnambula* with me?"

Roberta raised her eyebrow. "As in . . . ?"

Leanne grinned wide. "As in the original production. In Milan. In 1831."

"Oh sure." Roberta rolled her eyes. "What else am I going to do?"

"Celebrate your niece's wedding the best way we know how," Leanne said, still gripping Roberta's shoulder as their bodies shimmered out of sight.

Find out what happens when a jilted bride stumbles back in time to colonial Boston. When she's mistaken for a serving girl, she finds herself working alongside a widowed blacksmith who is as jaded and frigid as the icy waters in Boston Harbor. Can she melt his cold heart before time gets the better of them both? Start reading *Forged by the Past!*

Can we keep in touch? Do you want to read what happens when one woman finds her soulmate in the spirit world, but in order to claim him, she must give up everything she's every known and worked for? Claim *Honored by the Past*, a prequel novella, when you sign up to my newsletter to find out whether a sinfully gorgeous spirit can convince a jaded woman to leave her past behind for love.

. . .

Thank you so much for reading *Sirens of the Past!* If you loved seeing Dick and Cami's relationship grow, let your friends know. Help other readers fall in love with this couple by leaving a review.

251

Scan the QR code to start reading *Forged by the Past* and *Honored by the Past* today!

ACKNOWLEDGMENTS

I have a few amazing people to thank for this book. First and foremost, my amazing readers! You took a chance on a new author, and I can't thank you enough. I keep you in mind every step of the way.

To Jessi Gage, my friend and mentor, whose brilliant advice and critiques smoothed out the bumps along my author journey. A special thank you, also, to Sydney Rimpau, for being an early reader on this book.

Lastly, and always, to my husband, Ben, who makes one cute personal assistant. ;-)

ABOUT THE AUTHOR

Aimee Robinson is a lover of romance novels in all forms. Her absolute favorites, though, are the ones that offer a little bit of something *extra*: time travel, guardian angels, good old-fashioned meddlesome grandmothers with a supernatural secret to hide, you name it.

She believes romance novels should transport you from the humdrum to the swoonworthy, preferably while being curled up on the couch with chocolate and tea (or wine...or both!). Aimee's overactive imagination lends itself to fun tales with emotional adventures, sexy snark, and happily ever afters.

When not writing or reading, Aimee enjoys spending time with her husband and keeping up with her two young sons.